Praise for th

"Seriously funny, wick

MW01616810

— Janet Evanovich

"Archer navigates a satisfyingly complex plot and injects plenty of humor as she goes....a winning hand for fans of Janet Evanovich."

— *Library Journal*

"Davis's smarts, her mad computer skills, and a plucky crew of fellow hostages drive a story full of humor and action, interspersed with moments of surprising emotional depth."

— *Publishers Weekly*

"Archer's bright and silly humor makes this a pleasure to read. Fans of Janet Evanovich's Stephanie Plum will absolutely adore Davis Way and her many mishaps."

— *RT Book Reviews*

"Funny & wonderful & human. It gets the Stephanie Plum seal of approval."

— Janet Evanovich

"As impressive as the amount of sheer fun and humor involved are the details concerning casino security, counterfeiting, and cons. The author never fails to entertain with the amount of laughs, action, and intrigue she loads into this immensely fun series."

— *Kings River Life Magazine*

"Slot tournament season at the Bellissimo Resort and Casino in Biloxi, Miss., provides the backdrop for Archer's enjoyable sequel to *Double Whammy*...Credible characters and plenty of Gulf Coast local color help make this a winner."

— *Publishers Weekly*

DOUBLE
DOSE

DOUBLE DOSE

A DAVIS WAY CRIME CAPER

Gretchen Archer

DOUBLE DOSE
A Davis Way Crime Caper

First Edition | January 2023

Gretchen Archer
www.gretchenarcher.com

Paperback ISBN-13: 979-8-9872011-0-7
Kindle ISBN-13: 979-8-9872011-1-4

Printed in the United States of America

Friday, 8:59 A.M.

I was called to the principal's office at Willow Academy for Exceptional Children at nine o'clock in the morning on a breezy Friday in June. I'd just left Willow. I'd walked my daughters to the front door and signed them in at eight fifteen and had been at my desk for no more than ten minutes when the school called. "Are the girls okay?"

"They're fine, Davis."

First-name basis. That's how often I spoke to Cricket Robinson, gatekeeper and head Band-Aid dispenser at Willow, where my twin daughters, Bexley and Quinn, attended preschool. "They've barely been there long enough to put their backpacks in their cubbies," I said. "What could have happened already?"

"I'd rather not say over the phone."

"Cricket. Are the girls okay?"

"They're fine. But Mrs. Wellesley needs to speak to you. Could Mr. Cole come too?"

"I doubt it." My husband, Bex and Quinn's father, Bradley, was almost two hundred miles away in Jackson, Mississippi, attending a meeting with the Mississippi Gaming Commission. "He's out of the office and won't be back until much later today."

"Could you come now?"

"Not unless it's an emergency." I had a convention, a convention I'd just learned about the day before, checking into the Bellissimo Resort and Casino in Biloxi, Mississippi, where we lived and worked. "If the girls are okay, why can't it wait until Monday?"

"Davis." She lowered her voice to a whisper. "You might need your birth control pills before Monday."

Friday. Show and Tell.

Surely they hadn't.

My name is Davis Way Cole. I'm thirtysomething, pushing fortysomething, and on the short side at just over five foot two. My hair is almost red. Think cinnamon. My eyes, even though I checked the hazel box when I'd recently renewed my driver's license, are cinnamon too. I'm an undercover casino operative at the Bellissimo to my husband's President and Chief Executive Officer, which was why we lived there too, in the President's Residence on the twenty-ninth floor of the hotel. I went back to work full time when Bex and Quinn started Pre-K at Willow, the most prestigious, ludicrously expensive, and inconveniently located preschool in Harrison County, but only after climbing the waiting list we'd been on since before the girls were born. They attended preschool with the son of a United States Congressman. With other local casino executives' children. With the daughter of a famous romance author. And with two of country music legend Trace Adkins's grandchildren. (Who they recently brought for Show and Tell. He sang "Twinkle Twinkle Little Star" to Bex and Quinn's class. And my daughters took my birth control pills for Show and Tell? How did they get to the top shelf of my vanity, a shelf I could barely reach without a step ladder, to find my birth control pills? How did birth control pills even rate as Show and Tell material with Bex and Quinn? To my knowledge, the girls had no idea what birth control pills were. And also to my knowledge, they'd each taken a book for Show and Tell. *Don't Let the Pigeon Drive the Bus!* and *The Red Lemon.*)

Two weeks into their preschool careers, our daughters were suspended for a week after convincing their classmates that superpowers were transferred through bites. Everyone in their class went home with bite marks after Bex and Quinn told them if they ever wanted to fly, or be invisible, or turn broccoli into cupcakes, they had to bite each other. Which they did. They bit the stew out of each other. In the end, it cost us a generous donation to the school library. Four weeks later, Bex and Quinn were asked to leave Willow and never come back after tiptoeing past their teacher, the teacher's assistant, and the teacher's assistant's assistant, carrying their new shoes. Shoes a classmate had told them were ugly. They hid the shoes inside a toaster oven in the teacher's lounge. An unsuspecting Terrific Twos teacher, preheating the oven for her Lean Cuisine Cauliflower Crust Three-Cheese Pizza, set the shoes and the teacher's lounge on fire. It cost us a soccer field refurbish. That night, Bradley and I sat the girls down and didn't tell them they were on their last Willow leg and that they'd better keep little lids on it. Instead, we followed the school's sage advice and initiated a reward program. Rather than discipline them for what they did, we rewarded them for what they didn't do, which made no sense to us. For one, neither of us were raised that way, and for another, we knew our daughters. It wouldn't work. But we loved our girls, we wanted to be good parents, and we only went along because of the school's sly habit of reminding us at every turn that they'd forgotten more about early childhood development than we would ever know. For every day Bex and Quinn didn't come home from school with frowny face stickers plastered all over their Willow jumpers, they earned a scoop of ice cream. To be awarded on Saturday mornings. Ice Cream Breakfast with Mom and Dad, up to five scoops for keeping their little selves in check for seven little hours Monday through Friday, one of which they slept through. (They supposedly slept through.

Shoegate happened during nap time with three adults in the classroom who thought the girls were asleep.) When the ice cream didn't work, the school advised us to up the ante, suggesting the girls were too cooped up as a result of "living in a hotel," then went on to tell us one of Bex and Quinn's classmates, the daughter of the romance author, had a barn, three ponies, and a riding arena in her backyard. As a result of all the fresh air and exercise, the child was a model student who never caused a moment's trouble. So we spent an absolute fortune turning two thousand square feet of space we weren't really using into an enclosed glass patio. Complete with grass. And extensive landscaping. All the way to mini palm trees. We added a bike trail throughout. One corner held a multi-level princess castle, and another, a pretend beach with an elaborate sprinkler system that mimicked little waves. Our dogs loved it. Our daughters couldn't care less except for the indoor-outdoor room's hide and seek properties. And two weeks after we unveiled their new at-home playground, Willow School for Exceptional Children unveiled their own new playground we'd been forced to purchase for the school after Bex and Quinn, claiming a little birdy told them to, freed all the residents of the Spread My Little Wings display in the Critter Classroom. A Thrilling Threes teacher lost two square inches of hair when she had to have six stitches after a woodpecker attack. Since the library donation, refurbished soccer field, and new playground equipment, and in addition to Willow's Ivy-League-worthy tuition of twenty-two thousand dollars per child per semester, we'd purchased miles of new red velvet drapes for the school's massive theater stage, and I'd been coerced into chairing the Fall Festival Fundraiser. Bex and Quinn were only six months into their Pre-K careers, and we were going broke. And for their latest trick, they took my birth control pills for Show and Tell. I wondered what else the school could get out of us.

Whatever they want, don't pay it. It's extortion. You could hire a neurosurgeon and a microphysicist to home school the girls for what Willow is costing you.

My best friend and partner, Fantasy Erb—six feet tall, casually elegant, she looked like a live version of a chocolate-skinned Barbie, a woman who took no prisoners, and that could be because she was a former prison guard, arrived midway through my phone call. She gathered right away it was Willow on the other end of the line. She sat down at her desk to the right of mine, then pushed a hot cup of coffee and the note under my nose. I was on hold while Cricket discussed my case with Willow's headmaster, Barbara Wellesley, so I gratefully accepted the coffee but didn't write Fantasy back. Instead, I said aloud, "The girls took my birth control pills to school for Show and Tell."

Fantasy nodded slowly and thoughtfully. "New chef?"

"What?"

"The Mommy and Me tea last week," she said. "You said the cookies tasted like sidewalk."

"Because four-year-old children baked them."

"Donate a new chef to the school's cafeteria anyway," she said. "It'll get you off the birth-control hook."

"Where am I supposed to find a new chef?"

"In one of our twelve restaurants." She pointed above our sub-basement offices to the Bellissimo in general. "Or do what I've told you to do every day since the girls started at Willow. Tell the headmaster that kids will be kids, and if she doesn't want your money for teaching your kids, you'll find a preschool that does."

"And then what?"

Fantasy said, "Find a preschool that does," just as Cricket said, "Excuse me? Davis?"

How long had Cricket been back on the line? Had she heard us?

"Hold on, Cricket. Let me turn down the television." I smacked Fantasy's arm. "Okay. Shoot." Before she could shoot, security alerts flashed across Fantasy's and my phones and security emails dinged into our inboxes.

Fantasy read the subject line. "Hiccups?"

Cricket said, "Mrs. Wellesley has agreed to let Bexley and Quinn stay for the rest of the day, but only if you and Mr. Cole meet with her when school is out at three this afternoon."

"We'll do our best."

More security alerts dinged in. More hiccups. Since when were hiccups a security matter? Fantasy queued live casino video feed for the section reporting hiccups and sent it to the big screen on the wall directly in front of us. We watched, first with amusement, then with curiosity, then with increasing concern as an entire bank of video poker machines idled by while their players hiccupped. Many were hand-to-chest, as if to hold the hiccups in. Two women at side-by-side video poker machines were not only hiccupping but laughing uncontrollably at each other between hiccups. The other hiccupping players looked at each other accusatorily, as if the person next to them had started the hiccup war. Fantasy and I continued to watch wordlessly as a slot attendant approached the hiccupers, then like us tried to make sense of twenty people in one place, all with the hiccups at the exact same time, until she popped a hand over her mouth. Her eyes grew wide. Her head bobbed. Ten seconds later, it bobbed again. The slot attendant had the hiccups.

"Fantasy?" My eyes were glued to the screen. "Are hiccups like yawns? Can you catch them?"

"No."

I held my breath anyway, waiting to hiccup vicariously, when another security alert hit our inboxes. Blackjack Two, miles from the video poker machines, was reporting hiccups. Sixteen players, one pit boss, four dealers, and two cocktail servers had uncontrollable hiccups. Within ten minutes, everyone in the casino had hiccups.

Friday, 9:15 A.M.

We froze the casino until we could figure out what was going on.

No one in or out.

To make it more palatable for our guests who didn't like the idea of being held hostage by slot machines—most seemed to like it a lot—we loaded the slot machines with two hundred dollars of free play each and gave the table players the equivalent in table credit. That'd keep 'em busy for a while. The casino wasn't exactly packed, somewhere close to three hundred guests and thirty-seven employees by our count, and that was more about the two hundred and fifty pharmacists, pharmaceutical sales reps, medicinal chemists, and doctors with Good Pills Biopharmaceuticals, Inc. pouring in for their convention than anything else, but it wasn't five minutes later that Plethora, our five-star buffet, adjacent to and overlooking the casino, called Security to report an additional two hundred guests with hiccups.

"Why are there two hundred people having breakfast at the buffet at the same time?" Fantasy asked. "Is it Senior Discount Day?"

"No," I said. "They're here with the Biloxi Casino Exchange."

"Are you playing with me?" she asked.

"I wish."

The Biloxi Casino Exchange, a new and ill-advised community outreach program to promote goodwill between the city's competing casinos, facilitated sending patrons from one casino to another's spa. Or supplying them with box-seat tickets to another casino's headliner act. And since we'd voted against the program for numerous reasons, mostly because we were on great terms with eleven of our neighboring casinos and regularly traded amenities, and we felt sure the one casino we weren't on good terms with only wanted to use the program to spy on everyone else, starting with us, we only offered free breakfast buffets, because nothing happened during breakfast. Except for that day. It would seem we were serving Belgium waffles with a side of hiccups.

"Now what do we do?" Fantasy asked.

"We herd the Plethora people into the casino."

"They're high rollers, Davis. Two hundred dollars on a slot machine won't impress them."

I rolled my eyes, loaded all the slot machines and tables with an additional two thousand dollars per person in free casino play, then sent instructions to the Plethora manager to shuffle all the Exchange guests to the casino.

"There," I said. "Million-dollar problem solved."

"Not the hiccup problem."

We watched the wall-to-wall monitors featuring wall-to-wall hiccupers.

"What are we going to do, Davis?"

"For one, we forget about the Exchange guests. As soon as the hiccups stop, we'll send them back where they belong. And in the meantime, I guess we watch and wait."

"How long do hiccups last?"

"Five minutes?" I guessed. "Ten?"

She checked the time. "We're going on fifteen."

I consulted Dr. Google on my phone. "Hiccups generally last between one and two hours."

"Are we going to sit here and watch five hundred people hiccup for between one and two hours?"

"I hope not."

But we did, silently, for at least five more minutes, until I realized my head was bobbing in time with the hiccupers on my computer screen. I turned to Fantasy, who was blinking in time with the hiccupers on her screen. "Stop watching."

"I can't."

"Let's do something else."

"Like what?" She blinked away.

"Like figure out how everyone in the casino got the hiccups instead of waiting for their hiccups to go away."

She stayed rivetted to the hiccup show.

I waved a hand between her face and the screen. "See if you can find out why the conference people are in the casino so early."

"What will you do?"

"I'll see if we missed anything on their background checks." Which was somewhat of a way to kill time while we waited on the hiccups to go away, but wasted no time at all because the two-week-old security folder I found on Good Pills Biopharmaceuticals was empty. Apparently, we had a conference in house full of fine upstanding citizens, none of whom were wanted in multiple jurisdictions for multiple crimes. There were no records of prior misdemeanors, much less felonies, not a restraining order in sight, or even a lone unpaid parking ticket.

Unusual.

Two hundred and fifty model humans.

Fantasy pulled up the Bellissimo daily briefing and clicked the drug itinerary. "All the Good Pills people are in the casino because they're scheduled for a Welcome Breakfast at nine at the Plethora Buffet."

"Busy morning for Plethora." Which had ceased operations. Because every cook, server, busser, and dishwasher had the hiccups.

Fantasy nosed around a little more. "Listen to this, Davis. The Good Pills file is two weeks old."

The little red flag that lived in my brain stirred. "That's how old their security folder is," I said. "Two weeks."

"What does that mean?"

The convention was news to me—I'd only heard about it the day before—for which there could be multiple reasons. How could it be news to the Bellissimo at large too? I couldn't come up with a single good reason. "It's probably a typo," I said. "I bet it's a glitch and the date should be a year and two weeks ago."

"No." She tilted her computer screen. Every entry had the same two-weeks-ago date. "The drug people booked this conference two weeks ago."

The little red flag in my brain waved at me. "How does a company pull together a two-hundred-and-fifty-person conference in two weeks?"

"They don't." She clicked away, her eyes racing around the Good Pills itinerary page. "It says in the notes that Good Pills was booked at another Biloxi casino, but it fell through."

"On which end?" I minimized the blank security page on my computer screen and maximized the one for Special Events. I logged in. "Did the casino where they were originally booked cancel on them, or did they cancel on the casino?"

"It doesn't say."

"Which other Biloxi casino?"

"It doesn't say that either," she said. "I can only see their booking date and their schedule."

I found their conference folder in Special Events. Good Pills Biopharmaceuticals, headquartered in Elmhurst, Illinois, was primarily in the headache therapeutics business and had a market value of seven billion. What I didn't find was how or why their original Biloxi conference plans had fallen through. Had another hotel accidentally double booked conferences on top of each other? Did the deposit check Good Pills wrote another Biloxi resort bounce? Did one of our neighbor casinos know something about Good Pills we didn't? "What else is on their itinerary, Fantasy?"

"After the Welcome Breakfast, they have a presentation called, 'There's No Such Thing as a Sinus Headache.'"

"I beg to differ."

"After that," she read on, "workshops and breakout sessions. There's 'The Truth About Ice Cream and Brain Freeze,' 'Husbands Get Headaches Too,' and 'An In-Depth Analysis of 150 Different Kinds of Headaches.'" She turned to look at me. "How do you do an in-depth analysis of a hundred and fifty headaches in fifty minutes?"

I shrugged.

"You can't analyze a hundred and fifty anythings in fifty minutes."

No argument from me.

"Much less headaches," she said.

I nodded in agreement.

"Tomorrow looks just like today." She went back to the Good Pills conference agenda. "The breakout sessions include 'Botox: It's Not Just for Crow's Feet,' 'The Relationship Between Bubble Gum and Headaches,' and 'Is There a Link Between Scented Soap and Migraines?'"

I sat back in my chair. "Let's say it cost Good Pills fifty thousand in transportation for two hundred and fifty people round trip from Illinois to Mississippi."

"Okay." Fantasy sat back too.

"And they're paying us a hundred thousand for their rooms for two nights."

She nodded.

"Another fifty thousand dollars for our conference facilities and another fifty thousand, at least, in food and bar."

"Your point?"

"Good Pills is spending two hundred and fifty thousand dollars to talk about bubble gum? Those are the fakest workshops of all fake workshops ever." Back at my computer, I nosed behind the conference tab in the Special Events folder. "Whatever they're here to do it has nothing to do with scented soap. And why is this the first we've heard of them? Who signed off on this?" Before I could begin to look for the person or persons responsible for letting Good Pills sneak in our back door at the eleventh hour, the words INCOMING VIDEO CALL flashed across the big screen in front of us. It was our boss, Jeremy Covey. Instead of hello or good morning, he said, "What are you two doing sitting at your desks while the whole casino has the hiccups?"

"What should we be doing?" I asked. "Running through the casino yelling 'BOO' at everyone to scare the hiccups out of them? This is a little unprecedented. It's not like we have a page in our operating manual to tell us what procedures to follow when the whole casino has the hiccups."

He blew out a breath of frustration.

"Where are you?" Fantasy asked.

"I'm in the cage," he answered.

The cage was casino accounting. Casino accounting was where all casino banking transpired, but it wasn't slam-bang in the casino. It was casino adjacent. "The cage doesn't have hiccups?" I asked the fifty-five-inch image of the Bellissimo's Vice President of Security on the wall monitor in front of me, and it was fifty-four inches too much. Or maybe it was just bad lighting. The camera angle was that of him looking into a shiny Christmas tree ornament, all nose. In real life, his nose fit well on his extra-large head—think beach ball—above a frame large enough to hold a head that big. And he had about as much hair on his head as a beach ball too, which was to say none, and that was why we called him No Hair. If we kept it up with the video conference much longer, we'd have to change it to Big Nose.

"No one in the cage has the hiccups," No Hair's huge nose said.

"We're scanning the casino and can't find anyone who doesn't have them," I said. "Which means there's a possibility that whatever's causing the hiccups could be coming through the air vents. How is the cage spared? Isn't it on the same system?"

"The cage is sealed, Davis. On its own heat and air."

Right. So a small thief couldn't crawl through the ductwork and nab a large amount of money.

"Did you know about the Good Pills conference, No Hair?" I asked.

"I saw it on the schedule a few weeks ago," he answered.

"So you signed off on it?"

"No," he said. "I thought you did."

"I did not."

"Then who did?"

We both scratched our heads.

"Did you know this conference was booked at another Biloxi casino until two weeks ago?" I asked.

"Which one?"

"That I don't know."

We scratched our heads again.

"Do we think there's a direct connection between the pharmacists and the hiccups?" I asked.

"I have no idea what to think other than the obvious," No Hair said. "Someone wants us looking at hiccups and nowhere else."

"What do you mean?" Fantasy asked.

"How many surveillance screens do you have dedicated to hiccups?" Fantasy and I glanced at the dozen big screens that lined our office walls on both sides of the huge screen in the middle that was full of his nose, all featuring hiccupping casino guests. "Where aren't we looking?" he asked, knowing where we weren't looking, but posing the question so we'd ask ourselves.

The Bellissimo covered 3.2 million square feet. The casino was only forty-five thousand square feet of it. We weren't looking at the front desk, the hotel lobby, the shops on the mezzanine, the restaurants, the spa, the salon, the grounds, valet, the entrances, the exits, the receiving docks—the receiving docks! At nine o'clock on Friday mornings, cash arrived by armed courier to be transported to our vault so we'd have enough on hand for the weekend. Depending on how busy we were or weren't—if it was pouring rain out on a weekend we had a golf tournament scheduled and half our guests canceled, or if the Red Hot Chili Peppers were in the house and their fans were pouring in—the amount of additional cash we received on Fridays could be anywhere from five hundred thousand to five million dollars. On Monday mornings at nine on the dot, the extra cash went back to the bank to wait for the next Friday. I glanced at the time. It was 9:20. My fingers flew across one of the keyboards in front of me while the little red flag in my brain danced a jig.

"Are you pulling up the receiving dock, Davis?" No Hair asked. "Are you contacting casino surveillance to see if they might be keeping an eye on anything other than hiccupers, Fantasy?"

It was with enormous relief that I watched warp speed video of the courier truck delivering the weekend cash, then walking it straight through the casino, past the cage, and into our vault. The only hiccup was, well, hiccups. Four armed couriers arrived without them and left with them. Fantasy found a little more. The five casino surveillance operators in their offices a floor above the casino who were supposed to be watching every bank of slot machines, every craps table, and every transaction at the casino cage, weren't. They were slumped over their desks, either fast asleep or otherwise—it was impossible to tell from our vantage point—circled by fifty destroyed surveillance screens.

"No Hair," I broke the bad news, "surveillance is down."

"What's that supposed to mean?"

Before I could answer, my phone buzzed with an incoming text message from Ms. Kelsey, one of Bex and Quinn's teachers at Willow School for Exceptional Children. It would seem my exceptional daughters, in addition to taking my birth control pills for Show and Tell, had also smuggled a rabbit to school. *Davis, please have someone pick up your rabbit.*

I didn't have a rabbit.

Friday, 9:30 A.M.

Any doubt I had that the Bellissimo was in the process of being compromised flew out the window. The little red flag in my brain jumped out after it, her work done. Five hundred people with the hiccups was a curiosity, for sure, and cause for concern, but our surveillance department incapacitated was confirmation.

I put in an alert requesting all available Security to get to Surveillance as quickly as possible, but don't go through the casino to get there, then accessed the cloud speaker in their cramped office. "Hey! Surveillance!" One groggy head lifted an inch. "Wake up!" Another disoriented tech stirred. Fantasy leaned over my shoulder and into the tiny microphone dot at the top of my computer screen, and in a very practiced way threatened them with bodily harm if they didn't get up and moving that very instant. She didn't use her inside voice. Four bolted upright in their chairs, and the fifth, yelling, "Mom? Mom?" shot out of his so fast he wound up on the floor.

The last thing they remembered were donuts. A young man wearing a Bellissimo uniform knocked on their door with a tray of chocolate-glazed donuts so fresh and warm the chocolate was still glossy and dripping. After that, it was lights out. Apparently, their lights went all the way out, because while they slept, the fifty monitors surrounding them had been disabled by ten brutes with sledgehammers or maybe just one mercenary with a fixed-fire muzzleloader. Every OLED screen had received a punch to the gut, all were inoperable, most spiderwebbed from the middle out. The others, their thin glass screens completely annihilated, were nothing but colorful wire and dangling circuit boards. Our surveillance department was effectively closed and wouldn't be up and running again anytime soon.

On their way to be checked out at the emergency room at Merit Health on Reynoir Street, we interviewed the donut sleepers briefly by video call. Most were still yawning deeply. None remembered a thing after their first bite of donut—not one conscious thought, not a sound, not any activity around them, just wonderful dreamless sleep. One told us it was the best nap he'd ever had in his life and asked if we knew what the donuts had been spiked with so he could look for an over-the-counter version.

I logged in to the surveillance archives to make sure our cameras had continued to record. Not scanning the casino like they normally would with techs at the wheels, but at least recording. My rolling desk chair in fifth gear, my fingers flying across three different keyboards, Fantasy and I were glued to the images slowly appearing on our screens. The cameras had been tampered with too. Not disabled, but all had been haphazardly redirected. For every camera aimed at a ceiling, a wall, or at the dark door of a restaurant, there were two others still displaying casino activity. We sent those flying to the screens of our wall monitors and were in the process of scanning them for unusual activity during Surveillance's nap when my husband finally returned one of the many calls I'd squeezed in since discovering Surveillance compromised. I hit the speaker button because I didn't have time to relay it all to Fantasy afterward. She might as well listen in.

"Davis, are the girls okay?"

"Yes."

"Are you?"

"Yes."

"Is the Bellissimo on fire?"

"No."

"Then what's the emergency?"

"It's a rabbit, hiccups, and donuts."

"One more time?"

I told him one more time.

"A rabbit emergency? You've called a dozen times, texted nine-one-one two dozen, and had someone shove a note under the door of closed proceedings asking me to call you ASAP over a rabbit, hiccups, and cookies?"

"Donuts."

"Excuse me. Donuts."

"Bradley, Bex and Quinn smuggled a rabbit to school."

"They did not."

"They did."

"Where'd they get a rabbit?"

"That I don't know."

"The girls did not smuggle a rabbit to school. Keep going," he said.

"The casino has hiccups."

"A casino can't get hiccups."

"Well, it can," I said, "because ours does."

My husband, who looked like an advertisement for the state of California, or maybe Florida (sandy blonde, blue-eyed, perpetually tanned, built like a surfer), wore a suit like he was born on Wall Street (he was a casino attorney before he ran our billion-dollar casino), but he was actually a native Texan transplanted to Mississippi, where he remained a devoted Longhorns fan. He said, "Fourth and goal, Davis." And by that, he meant, move along and make it quick.

I moved along. And made it quick. "Surveillance ate bad donuts."

"*What?*" He inhaled big. I knew what that meant. I had a speech coming. "Davis." Two distinct syllables. I was right. A speech was on the way. "I've been gone an hour," he said, "a single hour. I stepped off the plane not fifteen minutes ago. I barely made it to the meeting on time. I attend one or two Gaming Commission meetings a year, only when absolutely necessary. I'm here because it's absolutely necessary." He took another deep breath. Reloading. "You've halted the proceedings of a closed meeting with a packed agenda to pull me out over a rabbit, hiccups, and donuts? In my life I've never heard of a rabbit, hiccup, or donut emergency. Before you interrupt the meeting again over anything less than a true emergency, first go look out the window and remind yourself why I'm here and what I'm up against."

I wished I hadn't led with the rabbit. And I didn't need to look out the window to remember what he was up against, what we were up against, and what the Bellissimo was up against. Bling-Bling. We were smack-dab up against Bling-Bling Biloxi. The new casino kid on the block. And by block, I meant same block, practically on top of us. And by new, I meant one day it wasn't there and the next it was.

Maybe Bling-Bling wasn't built in a day, but it sure felt that way.

Earlier that year, exactly six months earlier, we'd woken up to breaking news. In the blink of an eye, a Chicago slumlord, who also owned a thriving import/export business, a drug company, several construction companies, and a chain of dry cleaners in addition to two hundred dope-peddling hot dog stands scattered all over the city—think Chicago Mob Boss—had somehow managed to accomplish what the Bellissimo had been unable to for twenty-five years. He'd purchased the public beachfront on the west side of our property from the City of Biloxi after winning a trial in Chicago that had lasted two years.

Or maybe he didn't win it so much as he was acquitted on all charges (extortion, organized crime, racketeering, money laundering, drug trafficking, human trafficking, and outright murder), because for two long years the feds couldn't keep a witness alive long enough to testify against him. So with all of America at his disposal after walking away scot-free from six decades of Chicago mobbery, he chose to start fresh in Biloxi. And bought the property next door to us. Property we'd wanted forever. Property that had long been declared unsuitable and unsustainable for structural development in any and every way. Our intent was never more than to make it a luxury beach experience for our guests, and every year, like clockwork, we took another stab at it, upping our ante each time, only to receive the same answer again and again. A big fat no. But somehow a stranger from Chicago, a man who went by the name Jimmy "Tick-Tock" Russo, a man the feds couldn't pin a single charge on, a man with no connection to gaming or Biloxi that we could find, not only purchased the property, but talked someone into rezoning it for construction.

Something we'd been told could never happen.

It happened.

Hundreds of cement trucks stopped traffic both ways on Beach Boulevard the day Bling-Bling broke ground. At five in the morning. When the sun came up, we were shocked to see the footprint of a giant structure in place and the Gulf filled with hundreds of barges dropping off massive chunks of a prefabricated high-rise. Even their luxury hotel suite pods, finished all the way to wall-to-wall reclaimed hardwood flooring and marble shower stalls, were delivered by barge. Towering cranes parked on land reached their long talons out the Gulf to lift the guest room pods off the barges, then stack them on top of each other, all day and all night for a week. From foundation to ribbon cutting, Bling-Bling, looking for all intents and purposes like a space station with out-of-this-world amenities through their roof, which was taller than ours, ripping away our twenty-five-year-old distinction as Mississippi's tallest building by thirty-six little inches, went from nothing to open for business in just under six weeks. What we'd been told by our elected officials, the city council, and the developers would be a low-profile event venue built mostly on an enormous barge meant to lure Las Vegas headliners just steps from our casino resort—which sounded like a very good thing—quickly turned into a high-profile casino resort built on sand and slapped together like a game of Jenga.

A very bad thing.

And there went the neighborhood.

We didn't take it sitting down. Things grew so bad so fast between us and Bling-Bling that the city, tired of troubleshooting their ridiculous complaints about us (stop with the fireworks) and our legitimate problems with them (stop blocking all traffic to and from our resort with your construction), assigned a liaison. A casino liaison. Have you ever? A woman named Starling Halter, whose claim to fame was wearing halter tops two sizes too small, was hired by the City of Biloxi to keep the peace between us and Bling-Bling. She did nothing but stir it up. And *she* was why we had two hundred of Bling-Bling's high-rolling hiccuppers at our buffet that morning with her ridiculous Biloxi Casino Exchange program. Things were ten times worse with her than without her. But Bradley hadn't stopped what he was doing, which was running our resort and casino, to complain to the Gaming Commission about the large-breasted and ineffective babysitter the city had assigned. He was there because the survey said, or, rather, the surveyors said, Bling-Bling's twenty-floor parking garage, which had twenty floors of our west-wing hotel guests staring at a solid wall of mirrored glass instead of the Gulf of Mexico, and the ten floors above them gawking at Bling-Bling's parking garage roof, upon which they had a topless pool complete with topless bartenders and servers, was built out seven feet past the approved blueprints, landing it squarely six feet onto our property. And that was why Bradley and the entire Bellissimo legal team were at the Gaming Commission meeting in Jackson, Mississippi, that morning.

I'd interrupted.

"I didn't mean to snap at you, Davis." I could feel him running a frustrated hand through his hair. "Let's back up."

"Backing up," I said.

"Not one word you said made sense. We don't have a rabbit. I've never even seen a rabbit at the Bellissimo. I've never seen a rabbit in Biloxi. You drove the girls to school. If there was a rabbit in the car, how did it get there and how did you not know?"

"I have no idea how it got there, Bradley, and I didn't know it was there because it's like I'm sixteen again and just got my driver's license. I'm a little rusty. I was watching the road, not looking for a rabbit." (I hadn't driven since before the girls were born, mostly because I didn't have a car—long story—but got a brand-new car for my birthday. Which coincided with the girls starting preschool at Willow. It was perfect timing, because Bex and Quinn arriving to school by Bellissimo stretch limo seemed a little ostentatious. Didn't want to start out on the wrong foot. As if a brand-new bright red Porsche Cayenne Coupe wasn't ostentatious on its very own.) "And not only that," I kept going, "they took my birth control pills for Show and Tell."

That piped him down for a beat, mostly because we already had our hands full in the kid department. When he found his voice, he said, "Keep going. Who has the hiccups?"

"Five hundred people in the casino. First it was a handful of players at a bank of video poker machines, then everyone at

Blackjack Two, and within ten minutes the whole casino plus two hundred buffet guests at Plethora had the hiccups."

"How?" he asked. "Why?"

"We don't know yet."

"Who is we?" he asked.

"Me and Fantasy."

"Where's Baylor?"

Fantasy and I immediately locked eyes. "Who?"

"Baylor," my husband said. "He works for you. The third member of your team. Is he there?"

I stole a glance at Baylor's empty desk to my left. "No."

"Where is he?"

I told the truth. "I'm not exactly sure."

"Well, get sure, Davis. And tell me who else has the hiccups."

"As far as I know, the hiccups are contained to the casino."

"As far as you know? You haven't checked?"

"No."

"Then why do you believe no one outside of the casino has hiccups?"

"Because we locked the casino doors."

That got him. "You are holding our guests hostage in the casino because they have the hiccups? Last I heard, hiccups weren't life-threatening. Unlock the casino doors."

"We're just asking them to stay put until we can figure it out. It's only been—" I checked the time "—it hasn't been long."

Actually, it had.

It had been almost an hour.

"Open the casino doors," he said. "Now, what about the donuts?" Bradley asked. "And tell me fast. Seventy people are waiting on me."

Before I could tell him that we'd had a major security breach in our surveillance department thanks to doped donuts, and for that reason alone the casino needed to stay locked down, Fantasy, still scanning archived casino video for the time Surveillance hadn't been watching, got a hit. She froze one of her computer monitors on the image of a thin woman with her hair pulled back in a high sleek ponytail who looked to be in her early thirties. Fantasy sent the photo flying to a big screen. The woman was wearing a power suit with ankle-strap wedges and a Michael Kors crossbody bag, all in shades of taupe. With a few more clicks, Fantasy filled every screen with images of the same woman with the same ponytail in the same suit with her hand in and out of the same Michael Kors crossbody bag. All over the casino and all over Plethora.

"I'll save the donut story for later," I said, my attention no longer on our call, but on the ponytailed woman on the big screens, "if you could have someone pick up the rabbit and my birth control pills."

"Who would you suggest?"

"Anyone," I said. "Let me get back to the hiccupers and you take care of the rabbit." Silence. "And my birth control pills," I added.

"Davis, I don't have time to make arrangements to have a rabbit and birth control pills picked up. I won't even be able to call you again until three o'clock."

"Why not?"

"Because that's our next break."

"You don't even get a lunch break?"

"They're bringing lunch in."

Beside me, Fantasy whispered, "Ask what they're having."

I waved her off. "Okay. I'll tell the school you'll send someone to pick up the rabbit at three."

"I will not," he said. "The rabbit isn't ours. Tell the school we will not be picking up someone else's rabbit."

He left me no wiggle room. And I had very little energy to worry about someone else's rabbit just then either, so I told him I'd do my best to work everything out and let him go, because Fantasy had the huge screen split with two additional images of the ponytailed woman. And she just might be the way I worked it out. Not the rabbit. Or my birth control pills. But the answer to our casino problems could very well be on the screens in front of me. One was a still shot of the ponytailed woman. What we couldn't see from a distance or from overhead camera angles, we could see on the big screen. A flesh-colored face mask covered her mouth and nose. Not all that unusual. On her hands, flesh-colored gloves. Somewhat unusual. Our facial recognition software couldn't see through the mask and there'd be no fingerprinting anything she'd touched because of the gloves. The screen to the right was the ponytailed woman in action. Fantasy clicked the video forward. We watched the ponytailed woman winding through our buffet and casino, slowing down every fifty feet or so to pull a twenty-dollar bill out of her crossbody bag, then both casually and strategically placing single twenties everywhere. Propped around ATM kiosks. Between slot machines. At empty breakfast tables. At empty bars. A few she dropped in wide aisles.

It was a casino.

Gamblers loved loose cash.

It wasn't enough money to turn in to Security, although most of the people who spotted the lonely twenties scanned their immediate areas to see if anyone was actively looking for cash they might have dropped before examining the bills, stuffing them into the closest slot machine, or tucking them into their wallets. Within five minutes, everyone who'd touched one of the twenties had the hiccups. Five minutes later, everyone around the ground zero hiccupers had the hiccups. Who was the ponytailed woman in the power suit dropping hiccupping twenties all over our casino? Before we could begin to answer the question, the word INCOMING VIDEO CALL flashed across our screens again, and our boss, No Hair, replaced the ponytailed woman's image. He'd made his way to the casino. We could see casino guests in the background, somewhat assembled, some in huddled klatches, others, exhausted from hiccups, stretched out in slot-machine chairs they'd dragged to the main aisle.

No one gambling.

Everyone hiccupping.

"Davis." Hiccup. "Fantasy." Hiccup. "Call a hiccup specialist."

I said, "No Hair, there's no such thing as a hiccup specialist."

"Then call—" hiccup "—a regular doctor." Hiccup. "I've had the hiccups—" hiccup "—for fifteen minutes—" he had a hand splayed on his bucking chest "—and this needs to stop."

From her phone, Fantasy quickly consulted Dr. Google. "Have you tried holding your breath?"

Between hiccups, he said they tried it until a lady passed out, then gave up.

Then she said, "Have you tried breathing into a paper bag?"

Between hiccups again, he told us there weren't paper bags in the casino.

She took a final stab at it. "Have you tried sipping ice water?"

I consulted Dr. Google for the second time that morning. "How about sugar? Have you swallowed sugar?" I read down the list. "Have you sucked lemons? Have you tried sitting down, pulling your knees to your chest, and rocking back and forth?"

He managed to say, "*What*? Have you—" hiccup "—lost your—" hiccup "—mind?"

He hung up on us, but not before flashing a thick stack of twenty-dollar bills he told us might be behind the hiccups, look into it, and not before we caught a glimpse of the ponytailed woman casually strolling behind him, seemingly without a care in the world and without hiccups, which Fantasy and I determined after watching her image frame-by-frame two more times. Who was the ponytailed woman in the power suit dropping hiccupping twenties all over our casino?

"Did you see No Hair's tie?" Fantasy asked.

"I didn't notice his tie because I was too busy watching him wave a big stack of twenty-dollar bills."

"Should we try to get him back and tell him to stay away from the twenties?"

"He already has the hiccups. He's already dosed himself."

"He was holding a lot of twenties."

"He may have the hiccups for a week, Fantasy, because he just dosed himself in a big way."

"Should we call him back and warn him?"

"I think it's too late."

Friday, 10:00 A.M.

With half the people in the casino there for the Good Pills Welcome Breakfast to kick off their booked-at-the-last-minute conference, we started our search for the ponytailed woman there. It was something productive to do while we waited on the hiccups to stop and worried about No Hair.

Of the two hundred and fifty attendees, half were pharmaceutical sales reps. The healthy people in the waiting room at the doctor's office on their laptops with large rolling briefcases full of drugs at their feet.

"I don't even understand pharmaceutical sales," Fantasy said. "Doesn't it make more sense that a doctor would prescribe the best drug for the job instead of the drug their favorite salesperson is pushing? I mean, isn't healthcare an industry that shouldn't be swayed by sales reps carrying a tray of chicken nuggets for the nurses on their way to eighteen holes of golf with the doctors?"

I was at the end of my drug pusher list—mine had more men than women—having not found anyone or anything near the woman in the suit, about to move on to the Research and Development team. "You know what I don't understand? Drug commercials."

"Me neither," she said. "There isn't a pill on television I would swallow."

"It makes no sense." I clicked through the chemists and doctors in charge of clinical trials. "Who are the drug advertisements for? Do people really ask their doctors for a specific drug because they heard on television it would clear up their skin, totally ignoring the part that says they'll hallucinate about baby goats and their toenails will fall off?"

She said, "Beats me," as I reached the bottom of the Good Pills R&D team's barrel, all the way to a Dr. Wurtz. His was the last name on the list. Dr. Winford Wurtz. Which sounded interesting to me. I'd start there and work my way up. I clicked.

"I mean, what kind of trade-off is allergy relief for crossed eyes?" Fantasy asked. "Sure, your eyes don't itch anymore, but they're crossed."

I said, "That's what streaming services are for. You don't have to watch drug commercials." I clicked on Dr. Wurtz's photo. He looked like a mad scientist. He looked like Albert Einstein. He looked like he was a hundred years old, but his bio said he was sixty-three.

"You know what I saw last week?" she asked.

"No." Dr. Wurtz's bio also said he was five foot zip. Shorter than me. And I wasn't tall.

"A drug vending machine."

"A what?" His bio also said he was from Germany.

"It was a huge metal box at the grocery store where the pharmacy used to be," she said. "You hold your prescription up to a screen on the box, scan it, stand there five minutes, then your drugs drop out."

"Interesting." Dr. Wurtz worked for Krüger Chemicals in Nuremburg before Good Pills stole him away. "I wonder how long it will be before someone figures out how to break into the drug vending machine."

"Not long," Fantasy said, "if it hasn't happened already." She tilted her screen. "Could this be our twenty-dollar bill donor?"

She was still on her drug rep list. I glanced. "No. Unless she's lost fifty pounds."

Fantasy said, "She probably sells a pill for that."

I tilted my own screen. "What do you think of this guy?"

She looked. "He's cute. What about him?"

I clicked to another screen. "Before he worked for Good Pills, he developed synthetic nerve agents in something called fume cupboards in his basement."

"Are you making that up?"

"I'm not."

"Nerve agents as in chemical warfare?"

"No," I said. "Synthetic nerve agents, as in he holds a patent on a small fuzzy blanket dental patients hold to block pain when they're having a root canal. It takes the place of fourteen numbing shots with ten-inch needles."

"A pain killer blanket?"

"Exactly."

"I'll take ten."

"You can't buy them."

"Why not?"

"Apparently, the painkiller the blanket transfers is so strong, it lasts up to a week. People caught on and were scheduling unnecessary root canals so they could go straight to elective procedures, like cosmetic surgeries, with their dental painkillers in tow. Athletes were scheduling root canals before boxing matches and cycling events just for the painkiller."

"So they took it off the market?"

"Until Dr. Wurtz can find a way to turn the painkiller on and off."

"And he's here? At our casino?" she asked. "Do you think he packed any root canal blankets in his suitcase?"

"Maybe we should ask him." I rolled to another computer terminal just to my left to access the Bellissimo front desk system. "He checked in yesterday. That would put him in the casino for the Welcome Breakfast." I rolled back from the desk. "Let's go see the good doc." But before we could, and before we remembered we couldn't really go to the casino to speak to Dr. Wurtz unless we wanted the hiccups, the fifty-five-inch monitor on the wall screamed. "ARE YOU GIRLS THERE?"

It was No Hair. Backed up by a roaring crowd. And by roaring, I meant not only was No Hair yelling, but everyone we could see and hear behind him was yelling too.

"I CAN'T HEAR," No Hair boomed. "NO ONE IN THE CASINO CAN HEAR. WE'VE LOST OUR HEARING. GET A BIOHAZARD CREW IN HERE TO FIND THE SOURCE OF WHATEVER IT IS WE'RE DEALING WITH AND GET THEM IN QUIETLY OR WE'LL HAVE THE AUTHORITIES AND MEDIA BREATHING DOWN OUR NECKS. SHUT DOWN THE HOTEL. NO ONE IN OR OUT UNTIL WE HAVE ANSWERS. ESPECIALLY DON'T LET ANYONE NEAR THE CASINO. THEN FIND ME A LIP READER OR A SIGN LANGUAGE INTERPRETER AND GET ME BAYLOR."

"WHO?" I yelled back.

"DAVIS, I CAN'T HEAR YOU." No Hair pointed to his own ears.

Fantasy scrambled around the middle drawer of her desk, passed me a whiteboard, then tossed me a green marker. I wrote WHO? on the board, then turned it around for him to see.

No Hair yelled, "BAYLOR. BIG GUY WHO WORKS FOR YOU? SEND HIM. I NEED HELP WITH CROWD CONTROL. AND TELL HIM TO BRING SOMETHING SAFE FOR US TO DRINK."

The screen went dark.

After a long contemplative moment of silence, Fantasy said, "What are we going to do?"

"We're going to lock the front doors," I said, while in the process of electronically securing all entrances to the Bellissimo.

"I meant about Baylor."

I stole another glance at Baylor's empty desk. "He'll show up any minute."

"And if he doesn't?"

"He will."

Friday, 10:01 A.M.

Baylor, just Baylor, like Adele was just Adele, was the third and final member of my covert security crew. The muscle. And my muscle was on assignment. The problem was the three of us—me, Fantasy, and Baylor—were the only ones who knew. I hadn't asked for permission to dispatch Baylor to do my team's dirty work thinking I'd ask for forgiveness after we saved the day. It was never my plan to get caught beforehand, and it was all Casino Liaison Starling Halter's fault. If she'd even halfway done her job, I wouldn't have had to do it for her. But instead of being a neutral problem solver between us and Bling-Bling, which was exactly what we were told she'd do, and exactly what we needed, she singlehandedly started a war. A war we were fighting with Baylor on the frontlines.

Starling, on loan from the National Police Force Resource Center in Milwaukee, Wisconsin, was listed on their website as a Certified Urban Corporate Conflict Counselor. (What a bunch of baloney.) She landed in Biloxi with a suitcase full of halter tops and two arrows in her peacekeeping quiver: therapy babble and poking the Bellissimo bear that was already mad. She showed up six weeks before Bling-Bling opened, which was right after our new neighbors slapped a cease and desist order on us accusing the Bellissimo of being the source of all the anonymous gangster tips called into the Mississippi Bureau of Investigation, the Federal Bureau of Investigation, and the Organized Crime Divisions of the Departments of Labor, Justice, Corrections,

Homeland Security, and Defense—all of which I fully intended to deny for the rest of my livelong days—and right after we'd filed a million-dollar complaint against them when debris from their construction site destroyed our pool. Starling Halter's first official task was to help resolve the pool issue.

Her call was routed to my Bellissimo internal number, a dusty landline phone in a dark corner of my desk, a phone that almost never rang, and when it did, it was usually a wrong number, either a hotel guest trying to book a massage at the Bellissimo spa or an employee misdialing the payroll department. Most of the time I ignored it. I wish I'd ignored it the day Starling called. I might have answered her call out of sleep deprivation. It came at the height of Bling-Bling's stealth-of-night construction, which happened to be right outside the master bedroom of our twenty-ninth-floor Bellissimo home, and neither Bradley nor I had slept through the night for weeks because of the constant banging, clanking, and staccato sirens of tractors and trailers backing up. And I might have answered her call out of boredom. With guests canceling in droves since our pool was on the blink, I had nothing better to do. Then again, I might have answered the phone because I knew it wouldn't be Cricket Robinson at Willow School for Exceptional Children, because she didn't have my desk number. My primary vehicle for communication, my cell phone, was still hot from the call I'd just suffered through with her lecturing me about identical twin pranks the girls wouldn't stop pulling on their teachers. I was the last person in the world who needed that particular lecture, because Bex and Quinn tried those tricks on me all the time: switching beds, trading clothes, insisting they were both one or the other. "Why are you calling me Bex? I'm Quinn." Then from the other, "No, she's not, Mommy. I'm Quinn." (To which I always said, "Listen, girls. I was there when you were born. I know who's who.") But most likely, I answered Starling's call because I couldn't find another federal agency to call an anonymous tip into about the mobsters next door. So when I accidentally answered Starling's call, I was already tired, cranky, and talked out. I might have grabbed the office phone and said, "WHAT?"

She introduced herself at length, to which I responded briefly. "I'm in security."

"And your name?"

Instead of telling her my name, I said, "What can I do for you, Starling?"

"It's Officer Halter," she corrected me.

"I read your bio," I said. "We both know you're not an officer. You represent law enforcement, but you're not a sworn officer."

I regretted saying it as soon as the words left my lips—it wasn't necessary—but I was operating on two hours of spotty sleep, we'd had a week-long conference with two thousand attendees cancel that morning because Bling-Bling offered them a better deal, and Cricket Robinson of Willow School for Exceptional Children didn't speak twin. All on top of losing our pool.

Starling cleared her throat. "Let's move on, shall we?"

"Let's," I said.

She invited the Bellissimo to a conflict resolution roundtable with Bling-Bling at which she would mediate.

"No."

I accidentally did it again.

"Excuse me?"

"No, thank you," I said.

"Do you understand that if you're not willing to own your negative feelings for Bling-Bling and resolve your issues peacefully through me, a neutral party who only wants what's best for everyone, your chances of a mutually beneficial relationship with your new neighbors are slim?"

"My negative feelings?" Had I heard her right? "What do my feelings have to do with a galvanized rod missile launching off their thirty-two-story roof in the dead of night destroying a three-tiered infinity pool overlooking the Gulf that would have impaled one, or maybe forty, of our guests had it shot off their roof during the day? The damage is well documented. Maybe you should take a look then tell me how we're supposed to resolve it peacefully. We woke to an annihilated pool, a poolside patio restaurant destroyed, a flooded pool deck, hundreds of thousands of dollars in outdoor furniture and landscaping lost, with a twelve-foot-long galvanized flagpole buried two feet into what's left of a concrete pool floor. There's a crater at the bottom of what used to be our pool the size of a two-car garage. What, Starling, other than them owning their negligence and paying for the damage, would be a mutually beneficial ending?"

She inhaled sharply. "Do you understand those are hurtful words?"

"I understand Bling-Bling doesn't follow the rules, which I agree is hurtful. And dangerous."

"I understand it's easier to believe your own narrative."

"I believe a tragedy was barely averted and that we're down a swimming pool that's won a *Travel + Leisure* Luxurious Outdoor Spaces Award every year since it opened. Did you know Lisa Marie Presley's front team was here a month ago to look at our pool as a possible venue for her fifth wedding? That's out the window. Do you want to know how it happened, Starling? Ask the mobster who moved in next door. Have you seen *The Godfather*? He's my new neighbor. I'd encourage you to read up on him. Jimmy 'Tick-Tock' Russo just walked away as free as a bird after a three-year investigation and a two-year trial without a single conviction. Why? Because the feds couldn't find the dead bodies. Or the millions upon millions of dollars of ill-gotten gains everyone knows he is sitting on. Would you like to know where all that evidence is, Starling? Next door." I promise I tried to stop myself, but I couldn't. "Tick-Tock Russo moved the dead bodies and the dirty money to Biloxi. Look into it, would you? And while you're at it, take a look at their property. Bling-Bling was built under the sloppiest conditions you could ever imagine, and not one inch of their building is up to code, and that's how we lost our pool. The pool we need them to replace. Those are my beliefs."

She cleared her throat. Her tone was decidedly a notch less friendly when she said, "Spreading false and misleading information can have negative effects on your mental health."

I said, "You let me worry about my mental health."

There was silence. No snappy retort from either of us. It went on to the point of phone chicken. I won when she said, "I understand the Bellissimo doesn't want competition."

Maybe I hadn't won. Because that made me madder than I already was. "It has nothing to do with competition. We're already one of a dozen Biloxi casinos. We know all about competition. Competition is good for the marketplace. This isn't about competition."

She said, "What I'm hearing is the prettiest girl in class doesn't want a new girl moving in who might be a little prettier."

I pulled the phone away from my head and stared at it a minute, then asked, "Are you even a real counselor?" to which she snapped, "You can't choose your neighbors. But you *can* choose how you respond to them."

"We were lied to by the city, the county, and the state of Mississippi about who and what our neighbors would be. How do you suggest we respond to lies?"

She said, "Labeling and name calling hurts you more than it hurts anyone else."

I rolled my eyes around and around. "Hurt will be the least of it. People are going to die when Bling-Bling's building implodes."

She said, "Do you understand that if you'd change your perspective and take a more positive approach, everything else might fall into place?"

"I'll tell you what's going to fall, Starling. Thirty-two floors of their hotel are going to fall. They're going to collapse on top of their casino. Thousands of people will die. That's what I understand."

She said, "My job is not to listen to your conspiracy theories."

I said, "What exactly is your job?"

She hesitated a beat before rushing out her next words. "This is a one-time offer. Meet me at the coffee shop in your lobby and I'll explain my job to you."

"Are you talking about Beans? Our coffee shop?" I asked. "You're in our lobby?"

"I am."

I thought about it a minute, then said, "Sit tight."

I hung up.

Fantasy, who'd slept all night, therefore probably in a much better humor than me, was at her desk to my right dealing with her own drama, paying no attention to mine, because I went on and on about Bling-Bling every day. She was on the phone with Reggie, her freelance sportswriter husband who worked from home, explaining bleach. "It's your own fault, Reggie. You don't pour bleach straight into the washing machine. You carefully pour it into the bleach dispenser." Silence. "No, I can't fix it." Silence. "Because some things can't be fixed. You have seventy other football shirts." Silence. "Sorry. Jerseys." Silence. "It's one word, Reggie. Heirloom. And the H is silent. You're saying it like two words, 'hair' and 'loom,' like you say, 'sand' and 'witch' instead of sandwich. And wouldn't your football shirt be a collectible? Which is different than an heirloom?" Silence. "JERSEY. Football JERSEY. Sorry." Silence. "Anything can be replaced." Silence. "Well, I'm not dead. Get another shirt with his name on it and I'll sign it for you."

Baylor, just Baylor, was on my left and on his phone too watching his newborn son sleep via a smart baby monitor.

"Baylor."

He held up a finger. "I'm sleep tracking Little Dude, Davis."

Baylor, a new and nervous parent, was forever watching his son on his phone or on one of the ten surveillance monitors he'd installed all over, under, and around his condo, because he lived in fear of his son being kidnapped. And held for casino ransom. "I'm one of seven people who can get into a vault of a billion-dollar casino, Davis. I have to protect my son." I understood his concerns—I was pretty much in the same boat—but I hadn't hired a data protection company to scrub me from the internet or turned my home into Fort Knox.

"Take your phone downstairs and sleep track Little Dude at Beans."

Still glued to his phone, he said, "I don't like coffee."

I reached for the closest thing I could find, which was a small square sticky-note pad, then tossed it, aiming for his head, and told him to try a latte. He caught the pad midair without taking his eyes off his phone and threw it back. I didn't catch it. "Go." I rubbed my nose, then bent for the sticky-note pad that had bounced off it. "Starling Halter is waiting at Beans. Go meet with her."

"The liaison chick?"

"That's her."

"Why can't you go?"

"Because I work undercover." Which was true. Fantasy and I both kept low Bellissimo profiles so we could sneak around, especially me, because there was another element to my job, that of dressing up in designer duds and convincing the media and the public I was actually the owner's wife. For that reason alone, I stayed behind the curtain. "You don't work undercover." Also true. Baylor wandered the halls regularly and everyone knew he was high on the security ladder, but no one knew exactly how high. "I don't want the casino liaison to know who I am," I said. "I don't mind her knowing who you are."

"What am I supposed to meet with her about?" he asked. "The dead bodies you think are buried in the walls at Bling-Bling?"

To which I said, "I doubt they hid dead bodies in the walls."

"Have you been up all night with your binoculars again, Davis?" Fantasy asked.

I'd upgraded to a telescope. Two, in fact, which I didn't share, instead telling Baylor, "Talk the liaison into going next door to Bling-Bling for a big fat check to repair our pool."

"How much?"

"A million dollars."

"And if I can't squeeze a million dollars out of her?"

"You're not asking her to dip into her savings. You're asking her to squeeze a million out of Bling-Bling."

"And if I can't—"

"Then sit there and listen to her psychobabble until you can. You might learn something."

We didn't see Baylor for the rest of the day.

The next morning, while the three of us sat at our desks wondering what we'd do that day other than run background checks on job applicants because so many of our employees were being snaked by Bling-Bling, I asked Baylor how it went.

"She's smart."

"That's how it went?" I asked. "She's smart?"

"And she's nice," he said. "She just wants everyone to get along."

"What about our pool?" I asked.

"What about it?" he asked back. "Aren't you in charge of the pool?"

"I am *not* in charge of the pool."

Fantasy leaned into the conversation. "Did she say why she doesn't wear clothes?"

"She wears clothes," Baylor said. "She had on pants and a flower shirt thing. No sleeves."

"It's called a halter top, Baylor," I said. "It's her signature article of clothing."

"That's kinda cool because her name is Starling Halter. Get it?"

I got it.

"Did you discuss our pool at all?" I asked.

"What about our pool?" he asked back.

Deep down, and, I had to admit, on top too, I loved Baylor. He reminded me of a child star who'd survived a uniquely challenging childhood most would struggle to find their way past, but then exceeded everyone's expectations on the other side when he grew up to be a law-and-order guy instead of a street thug living under a bridge. Either that, or a puppy. Baylor reminded me of a puppy too. Cute, funny, never met a stranger, but had to be supervised, reined in, and held back from jumping into the mail truck because he thought it'd be fun to ride around the neighborhood all day. Then grew up to be a K-9 police dog. Who still chased the mail truck. In many ways, having skated by on his boyish charm, good looks, and million-dollar smile since reaching the age of accountability, part of him still stood at the edge of adulting unwilling to take the final step. I knew very little of Baylor's past, because he knew very little of it. It wasn't like he kept secrets. It was more like he didn't know. Left on the steps of a New Orleans parish orphanage as an infant, then two-plus decades later plucked from Bellissimo vault duty by No Hair to join my team, I could only fill the blank space past his semi-formal education with extreme sports, tequila, and women. Until he met a girl who would change his life forever. Although he still loved extreme sports and tequila. He was fiercely loyal, reliable when it counted most, and a deadeye with firearms. Any firearm. But still, after Fantasy and I doing our best to raise him right since we'd been given custody of him, and after becoming a father, which one would think would dropkick him to maturity, he continued to say things like, "What about our pool?"

"What about our pool, Baylor? It's destroyed," I reminded him.

"I know."

I took a deep breath of patience. "Did Starling say she'd go to bat for us with Bling-Bling so they'll pay for the rebuild of our pool?"

"She didn't say anything about the pool. But she did say you have anger issues. Probably because deep down you don't like your dad."

The room grew so quiet, I heard my own head slowly turning his way in time with my jaw dropping. Nothing could be further from the truth. There were certainly times my mother and I butted heads, but I worshiped the ground my father walked on. Baylor watched me take the slap to my heart, backing away, holding both palms up in surrender. "I didn't say it. She did."

I stood slowly. I turned for the door. Fantasy asked my back where I was going. I waved instead of answering. Ten minutes later, I was sneaking in the private door of my husband's office on the executive floor. I caught him on a conference call about the subject of the day, our wrecked pool. He gave me a wink and a nod. The wink was all for me. The nod was to a chair.

I sat.

Biloxi's newly appointed mayor, Celeste Reed, was mid-sentence. "—had dinner last night with our new liaison, Jimmy Russo's daughter, and your Baylor."

I sat up straighter. Bling-Bling Jimmy "Tick-Tock" Russo's daughter? In all my research of Jimmy "Tick-Tock" Russo, I hadn't come across a daughter. And Starling the haltered liaison? And Baylor? Our Baylor?

Dinner?

"How'd it go?" Bradley asked.

"Good stuff," I heard our chief of police, recently appointed by our recently appointed mayor, Hugh Warner, say. "I had the Eggplant Josephine."

"I meant was any progress made," Bradley said, then hit the mute button on his phone to quickly ask me, "Did you know Baylor went to dinner with the mayor, chief of police, the Bling-Bling daughter, and the new casino liaison person last night?" I shook my head no. He disabled the mute feature on his phone. "What about our pool?"

"What about it?" the mayor replied.

"Bling-Bling's construction destroyed it. We've canceled all pool events for the season," he said, "including concerts, weddings, and poolside gaming. Guests are choosing other resorts because we've lost our primary outdoor amenity."

"And I'm so sorry about that, Mr. Cole."

"Can the casino liaison assist?"

"Can she replace your pool?" A short laugh from Mayor Reed. "I don't think so."

"Let me put it another way," he said. "Can the new liaison facilitate Bling-Bling accepting responsibility for our pool?"

"Mr. Cole," the mayor said, "do you want to accept responsibility for *their* pool?"

He looked away for an exasperated beat. "For the *damage* to our pool," he said, "caused by their negligence."

The mayor said, "That is not within the purview of her responsibilities. Or mine, for that matter. So don't ask me to replace your pool either."

"How about the building permits I've repeatedly requested from your office, Mayor Reed. Are those within the purview of your responsibilities?"

"Tell me again what you'd like to see, Mr. Cole."

"Again, Mayor Reed, everything." Bradley had asked the city for the same documents so many times he had the list memorized. "The site design, building use permit, parking permit, signage permit. The stormwater management permit—" he picked up speed "—site erosion control permit, construction erosion control permit. All of it," he said, "plus the property survey maps."

"My people still can't lay their hands on any of it," Mayor Reed said. "We don't know where the Bling-Bling paperwork took off to. And at the same time, we don't understand or, frankly, appreciate your interest."

Bradley looked at me in a can-you-believe-this way. "Their property bumps up against ours," he said. "That's reason enough for my interest. Which is aside from the fact that I'm asking for public records well within my rights. I find it hard to believe your people can't find a single building permit issued to Bling-Bling. I find it even harder to believe you aren't more concerned, Mayor Reed. Are there building permits?"

"Of course there are," the mayor said. "Somewhere."

Out of nowhere, Police Chief Warner said, "That Starling's a real looker. And she sure took a shine to your boy."

"What does that have to do with building permits and survey maps?" Bradley asked.

"Maybe the smokin' hot new girl can find them for you if your boy Baylor asks real sweet," the chief suggested.

"Chief Warner." His boss's tone was crisp. "Don't be inappropriate."

"'Scuse me, ma'am."

"And don't interrupt."

"'Scuse me again, ma'am."

"Mr. Cole," the mayor patronized, "we understand the Bellissimo wanted the property that was sold to Bling-Bling. As I've explained to you repeatedly, that was a simple oversight on the part of my new administration, and we're very sorry, but what's done is done. And we understand Bellissimo feelings were hurt as a result. So much so that there've been certain members of your internal security team, or possibly just one member, who have leveled grave accusations at Bling-Bling, which naturally, has upset them."

I squirmed in my seat.

"And I understand your private residence is on the west side of the Bellissimo and Bling-Bling is blocking your view," the mayor went on, "for which, again, we're very sorry. My suggestion to you would be to embrace your new view and, like us, see progress. And we understand you will experience a *temporary* migration of employees and loss of guest traffic because a new casino is opening, Mr. Cole, a situation we feel certain will correct itself in due time. But you need to understand our new casino liaison's job isn't to build you a new pool or speed up the wheels of municipality management. My advice to you is to file a claim with your own insurance company to repair your pool, and I'd rather you not bother Starling Halter with your requests for documents not pertaining to your own business, but to that of your new competition's. Her job is to help you love your neighbor. Not find blueprints. Reach out to her. I promise, she'll help you cope with all the changes you're dealing with, because not only is change good, it's inevitable."

Shaking his head in disbelief with his finger poised over the button to disconnect the call, Bradley said, "I'll take it into consideration." He thanked them for their time, told everyone to have a nice day, then hung up.

We sat quietly, our eyes locked across his desk, sharing the same thought: something was up. There was more to the Bling-Bling story than we were being told. It was as if the city was aiding and abetting Bling-Bling, or at the very least, turning a blind eye. Probably because they didn't want to be fished out of the Gulf wearing concrete boots. Our new mayor, appointed by our old governor by executive declaration when our duly elected former mayor dropped off the face of the earth, wouldn't help. And she'd plucked Biloxi's new chief of police off the evidence locker desk. He was so out of his league, he couldn't help. It almost felt conspiratorial. But to what end? If their goal was for the Bellissimo to close, they were well on their way to getting their wish. We couldn't, for the life of us, come up with any other motive the city could possibly have for allowing Bling-Bling to slap up their ticking time bomb of a building, for all the stonewalling with us, and the worst, promising help was on the way then sending it in the form of Starling Halter, who so far wasn't helping at all.

Bradley stood. He walked around his desk, kissed the top of my head, and took the seat beside me. "So much for the liaison," he said. "Apparently she's not in the pool repair or document recovery business."

"Now what?" I asked.

"We wait this out. We watch. We protect the Bellissimo as best we can. It isn't personal, Davis. It's business."

It felt personal.

"What about Starling Halter?" I asked.

"What about her? You heard Chief Warner."

"I did. Try the Eggplant Josephine."

"That, and she likes Baylor. Put Baylor on liaison detail."

"I already did."

"Put him on permanent liaison detail."

"That's not a bad idea."

"I'm full of good ideas," he said. "Is that why you're here? In search of a good idea?"

I turned to seriously look him in the eye. I started and stopped twice, wondering, with all he had on his plate, if I should even bother him before I finally said, "Bradley, do I have anger issues?"

With a flash of surprise at the odd question considering the gravity of the conversation we'd been in the middle of, the anxiety on his face fell away to be replaced with a look of deep concentration. "Well." He tapped his chin. He studied me. "You get mad at my mother."

"Bradley, everyone gets mad at your mother. Your mother probably wakes up mad at herself every day of her life."

"And Willow." He let the mother business go. "You get mad at the school."

"So do you."

"Are you saying I have anger issues?" He pointed at himself. "I thought we were talking about you."

His phone rang.

We stared at it until it stopped.

"No." His attention was mine again. "You don't have anger issues per se."

I let the per se part go.

"Why?" he asked. "Who said you had anger issues?"

"Starling Halter."

"Her again." He shifted in his seat. "Forget her. It sounds like we won't get any further with the liaison than we're getting with the mayor. Let Baylor handle Starling Halter."

I took his advice.

In fact, I took it and ran with it.

Back at my desk, I scrolled through the caller ID log on my desk phone, found the number Starling had called from the day before, wrote it out in fat black Sharpie, and taped the note beside the phone. Starling wasn't my problem, and that started with not taking another call from her. It wasn't an hour later, while I was on my cell phone with the Fisheries Division of the Mississippi Department of Marine Resources because strange creatures were either making their underground way or jumping from the Gulf into the gurgling ocean water seeping into the massive hole in our pool floor, that Starling's number popped up on the caller ID of the desk phone.

The fisherman said, "I have no idea why the water is gurgling. Gurgling means bubbles. Bubbles mean air. Air means digging. Are you digging?" I gave Fantasy all the signals to take the Starling call and told the fisherman, "No, I'm not digging." Fantasy answered the Starling call with, "Make it quick," as the fisherman said, "Could they be air pockets rather than bubbles?" I said, "I wouldn't know," as Fantasy said, "Who?" The fisherman asked if the creatures in the gurgling air pocket bubbles had tentacles, which meant they might be baby octopi, then asked me if I was familiar with baby octopi. I wouldn't have been able to come up with an appropriate answer if he'd given me a week, so I said, "Could I put you on hold for a minute?" just in time to hear Fantasy say, "He's unavailable." She tapped an impatient foot. "Because he isn't available." She rolled her eyes. "He's at lunch, okay? He's out of the office." She twirled a crazy finger at her temple. "What are you talking about, Sterling?" I could hear Starling's tinny voice through the receiver but couldn't make out what she was saying. "Sure thing. I'll call you Starling if you want me to." Then Fantasy listened at length. I was about to grab the receiver from her and put the call on speaker so I could hear what the liaison was saying when she stopped me with, "That's none of your business. If you want to know if Baylor's married, ask him." Starling probably said something to Fantasy about feeling her feelings, then Fantasy said, "No, I will not give you his address." Starling probably said something to Fantasy about centering herself, then Fantasy said, "No, I will not give you his cell phone number either." Starling probably said something to Fantasy about checking in with her inner child, then Fantasy said, "I'll have him call you."

She hung up.

I made a list of everything I could remember overhearing Bradley tell the mayor he needed: learner's permits, burn permits, health permits. When Baylor finally did drag back in from lunch with Little Dude, which was him eating enough Taco Bell for a family of five while watching the baby sleep, I passed the list to him. "Starling wants you to call her. Set something up."

"Like what?" He stared at the list.

"Maybe not dinner, since you had dinner with her last night."

Fantasy leaned past me. "You what, Baylor? You had dinner with Sterling?"

"I did not."

"I know for a fact you did," I said. "Why would you lie about dinner?"

"Who lies about dinner, Davis? Starling was late, okay? I had dessert with her," he said. "That's different from dinner."

"So who'd you have dinner with?" Fantasy asked.

"Celeste the mayor, Warner the chief, and the Bling-Bling woman."

"The Russo daughter?"

"I only had dinner with her. No dessert," he said.

"You had dinner with one and dessert with the other?" Fantasy asked. "Which one was with Sterling?"

"Her name is Starling," he said. "And mind your own business, Fantasy."

She said, "Your business is my business, Baylor."

I added, "Mine too."

He said, "Is not."

I gave the list a nod. "Call her back, set something up, and tell her we need everything I wrote down on Bling-Bling."

He perused the list again. "There's no such thing as a pollution permit. That doesn't even make sense. A permit to pollute?"

A week later, back at our desks in our sub-basement offices, Baylor, who'd been missing in action the whole week, because when he wasn't with Little Dude, he'd been with Starling who'd been feeding him a steady diet of parenting psychobabble including, "Be the baby. Walk a mile in the baby's booties," had nothing for us. No hint of compensation for our pool. Not a single Bling-Bling building permit. "Give me a minute," he kept saying. "I'm making lots of personal progress."

"It's been a week, Baylor. You've made enough personal progress."

"Davis, emotional growth takes a lifetime."

"That's it." I smacked the gavel down. "We're done with Starling."

"How can you be done with her?" he snapped. "You've never even met her."

"I saw her on television last night with Bling-Bling's Vice President of Food and Beverage. Does that count?"

"You need to reflect on repairing your relationships."

I turned to Fantasy, who'd stayed out of it, in a help-me way. She leaned past me to make eye contact. "Baylor, you're done with Sterling."

He said, "Her name is Starling."

She said, "You're done with her too."

I jumped back in. "Baylor, how can it not be obvious to you that she cares nothing about helping us and everything about sidetracking us with her psycho gibberish?"

"Sidetrack us from what?" he asked.

"From all the dead bodies and dirty money next door."

To which he said, "No one believes that except you."

So I said, "That's not true."

Then he said, "Davis, it is. The FBI crawled all over every square inch of Bling-Bling and didn't find a single dead body or ten dollars of blood money. Much less the stack of dead bodies and millions of dollars you say are there. You have trust issues."

My trust issues and I rolled our eyes Fantasy's way for support.

She pressed her lips together, looked away, and hummed.

"Fantasy!"

"Davis, I believe that you believe Tick-Tock hid all the evidence against him somewhere at Bling-Bling."

"Which is entirely different than you believing it too, Fantasy. If you don't believe the evidence is there, it's like not believing in me."

"See?" Baylor said. "Trust issues."

I sat on my trust-issue-riddled hands for the next five weeks, Starling having hissy fits because Baylor was suddenly unavailable to her and retaliating by ramping up the "Bling-Bling's the BEST!" rhetoric to a level I never dreamed was possible, all in a misguided effort to welcome Bling-Bling to Biloxi, which I believed was really to make us mad enough to give her access to Baylor again, until, as scheduled, Bling-Bling opened. In the meantime, I took on the pool job. I hired the only construction company I could find that could start work on rebuild of our annihilated pool immediately, Rivera Outdoor Elegance from Gurnee, Illinois. The foreman, a man named Dunk, looked like Popeye and had a five-pack-a-day voice. He and his crew of seventy moved in and took over the fourth floor of our hotel. The first thing they did was slap up a tent in our backyard large enough to cover a small city. To the tune of one and a half million. Dollars. While I was at it, I hired structural engineers to covertly kick the tires at Bling-Bling and tell me if their building was as dangerously unsound as I suspected. To the tune of two hundred thousand. Dollars. (They gave Bling-Bling a C-minus on physical integrity and predicted that if it didn't cave in or burn to the ground first, because their fire code violations were so flagrant, in one to three years, the entire resort would start slowly sinking into the Gulf.) And I quietly hired a team of surveyors to establish the boundary lines between us and our annoying neighbors. To the tune of fifty thousand. Dollars. It was when the surveyors presented their findings I learned Bling-Bling's parking garage, upon which they'd built their topless pool, had spilled six feet onto our property, at which point I finally had something solid to take to Bradley, which in turn finally gave us a leg of our own to stand on.

No thanks to Starling Halter.

Several days later, my team was called to Legal. The three of us sat at one end of a long conference table while ten of them menacingly circled the other.

The man in the middle said, "Mrs. Cole. Did anyone on your team ask our pool construction crew to keep an eye out for dead bodies?"

I looked at Fantasy, who shook her head no, then to Baylor, who also shook his head no, so I said, "No."

A suit on the spokesman's right said, "Did anyone on your team ask the structural engineers working for us to keep an eye out for money laundering inside Bling-Bling?"

I went through the same routine again, asking my team if they'd had the nerve to ask engineers on our payroll to look for millions in funny money being circulated through the casino next door. Fantasy and Baylor denied that too. So I said, "No."

Then the suit to the left of the spokesperson said, "Mrs. Cole, did anyone on your team ask our surveyors to use infrared technology to search for hidden rooms at Bling-Bling?"

And for the third time, after confirming neither Fantasy nor Baylor had asked the surveyors to find the evidence Chicago's Organized Crime Unit of fifty dedicated federal agents couldn't, I said, "No."

After lots of shuffling in their seats and throat clearing, mostly because their boss was my husband, we were told in no uncertain terms to shift our focus completely away from Bling-Bling and totally back to the Bellissimo until our team could get an audience with the Mississippi Gaming Commission in Jackson to present our findings regarding six feet of their parking garage on our property and advise the commission of our litigious intentions. In the meantime, back off before we found ourselves in serious defamation territory. Bling-Bling wasn't our problem. We were told to mind our own Bellissimo business. Ignore what might or might not be going on next door.

How? How were we supposed to ignore what might or might not be going on next door? Not only was I convinced old Tick-Tock, who had yet to show his face in Biloxi, was hiding all the evidence against him the feds couldn't produce in Chicago, I was equally convinced there was a reason he chose to reestablish himself in Biloxi. He could have relocated his nefarious operation to Vegas. Or Atlantic City. Or Detroit, St. Louis, or Philadelphia. But he chose Biloxi. For a reason.

I just didn't know what it was.

All I knew, and my only path forward, was based upon the fact that there couldn't possibly be an inch of their massive structure on the beach that was up to code. Fire alarms going off were one thing. Slowly sliding into the Gulf was another. But what if the wind suddenly blew the wrong way—it happened in the Gulf; we called it hurricane season—and their entire house of cards came crashing into ours? And how was I supposed to ignore what I believed to be an imminent danger to the public inside the gated walls of their resort? But the worst, the very worst, was the feeling that something wasn't right at Bling-Bling to the point of being really wrong. Cases in that point: our mayor abruptly retired and we got a new one we did not choose a year earlier, our former police chief was demoted to beat cop and replaced by a man who didn't know what day of the week it was, the land next door to us was sold in a pocket deal to strangers from Chicago who slapped up a jalopy of a building under the cover of night, our pool was mysteriously destroyed, we were assigned an ineffective negotiator who, as it turned out, had morphed into nothing short of a Bling-Bling ambassador, and in light of all that, we were being told by Bellissimo Legal to walk away.

That night after we put the girls to bed, a chilled bottle of pinot grigio between us, I asked my husband, "Do you know something I don't?"

Bradley scratched his neck. An affirmation if there ever was one.

"So many things, Davis. I know so many things you don't."

"Like what?"

"Like how to change a tire."

"I could change a tire if I had to."

"Yes, but you don't actually know how to change a tire."

"You take the bad tire off and put a good tire on."

"Where's the spare tire in your new car?"

I let that slide. "What else?"

"I understand the offside rule."

"I've never even heard of the offside rule," I said. "What else?"

He stared into his wine glass, then at me. "Where are we going with this?"

"Do you know something about Bling-Bling I don't?"

"Do I *know* something about Bling-Bling you don't? I doubt it."

"Do you suspect something about Bling-Bling I don't?"

"Such as?"

"Such as Jimmy 'Tick-Tock' Russo isn't running the show."

"What's that supposed to mean?"

I leaned in and whispered, "Maybe he's dead."

Bradley leaned in and did not whisper. "Davis, where is this coming from?"

"The one and only time I talked to the liaison, Starling, I asked her if she'd seen *The Godfather*. That was weeks ago. In that time, I've come to realize I haven't seen The Godfather. No one's seen The Godfather."

"Everyone's seen *The Godfather*."

"Everyone's seen the movie, but no one's seen Tick-Tock Russo. I sure haven't. Have you?"

He didn't answer, which was answer enough.

"All this Bling-Bling business on television," I said, "and not one appearance from him."

Bradley stared at his wine.

"Do you know, Bradley, that the most recent picture of Russo I can find is him leaving the courthouse in Chicago after all charges against him were dropped?"

Bradley stared through his wine.

"Have you seen him around town? Has anyone?"

"Davis." Bradley stared over his wine. "Don't let this be your new thing. We have no reason to believe Tick-Tock Russo isn't alive and well. Just because you haven't seen him doesn't mean he's dead. Please don't start that rumor."

I leaned in. "Something's going on at Bling-Bling, Bradley. You know there is. And one of these days, their problems will be our problems."

He moved the wine bottle so it wasn't between us. He chose his words carefully. "Legal's directive to cease and desist all inquiries pertaining to Bling-Bling came straight from me."

I didn't doubt that. Legal worked for him. We all worked for him. "Why, Bradley? When you know as well as I do something's not right at Bling-Bling."

He polished off the wine in his glass and reached for the bottle. He topped off my glass and poured himself another. "Because we have our own business to run." Then came a small speech, the subjects he covered being those of counting on me to keep myself out of harm's way for our daughters' sakes, for his sake, a subject he stayed on a while before moving on to expecting me to set a good example for my team by doing my job and only my job.

"So, let me get this straight, Bradley. You think everything is on the up-and-up at Bling-Bling?"

He said, "I think what matters is keeping our own resort open, Davis, and on a more personal level, I think you need to back off. You're looking left when you should be looking right. You're looking up and you need to be looking down. You're looking over and you need to be looking under."

Was he saying I'd overlooked something or was he saying I needed to look under something? If so, what would that be? Under the sea? Under every rock? Under our noses?

Undercover.

He meant undercover.

I was pretty sure he meant undercover, but he'd also issued the edict for me to not leave him raising Bex and Quinn alone and to keep my focus on the Bellissimo. I took that to mean he didn't want me undercover at Bling-Bling. But I also took it as permission to send someone else. So I sent Baylor. Without formally running it by anyone. And by anyone, I meant him, Bradley, Bellissimo President and CEO, also my husband, or the Bellissimo Vice President of Security, also our boss, No Hair, who both, along with Legal, told me to mind my own Bellissimo business. Well, the welfare of the Bellissimo was my business. Public safety was my business too.

I set about minding my business.

The next morning, I said to my team, "I have an idea."

They replied, "Oh, no."

I said, "Hear me out. I think we should quietly dig a little deeper. Get a better feel for Bling-Bling. Find what we might have overlooked."

"Like what?" Fantasy asked.

"Like hard evidence," I answered.

"Hard evidence of what?" Baylor asked.

"Don't start with the dead bodies and dirty money again, Davis," Fantasy said. "You're going to get us all killed."

"No one who isn't already dead is going to die," I said. "But what if we had their building condemned? That would take care of everything else. Like when Al Capone was nailed for not paying taxes."

Fantasy picked up her phone.

"Who are you calling?" I asked.

"My lawyer," she said. "I need to update my will."

Big chickens. Both of them. But they agreed to go along with it only because they agreed with me that having already been told by our own covert contractors that Bling-Bling's building was unstable wasn't enough. Being told wasn't proof. We needed proof. "Baylor," I said, "you're going undercover."

"Cool," he said.

The first day, Fantasy and I decked him out in jeans, a t-shirt, ballcap, and sunglasses and sent him for ice cream at Ben and Jerry's in Bling-Bling's food court. Every flavor. So he could listen in on food court conversations to get a feel for the place. The next, we dressed him up in a sports jacket and khakis with spiked corporate hair to play Keno all afternoon, chatting it up with the Keno girls to hear what the staff had to say. Then the day after that, disguised as Harley Davidson's number one fan in distressed leather to sit at the bar in their high-stakes poker room and pry information out of their patrons. The disguises served two purposes: so Bling-Bling wouldn't recognize him and so our least favorite Kumbaya Liaison and Bling-Bling's biggest fan, Starling Halter, wouldn't either. If Bling-Bling caught Baylor snooping, the jig would be up. If Starling Halter spotted him—the same Starling Halter who rang our office phone off the desk and showed up almost daily demanding to see or speak to Baylor—she might abduct him and we'd never see him again. Because she'd become borderline obsessed.

So far, Baylor had helped us build a nice dossier on our frustrating neighbor we were supposed to be ignoring. We had photos of deep and winding cracks in their brand-new walls, video of a bank of elevators that never stopped on the right floors, and documentation of a wide swath of crumbled foundation under their casino. Bling-Bling's security would catch Baylor snooping around soon enough, but until they did, we had him gathering intel on their death trap of a building and—bonus—their sloppy casino practices. We had video footage of cash payouts to slip, trip, and fall victims of their uneven casino floor, restaurant health code violations that bordered on criminal, and lots of documentation about an unusual group of employees they called casino hostesses. We called them prostitutes. When we had enough loosey-goosey gaming shenanigans and sloppy-structure evidence to keep all three of us awake at night—Baylor said it was Little Dude keeping him awake, not Bling-Bling—and thinking enough time had passed with me keeping my Bling-Bling nose clean, I quietly asked Baylor to start snooping into the money end of things.

"They're not laundering money, Davis. There's no evidence of it at all."

"I didn't mean that." (I'd meant that.) I went on to tell him I was talking about pesky little matters like where'd they get the money to build the monstrosity outside my bedroom window in the first place? There was no documentation of financing on the property, the building, its contents, or their enormous operation. Who had that much cash on hand? Not only did we not know where the money came from, we didn't know where all the money they were generating was going. They certainly weren't paying it out in the casino. We had yet to hear a word about a big win, and oddly enough, were seeing a slew of foot traffic from their casino to ours, but the players only stayed at our house long enough to win enough money to take back to theirs. Where they lost it again. If they kept it up, someone would circulate a petition asking for a skybridge soon. And what was up with Bling-Bling's secret gaming room under the main casino? Baylor knew it was there, because he watched black suits sneak in and out of the Private Gaming elevator on a loop, but he couldn't figure out exactly where it went. And what went on when it arrived at its unknown destination, because he hadn't seen a high roller enter the Private Gaming elevator even once. Just the Bling-Bling suits. Never Tick-Tock Russo. Just his henchmen.

"Maybe Bling-Bling's high rollers use another entrance," I said.

"Nope," Baylor said. "I've looked."

"Maybe that's where Tick-Tock Russo is hanging out, Baylor."

"In the private gaming room in their basement?"

"You just said you haven't seen him one single time."

"Not once," he said.

"Maybe you're not looking hard enough."

"I'm over there all day every day, Davis."

We thought about it a minute.

"Maybe the private gaming room in the basement is where they switch out the games."

"Could be," I said, because Bling-Bling's slot machines were completely electronic. No old school three-reel slot machines anywhere. With the push of a control button, Bling-Bling could have everyone playing the same game. All over the casino. It was the latest and greatest in electronic gaming. And unfortunately for us, the players loved it. In spite of the fact that they never won. "But I doubt it."

"Could the old guy still be in Chicago?"

"Why would he be? His operation is here, Baylor. Find him."

With all that going on, we only saw Baylor when we tracked him down. When he wasn't at Bling-Bling or fending off Starling, he was with his new baby, which was where everyone else (my husband and my boss) assumed he was when he was nowhere to be found, and that was time he (understandably) refused to give up.

"Little Dude needs me."

"I know," I said.

"You don't understand—"

"I do understand."

"No, you don't."

Since the day that child was born, he'd insisted Fantasy and I didn't understand. Fantasy had three teenage sons. Their names all started with K. I had too-smart-for-their-own-britches preschoolers. I think we understood. Right up until the day our surveillance techs ate doped donuts, our casino hiccupped their way to hearing loss, and our boss, No Hair, demanded I send Baylor to help. An hour into that long morning, I didn't understand a thing.

Except I needed Baylor back.

Friday, 10:02 A.M.

After trying to reach Baylor several times by phone with no luck, I went back to the rest of the punch list hearing-impaired No Hair had screamed at me. I disabled Wi-Fi in the casino. Then asked more than twelve hundred guests and eighty hotel employees to shelter in place. After that, I called in backup security at double overtime pay and gave them their marching orders—five on guard at the locked front doors, two guarding each of the side-door entrances to the casino, and one on every hotel floor. To keep the peace. All those chores completed, I stared at the phone wondering how to quietly make a biohazard call. I was so vague with the Mississippi Department of Health they gave up and put me through to Mississippi Environmental Protection Agency, who couldn't make heads or tails of my request for a biohazard team for no apparent reason either, so they pawned me off on the National Response Center.

"You're in Biloxi, Mississippi?" a woman asked.

"Yes."

"Is this about red tide?"

We were on the beach. "Sure."

"You're calling about something in the water?" she asked.

"You bet," I said.

"Reports of dry coughs? Itchy eyes?"

Close enough. "Yes."

"Can you see it in the water? Describe the water."

"It's wet."

I listened to her inhale quickly and exhale slowly. "How big a crew do you think you need?"

"What are my choices?"

"Ma'am, do you think there's a threat to public health?"

"The public at large? No." There was definitely a threat to the Bellissimo's health, but that wasn't what she'd asked. And I didn't want the National Response Center sending an army large enough to clean a nuclear waste spill. It was hiccups, and temporary, I hoped, hearing loss.

"Can you give me any details?" the woman asked.

"I can't."

"Why not?"

"Because I'm an operator in the call center. I don't have details." But really because I didn't want to alarm the National Response Center to the point of them issuing some manner of dire warning that would have Starling Halter with her favorite news crew on our doorstep before the biohazard people. At which point, I'd worn down the lady on the phone. She said, "We'll send a response team."

"Thank you."

Fantasy, who'd been busy taking a harder look at Dr. Winford Wurtz while I'd hemmed and hawed with government agencies, said, "Listen to this." She told me that in addition to the patent he held on painkiller dental blankets, Dr. Wurtz was also the architect of no-show socks that promoted hair growth. The socks had been taken off the market after numerous consumer complaints of leg hair growing so fast and thick that users were forced to visit waxing salons almost daily. It would seem the no-show socks promoting hair growth worked too well. And from the bottom up. By the time users had any significant hair growth on their heads, they looked like orangutans everywhere else. I wondered why someone hadn't thought to tape the no-show socks to their heads. Or tuck them inside a ballcap. Wouldn't that work? Regardless, we felt certain Dr. Wurtz was someone we wanted to speak to. If anyone knew what manner of magic to sprinkle on donuts to bring on deep sleep or on twenty-dollar bills to bring on hiccups and hearing loss, it was him.

I minimized the screens I had open to access an internal Bellissimo program showing the keycard activity in the hotel. I found Dr. Wurtz's keycard was used to enter his guest room at eight thirty the night before, but no indication the keycard had been used to exit.

Late sleeper.

And with him still in his hotel room, we wouldn't have to go to the casino.

"For better or for worse, let's go see the doctor." I stood. Slowly.

Fantasy stood. Slowly. Neither of us anxious to leave the safety of our sub-basement offices. "Maybe we can score a few painkiller blankets."

We geared up. For her, that was a Glock 19. For me, it was a Ruger LCR. At the door, preparing for the great unknown, we put it off another ten seconds when my phone buzzed with an incoming text message. I hoped it was Baylor returning my calls, but it wasn't. It was Cricket Robinson. At Willow School for Exceptional Children. *Davis, we really need you to pick up your rabbit. Mrs. Wellesley is highly allergic so we can't keep it in the office. Because of health regulations, we can't keep it in any classrooms or the cafeteria. The rabbit is unusually large and very loud. When it isn't grunting or wheezing, it's grinding its teeth, and if anyone makes eye contact with it, it gets nervous and thumps its big back paws for the next fifteen minutes. It's too disruptive for the Music and Movement room, the Literacy room, or the Dramatic Play room. We put it in the Fitness is Fun room, then had to call the fire department to get it down from a ceiling light fixture because of its ability to propel itself so far, so fast, and so high. Davis, your rabbit is derailing our curriculum and upsetting our entire campus. Are you on the way?* I texted back. *Cricket, the rabbit isn't ours. We have two dogs, Cotton and Candy. We don't have a rabbit. I don't know what makes you think Bex and Quinn brought a rabbit to school in the first place. It sounds to me like another student brought the rabbit and my daughters, being easy targets because of prior misunderstandings, are being blamed.* She texted back. *Bex's backpack is empty except for a collar embroidered with dancing carrots. The tag says Wilhelmina Bunny Girl. Quinn's backpack is full of hay, a cucumber, and radishes.*

Fantasy, reading over my shoulder, said, "Turn off your phone."

"I can't do that." By then, we'd made our way to the bank of hotel elevators. Holding our breath. We stepped into the empty elevator car and punched the button for the fifteenth floor. "What if the school really needed me? What if one of the girls had a fever? Or was hurt on the playground? I have to keep my phone on."

"Who is your call-in-case-of-emergency person?"

"You."

"Leave your phone on."

Too soon, the elevator stopped and the doors parted. We stuck our noses out looking for green vapors, purple mist, or black bubbles in the air. A man in a blue security blazer with a welding helmet on his head and leather driving gloves on his hands waved.

"That's not at all alarming," Fantasy, waving back, said through her teeth.

"Let's hope everyone on this floor is still asleep," I said through mine.

We were almost to room eighteen-fifty without passing a hiccupping or hard-of-hearing soul, or for that matter, anyone else who looked like a hotel guest. The only people we passed were members of our customer comfort staff, and they weren't pushing their cleaning carts. They were clutching their personal belongings, heads down, hugging the wall, and slinking for the service elevator. Right behind them were two in-room dining servers, loosening their neckties and unpinning their name badges on their way out.

I said, "I guess they don't want to shelter in place."

Fantasy said, "It's a mass employee exodus."

My knuckles were resting on the door to Dr. Wurtz's room, but I couldn't bring myself to knock.

"What?"

"Do we really want to go into this room? This man is obviously the source of some manner of invisible dust that causes REM sleep, hiccups, and hearing loss. What else does he have up his sleeve?"

"Do you mean what else does he have in his hotel room?"

"Where else would he hide it? There could be ten more disasters behind this door that could hit us all at once."

"You think if we go in this room we'll leave with three eyeballs, hives, and our knees will be on backwards?"

"That's exactly what I think," I said. "I don't know what hives are, and I don't want to find out."

"How about we talk to him through the door," she said. "We won't go in."

Before I could agree, my phone buzzed with an incoming text message. It wasn't Baylor, it wasn't Cricket Robinson from Willow School for Exceptional Children, but it was, perfect timing, my mother.

Whore R U!

She was, without exception, the world's worst texter. *I'm at work, Mother. Really busy. Can I call you later?*

IM at from dorm % calf git in.

You're at the front door of the Bellissimo? WHY?

Dim U reed the calf git in port?

You can't get in because we're having issues right now. Stay outside of the building and tell me WHY YOU ARE HERE.

Im leafing your farther.

Friday, 10:30 A.M.

Fantasy's knuckles were resting against Dr. Wurtz's guest room door. She knocked. When Dr. Wurtz didn't answer, she knocked with more enthusiasm. "Room service." He still didn't answer. She put her face to the crack between the door and the frame and said it loud enough for the people in the casino who'd lost their hearing to catch every word, "OPEN UP, DOC. IT'S ROOM SERVICE. WE HAVE YOUR ORGANIC PRUNE JUICE." Then to me, "The school again?"

"No," I said. "My mother."

"Why doesn't she ever call when we're not busy?"

"When are we not busy?" I asked.

"How long has it been since we were this busy?" she asked back. "And it's the two of us against the world."

It was. Bradley was in Jackson at the Gaming Commission meeting, No Hair was stuck in the casino, and Baylor was—I checked the time again—where was Baylor? Why hadn't he called?

"What do you want to do?" Fantasy asked. "Stand here all day knocking until the old guy answers or use our passkey and go in?"

"No," I said. "We're going to find Baylor and send him in."

"Why didn't I think of that? Let him slobber on himself and get blisters on his eyeballs. Call him again."

I called him again. "It's ringing." Baylor's morning assignment had been to pose as a restaurant critic and sample the omelets at Bling-Bling. There was something fishy about Bling-Bling sending their high rollers to us for breakfast. Why breakfast? Why send them to us for scrambled eggs from our buffet when they claimed to have world famous omelets at their Goody-Goody Omelet Café? "We'll get him off omelet detail and in this room. That way, if Bradley or No Hair asks about him again, we can say we have him chasing a mad scientist lead."

"And it'll be true."

Baylor's voicemail answered. "Yo," it said. Then, "Go."

"Baylor, where are you?" I asked his voicemail. "We have a situation and it's all hands on deck. Call me the very instant you get this message."

"Now what?" Fantasy asked.

"Let's go back downstairs and dig up masks and gloves and go in the doc's room ourselves."

"I thought we just decided to send Baylor in."

"He didn't answer."

"Wait." Her arm shot out to stop me. "Didn't he say he had a thing today?"

He had. As I was electronically building his food critic dossier, he said he'd rather do it another day.

"Why?" I'd asked.

"Because I'm busy tomorrow."

"Doing what?"

"I can't remember, but something."

"Baylor, Bling-Bling is sending their high rollers to us for breakfast. Which means you need to be there for breakfast."

"Why?"

"Because there has to be a reason they want their high rollers here instead of there that early in the morning. Figure out what it is while you're eating omelets, then after you'll have plenty of time to do your thing."

"If I remember what my thing is."

"Does Little Dude have a doctor's appointment?"

"That was last week."

"Does Little Dude have his tummy time class?"

"That was yesterday."

"Is Little Dude having another photo shoot?"

"That's next week."

"Then what, Baylor?"

"I can't remember."

"Go to Bling-Bling and eat omelets. It'll jog your memory."

As Fantasy and I made our way to the fifteenth-floor elevator, I wondered if the forty omelets he'd had time to eat had jogged his memory, and if that was why he wasn't answering his phone, because he'd remembered his thing without bothering to tell me. But before I could run it by Fantasy, my phone buzzed in my hand.

Fantasy said, "Do you think it's the school or your mother?"

I'd momentarily forgotten my mother was at the front door waiting to come in. And I'd really forgotten her news, that she was leafing my farther. By which she meant leaving my father. A preposterous notion I didn't have the bandwidth for right then and there. "Neither. It's No Hair." And he was FaceTiming. He wanted to see us. Or he wanted us to see him. Before I answered, I flipped my phone around to show Fantasy. Her face, registering that No Hair, who hated FaceTime, was FaceTiming, said, *what now?* My phone between us, I hesitantly accepted the call. And there was No Hair, his face as orange as an Oompa Loompa's. As orange as a basketball. As orange as the worst spray tan ever. His dark eyes blazed at us, the only thing on the screen that wasn't deep burnt orange.

Fantasy leaned in and yelled slowly, exaggerating each word, "WHAT HAPPENED? WHY ARE YOU ORANGE?"

No Hair didn't yell back. "I have carotenemia from Starbucks, Fantasy. Almost everyone in the casino has carotenemia from Starbucks."

She looked at me. "Is that iced coffee?"

I shrugged. "I've never heard of it."

"Davis?" No Hair spat my name. "Did I not tell you to have Baylor bring something safe for us to drink? I didn't ask you to send a Starbucks truck."

I had no idea what he was talking about. "No Hair, I have no idea what you're talking about."

"The Starbucks truck that rolled up to the marina entrance of the casino? You don't remember sending it? After I said lock everything down?"

"No Hair, I still have no idea what you're talking about. I'll admit I didn't lock down the marina, because there is no locking a marina. I locked the bank of doors that lead from the marina to the casino."

"One of your pool guys unlocked the marina doors that lead to the casino. For Starbucks."

"Do you mean one of the construction guys repairing our pool?" I asked. "Those aren't my guys. All I did was hire them. I'm not in charge of them. And I'd like to know what they're doing with the keys to our casino doors."

"I would too," Orange Crush said. "What I do know is someone on the pool crew unlocked the doors, then Starbucks started passing out frozen hippie juice. That was fifteen minutes ago. Now we're all orange. From your Starbucks truck."

"Not my Starbucks truck. I didn't send it. And I've never heard of frozen carrot coffee."

"Carotenemia is a condition. Not a carrot drink. The casino is crawling with pharmacists who say we've been exposed to massive doses of beta carotene. They assume it was delivered via the free caffeine punch from the Starbucks truck you sent."

"You drank coffee?"

"I drank water, Davis. Everything your Starbucks truck brought was dosed with beta carotene. Even the water. And everyone drank something from them. Take a look." He flipped his phone around and gave us a slow panoramic tour of the main aisle of the casino, almost everyone gathered there a shade of orange. I scanned quickly, looking for the ponytailed woman, who I couldn't find, so I took screenshot after screenshot of the orange crowd to look for her later, then disabled FaceTime because my eyes were burning from all the orange just as he said, "Thanks a lot."

"No Hair," I said, "I didn't do this. I didn't send a Starbucks truck. I don't even know what a Starbucks truck is."

"Like a food truck, Davis. A fully staffed rolling Starbucks."

"Does the carrot business have anything to do with the rabbit?"

"What are you talking about?"

"You know," I said. "Rabbits and carrots."

"*What?*"

I thought it best to back away from the subject of the rabbit. I switched gears. "You aren't yelling. Does that mean you can hear?"

"Everyone's hearing has returned. Can you hear me, Davis? Because I'd like to thank you again for a casino full of people with fireball orange skin." Then he yelled again. "WHERE IS THE BIOHAZARD TEAM I ASKED FOR?"

"They should be here any minute," I told him.

By then, we'd reached the fifteenth-floor elevator landing. I put an arm out to stop Fantasy from calling the elevator because I didn't want to drop the call. "Does anyone still have the hiccups?"

"No hiccups," he said, "and we can hear, but we're orange."

I checked the time. "That was an hour of hiccups and an hour of hearing loss. Chances are you'll only be orange for an hour."

The Great Pumpkin thanked me for weighing in with my expert opinion and hung up just as a security alert flashed across my phone screen. The biohazard team had arrived. They were at the front entrance, with, I remembered again, my mother. Before I could call Security and ask them to let both in, my phone rang in my hand. It was my father. Probably to tell me my mother was leafing him. Make that leaving. A text message popped up before I could decide whether or not I should take my father's call. It was Cricket at Willow School for Exceptional Children. *Davis. Your rabbit?*

Not my rabbit.

I fell onto the upholstered bench between tables loaded with floral arrangements across from the elevators. I needed to take a breath. Fantasy plopped down beside me. I hesitantly sent a text message to my mother.

"Who are you texting?"

"My mother," I said. "I'm going to ask her to pick up the rabbit."

"And your birth control pills."

"And my birth control pills."

"Isn't it a bit of a long drive for your mother? All the way from Alabama just to pick up your rabbit?"

"Not my rabbit," I said, "and Mother's at our front door."

"Please tell me you're lying."

"I'm not." I texted. *Mother, are you still waiting to come in?*

She responded immediately. *Wafting om U. Tickling me thumps. Lice I half noting bester to do whiff my thyme.*

Did you drive here, Mother?

Not. I ditch hiked. If course I droves.

Do you remember Grandparents Day at Bex and Quinn's school?

Yas.

Do you remember how to get to their school?

May bee. Wife?

I couldn't ask her to pick up a rabbit and my birth control pills, so I asked her to pick up the girls. By default, she'd pick up the rabbit and birth control pills. *Bex and Quinn need to be picked up.*

Now I's youth Gurl Fridays?

I'm not asking you to be my Girl Friday. Whatever that is. I'm asking you to be my mother. I wouldn't ask you to pick them up if I didn't need your help.

That'd get her.

Fantasy, beside me, privy to every mangled word my mother dictated to her impossible first-generation voice-assisted phone, said, "Why don't you just call her? Wouldn't that be easier than the hieroglyphics?"

"If I called her, she'd launch into the story about why she's leafing my dad."

"She's leafing your dad? What does that mean, leafing?"

"Leaving."

Fantasy's head fell back. The wall caught it. "Oh, boy."

My phone buzzed again. It was Mother. She was on board. *I fill git my grant daughters bee cause I loft them. End bee cause their r 2 many mans hear and I am stick of mans. I nevermore wash to sea a nothing mans in my like. End bee cause their is a women hear whiff her beasts spelling out brothering neveryone bee cause sheet kneads to seethe U.*

"Beasts spelling out brothering neveryone kneads to seethe?" Fantasy, still with her head tipped back, kept one eye on my phone for, I suppose, the comic relief of it all. "What the hell?"

"A woman with her breasts sprawling out bothering everyone because she needs to see me," I translated. "Wonder who."

"Casino Liaison Sterling Halter." She shook her head. "That's all we need."

"Her name is Starling. And I wonder why she's asking for me and not Baylor."

"Why won't that woman give it up with Baylor? It's like she thinks he's the only man-child out there," Fantasy said. "With her big boobs she could get any man-child she wanted. Why Baylor?"

"Who tipped her off something was wrong here?" I wondered aloud.

"How do we know anyone tipped her off? She shows up all the time for no reason whatsoever."

"She shows up hoping she'll run into Baylor."

"Again," she said, "defying logic. And who are the too many mans at the front door your mother is stick of?"

"The hazmat team."

I held my phone like a bomb, waiting for it to go off in my hand again, and when I wasn't on the receiving end of more bad or unintelligible news, I initiated normal human contact with Hospitality. First, I felt them out.

"Hospitality," a woman said.

"This is Davis Way Cole. How are you today?"

"Fine, Mrs. Cole. How are you?"

So whatever was going on in the casino, news hadn't made its way to the second-floor administration offices. Our hotel employees knew something was up because they'd been issued a shelter-in-place order. And Starling Halter had to know it wasn't just another winning day at the Bellissimo, because she was at the front door and couldn't get in. But if Hospitality was still answering the phone as if nothing was wrong, that meant our administrative offices, somewhat isolated at the end of the hall on the executive floor, didn't know yet. "I'm great," I lied. "Are you familiar with the VIP Host offices just outside of the casino?"

"Of course," the woman said.

"Great again." The VIP Host offices would be empty. Mostly because the VIP hosts stayed up late with VIPs and neither group sobered up or showed up the next day before mid-afternoon. "Did Food Services deliver hospitality trays to you this morning?"

"They did," the woman said.

"Could you send a few to the VIP Host office?"

"How many is a few?"

I didn't know how large the hazmat crew was. "Enough for twenty guests."

"Of course."

"Or fifty."

"I'll send plenty," she said. "When?"

"Now."

I hung up because I was receiving a text message from a blocked number. *I have something of yours.*

I showed it to Fantasy. "Maybe someone stole your rabbit."

My phone buzzed again. *Loves omelets.*

Nope. Someone stole my Baylor.

The final text arrived. *Drop the nonsense with the Gaming Commission and I'll return him.*

Friday, 11:00 A.M.

We made our way from the fifteenth floor of the hotel to our sub-basement offices delicately, which was to say we walked down fifteen flights of fire-exit stairs to trade the questionable air inside for fresh air outside at the hotel receiving dock, then around the side of the hotel to enter the building again through Groundskeeping's door.

Deserted.

So our hotel employees had tipped off our operating crews.

Great. Next, the administrative offices would find out and there would go Guest Services, Human Resources, Hospitality, Special Events, Marketing, and Casino Operations.

"How many employees are supposed to be on the clock right now?" Fantasy asked.

"Friday morning? I'd say somewhere between five and six hundred."

"How many do you think are still here?"

"Somewhere between five and six. Counting us."

We rode Groundskeeping's elevator to the sub-basement. We could have saved ourselves ten minutes by returning to our offices the way we'd left them, but we needed the extra time to breathe. To process. To figure out our next move. We were clueless as to the source of the contamination in the casino because one problem's origins were different from the next. We lost Surveillance to doped donuts. It would seem the hiccups came from the twenty-dollar bills the ponytailed woman dropped. Based on what we knew of the hearing loss—sudden onset, sudden end—it was most likely some manner of supersonic sound wave emitted through the casino's speaker system that blocked auditory receptors. And the beta carotene that turned everyone's skin orange came straight from a Starbucks truck. If Starbucks wasn't safe, what was?

The strategic orchestration of it all was mind-boggling.

Just how deeply had we been infiltrated? Who was behind it? What was the point? To distract us? From what? And what was next?

We had no idea.

What we did know was that we were in charge. The twelve hundred hotel guests sheltering in place, the five hundred people trapped in the casino, a dwindling number of our employees, and the third member of our team, Baylor, being held hostage at Bling-Bling, were counting on us to find who'd compromised our entire organization, put a stop to it, and make it right. The enormity of our predicament made for the long walk back to our offices, hoping, with each step, we'd find a solution.

We didn't.

And when we couldn't put it off any longer, we dragged our feet down the long dark sub-basement hall. We pressed our palms against our recognition keypads, were approved by our security system, then tentatively stepped through the door. In case our offices had been poisoned in our absence.

"How long do we think Bling-Bling's known Baylor was snooping around?" I asked.

"I'd say ten minutes," she answered.

"I bet not."

"What do you bet?"

Our first stop was the break room. We needed caffeine fortification. And because we were still shell-shocked by the sight of our orange boss, we threw out the coffee in the canister and brewed a pot with fresh grounds from a vacuum-sealed bag. "I bet they've known for weeks."

"No way."

"What if they have, Fantasy? What if they've been waiting until today to nail him so they could use him as a Gaming Commission pawn?"

"I'm not buying it," she said. "He did something stupid and got caught sometime this morning because he's Baylor. They ran facial recognition on him, realized who he was, and took advantage of the fact that it just happened to be Gaming Commission day."

"Either way, Bling-Bling has no manners. If they did, they'd have kicked Baylor out and told him to never come back instead of holding him hostage."

"For sure," she said. "This isn't vintage Vegas with a backroom full of goons with baseball bats. What's wrong with Bling-Bling?"

"They caught someone spying on them." I filled two mugs with hot coffee I hoped wasn't laced with anything. "What do we do when we catch someone spying on us?"

"We kill them."

"No, we don't," I said.

"I meant we want to kill them."

"We question them, Fantasy. And that's what Bling-Bling is doing with Baylor. They're holding him and questioning him about the Gaming Commission business. The bad news for them is they picked the wrong person to question. He doesn't know a thing about the lawsuit. I doubt Baylor even knows today is Gaming Commission day. Much less the details."

"I didn't know today was Gaming Commission day," she said, "and I don't have details. What about Gaming Commission day could be so important to Bling-Bling that they'd hold Baylor hostage?"

"A lawsuit." I sipped my coffee. It tasted like it was supposed to. Not that I'd be able to taste something that would make my fingernails melt. I drank it anyway. Fingernails be damned. "We're suing them."

"I knew that," she said, "but don't we sue people all the time who aren't this rude about it?"

"No," I said, "we don't sue people all the time. I can't remember the last time we sued anyone. People sue us all the time."

"Right. The hotel towels are too soft. The restaurant baguettes are too hard. Why are we suing Bling-Bling again? Because they destroyed our pool or because we don't like their topless pool?"

"They're never going to pay for our pool, and we don't care about their pool except for the fact that the parking garage that's home to their topless pool is six feet on our property."

"What does the Gaming Commission have to do with it?"

"We have to advise them of casino-to-casino litigation before we file."

"Why?"

"So they can assign a mediator in hopes of keeping the peace."

"Ah," she said, "just what we need. Another mediator."

We quietly sipped coffee.

"Are we asking Bling-Bling to lose the parking garage?" she asked.

"No. We're asking them to move it to the other side of their hotel because it's six feet on our property. And bonus, our guests on the west side of the building won't be looking at their topless servers and sunbathers."

"That doesn't sound very mediatable."

"I agree," I said.

"And it doesn't sound cheap."

"Which is why they're holding Baylor," I said. "It saves them millions if we don't file the lawsuit."

When we couldn't put it off another minute, we stepped through to Control Central, the electronic cave where our day started and where we'd left everything on, except everything was off.

Power surge?

We were well protected against power surges.

It was something else.

"Who turned everything off?" she asked.

"No one," I answered. "No Hair's in the casino and Baylor's next door. There isn't anyone else who can get in our door to turn everything off."

We began flipping ON switches. Me, at the five computer terminals at our three side-by-side desks. Fantasy, at the control board of the twelve video monitors on the wall.

"What do you think would be the easiest way to get Baylor back?" I asked while entering passwords. "Negotiate," I answered myself as my passwords were rejected. "Neither of us can negotiate his release, if for no other reason, we can't stop what we're doing long enough to negotiate the release of a balloon." I entered what I knew for a fact were my passwords a second time. "We need Starling."

"Have you lost your mind?"

"She's here," I said. "At our front door. Bling-Bling loves her—" finally, third time's the charm, the system took my passwords "—and she loves Baylor. If we could rope her into negotiating his release, it'll give her something to do so she won't tell anyone we're locked down tight except for a biohazard response team. If she hasn't already." My computer was taking forever to load. Dots, dots, and more dots. So were the big screens on the wall. All twelve screens were finally up after Fantasy logged on three times just like I had but displaying static. "What is wrong with our system?"

"It's slow," she said, "although I can't imagine why. Gaming has ground to a halt, there's nothing else in the casino draining the system, no one's checking in or out of the hotel, and we don't have enough employees left at computer terminals to slow it down."

I turned away from my monitors hoping that when I looked again everything would be fine, along the lines of what my grandmother always said, a watched pot never boiled. "What time is it? Eleven thirty? Do you realize we've accomplished exactly nothing? We stopped looking for the dental blanket doctor after we stopped looking for the ponytailed woman dropping the twenties in the casino who kicked the whole thing off, and now we have to stop looking for both to talk Starling into rescuing Baylor."

"It's just after eleven, Davis. And Sterling will never agree to do us a favor."

"It's Starling." I rolled my chair around to look at my monitors. Our system still wasn't up and running. "And you don't know that." Frustrated with it, I backed all the way out, did a complete system reboot, and started over.

"Are you rebooting?" she asked. "I thought we were morally against rebooting."

"We are." Because of viruses, backdoor hacks, and losing valuable data. "Reboot anyway."

She did, her fingers flying over the control board. "She doesn't like us enough to do us a favor, Davis. She owes us nothing."

"She'd help us if there was something in it for her."

"Like what?"

"The very thing she keeps asking for and we keep saying no to."

"Baylor? We don't have Baylor."

"Television."

"A Prime Eight interview with us?" Fantasy laughed at the very notion. "No way."

"Not with us," I said. "With Baylor."

"Who isn't here."

"Starling doesn't know that."

Fantasy pressed control, alternate, and delete at the same time on the last of the big screen docks until they finally lit up. One by one. She breathed a sigh of relief. I was right behind her with my own sigh when I finally saw familiar welcome screens.

"I've got it," she said. "We call Sterling, tell her Baylor's in the casino and is ready to sit down with her for an interview. That'll buy us a little time because she'll need to round up her Prime Eight crew. When she gets here, we'll pour her a cup of Starbucks carrot coffee, then her boobs will turn orange."

The big screens finally pulled all the way up, all camera angles staring at empty hallways, stairwells, and closed doors. We hadn't left the cameras staring at empty hallways, stairwells, and closed doors. Fantasy immediately began redirecting them to the casino.

"Then what?" I asked.

"Then we tell her we'll fix her orange boobs after she delivers Baylor from Bling-Bling."

"Surely the Starbucks truck is long gone."

"And surely there are leftovers in the casino," Fantasy said.

"I'm not going on a carrot coffee scavenger hunt in the casino. Do you want to?"

"We'll get No Hair to do it."

"Not without telling him why. Do you want to tell No Hair we've had Baylor undercover at Bling-Bling, they're now holding him hostage, and we need Starling's boobs to turn orange so she'll get him back for us? Because I don't. Not only would we be in hot water with No Hair, but he wouldn't do it. He'd say as good as Baylor is at sneaking around, let him find his own way out."

"You know what? He might be right," she said. "How much time do we have?"

"Until this afternoon," I said. "Probably late this afternoon."

"How do you figure that?"

"Because the Gaming Commission doesn't weigh in on the cases presented until they've cleared the whole docket. Bradley said they had a packed agenda. So no doubt, it'll be late in the day."

To which she responded, "What the holy hell?"

All twelve cameras directed to the casino finally pulled up to the unnerving sight of orange people stripping off all their clothes and shoving them into large canvas bags held by Hazmats. My mother had been right all along. Wear nice underwear in case you're in an accident. And we were looking at an accident of gigantic proportions.

Fantasy redirected the cameras until they were aimed up and down the wide aisle in the middle of the casino where all the disrobing action was. My eyes couldn't find anywhere to land, because everywhere I looked there were half naked people, until one of the Hazmats raised his canvas bag above his head and sailed it into the crowd. That he'd put so much muscle into it granted him our undivided attention.

"Why did he do that?" Fantasy asked.

"I have no idea," I answered.

Next, the Hazmat pulled off his headgear and sent it flying after the canvas bag. We could see his face, and he wasn't smiling.

"What is wrong with him?" Fantasy whispered.

"I don't know," I whispered back.

Next, we watched him rip off the white rubber gloves covering his hands and forearms. He flung them right and left, scattering half-naked casino guests who were glued to the same Hazmat show we were, but they were ringside. The Hazmat squared his shoulders, took a deep and angry breath, then landed one booted foot forward, followed by the other, as he stomped his way to the Hazmat closest to him.

The crowd of half-naked casino guests took another giant Mother-May-I step back, but not before a woman in a teal bra and matching teal bikini panties, which didn't look all that bad against her orange skin, reached out an arm to warn the second Hazmat still stuffing clothing into a canvas bag that the first Hazmat was on the way. Hazmat Two turned around, took one look at his coworker, then ripped off his own headgear. Followed by his own gloves.

The space closed between them.

Hazmat One pulled his right arm back before propelling it forward to land a sucker punch straight to Hazmat Two's face.

Blood spurted.

Within seconds, what could only be described as a vicious brawl between the Hazmats ensued. It was an all-out Hazmat war. Six men and two women were trying to kill each other until a group of twenty or more underweared bystanders bravely stepped forward—a man in striped boxer shorts I recognized as a member of our own casino security team—and began pulling the Hazmats apart, but not without taking a few punches themselves.

Fantasy's hand landed on my arm. "What? Is? Happening?"

I clapped my hand over hers. "I. Have. No. Idea."

We watched until eight chairs were pulled from nearby slot machines and all eight Hazmats subdued and restrained in them with electrical cords yanked from the same nearby slot machines. Then one by one, from the largest male Hazmat to the smallest female Hazmat, they started crying. All eight sniffled, until tears spilled from their swollen eyes and fell on their battered faces. Before a full minute passed, they were boohoo sobbing all the way up and down the Hazmat line. Shoulders shook, tears flowed, and ugly crying reigned. Our orange casino patrons in various stages of undress began hesitantly inching forward, gaping in awe, until one by one, the Hazmats nodded off to sleep. Fantasy rewound and we watched the entire scene unfold again to make sure we'd seen what we thought we'd seen. And we had. One minute the Hazmats were gathering what they must have believed to be contaminated clothing from five hundred casino guests and employees, and the next, they were trying to kill each other, the next, crying uncontrollably, then the next, chins-to-chests asleep. The Hazmats did nothing but walk in the front doors with huge suitcases, walk fifty yards to the VIP Host office, gear up, enter the casino, and make the disturbing decision to ask the orange people for their clothing. Clearly, at some point in that process, something happened to the Hazmats. They'd been exposed to something mood-altering, sending them from one end of the spectrum to the other, then to sleep, but it was just the Hazmats.

Where would they have been exposed?

The VIP Host office.

The hospitality trays.

I slowly reached for my desk phone, the landline Starling Halter had first called me on. I dialed Hospitality. A recording answered. *Because of reports of problematic activity in the casino, Hospitality will close at nine thirty this morning. We regret any inconvenience and hope to be back at our desks tomorrow morning.*

If Hospitality closed at nine thirty, who had I ordered food trays from at ten thirty? And what had that person spiked the contents with? I slowly hung up the phone, knowing we had to stop everything and find the ponytailed woman in the suit who'd started it all and the doctor who we believed invented it all, but before I could, another security alert hit our phones.

Turn up the heat in the casino.

Someone else from Security responded. *Any changes to casino temperature must be authorized and approved by Vice President of Security.*

The first Security suit responded to the second. *The request is directly from Jeremy Covey, Vice President of Security, who is standing beside me in his shorts. He's cold. Everyone's cold.*

I had to grab the arms of my chair and hold on for dear life when the fifty-five-inch screen directly in front of us filled with our all-but-naked orange boss.

No Hair was one of the first people I met at the Bellissimo when I was hired. I'd been fired from the police force in my hometown of Pine Apple, Alabama, and it was my police chief father who'd done the firing. And while it was the best thing that could have ever happened to me, and my father knew it, things went downhill fast before they turned around. Biloxi and the Bellissimo had given me a fresh start on life. A do-over. Had it not been for No Hair's friendship, guidance, and protection those early days, I wouldn't have lasted a month. I might not have lived a month. I'd have never met my husband. I wouldn't have Bexley and Quinn. I wouldn't have my best friend in the world and the best partner anyone could ever ask for, Fantasy, and I wouldn't have my Boy Wonder, Baylor. And the thing was, I knew No Hair. I knew his loyalty, his intelligence, his street smarts, and I knew his heart. And I knew that as long as we'd worked together, I'd never seen him in the same tie twice. It was his thing: statement, novelty, and themed neckties. His wife of thirty-five years, Grace, once told me No Hair's passion for signature neckties went back to his Mississippi Bureau of

Investigation days, pre-Bellissimo Security, when he wore the standard-issue black suit, white shirt, and black tie. Every day. Grace said he hated the uniformed ordinariness of it all, so she began embellishing the backsides of his black ties, first with monograms in bright yellow or green thread, then I love yous and hearts in bright red, then, her needle skills advancing, multi-colored surprises: ducks on a pond, golf cleats and clubs, a sizzling steak beside a cold beer.

It stuck, No Hair's love of bespoke ties.

Earlier, after Fantasy mentioned No Hair's tie of the day, I'd backed up video footage from the casino to see for myself. The background of his tie that day was navy blue. Centered on the blue, in bright splashes of color like an abstract watercolor, was a mortar and pestle. In the middle of the mortar bowl were the letters Rx. To welcome the pharmacists for their convention. What I hadn't known, what I didn't want to know, and what I hoped to find a way to erase from my memory and never know again, was that under No Hair's suits, he wore tight boxer briefs that matched the ties. His back was to us, shouting directions, his massive orange arms flailing right and left, and stretched tightly across his considerable rear end was a much larger but perfect replica of the watercolor mortar and pestle with the big Rx I'd seen earlier on his tie. He turned around, looked straight into the eye-in-the-sky casino camera he assumed correctly we were watching, took a deep breath, and demanded to know when, where, and to what the Hazmats had been subjected that made them killing machines one minute and crybabies the next. He backed away for us to see the passed out Hazmats behind him, and that was when we saw his lone article of clothing. He'd picked up a green Starbucks apron and looped it around his neck for coverage. Only it wasn't Starbucks. The apron was the same green, the circle logo shaped the same, the same recognizable font, but without the creepy mermaid with two tails. Instead, it was a devil. With two pitchforks. Around it, the logo read STARTUP. Not STARBUCKS. At first glance and from a distance everything looked Starbucks and would certainly look Starbucks to No Hair, who didn't even drink coffee, and claimed if he did, he'd stand in line for an hour and pay what Starbucks charged for tutti-frutti coffee when hell froze over, but it wasn't Starbucks. Before our brains could even register what it meant, or why we were looking at so many green Startup aprons, how and why the people who wore the aprons in weren't long gone, or at least in their truck rather than inside our casino, No Hair's unnerving, Startup apron-clad image disappeared. Then every screen in Control Central of our offices followed. Our eyes darted from one blank screen to the next. We pounded keyboards. We hit ENTER on repeat. We unplugged and plugged in. Ten long seconds later, the screens, one by one, popped up displaying Bowls of Hygieia. An apothecary symbol. It was a snake with its body wrapped around the stem of a martini glass, its head peering into the glass, and its forked tongue hissing at the contents. It was the Good Pills Biopharmaceutical, Inc. logo. We never should have rebooted, because when we did, Good Pills swiped our operating system.

Friday, 11:30 A.M.

I blocked the Bellissimo's hijacked Wi-Fi from my phone so Good Pills couldn't track me, then did the same to Fantasy's before we set off to trade our offices for my twenty-ninth-floor home where I hoped to hack Bex and Quinn's Toddler Tablet, probably the only electronic device in all of Bellissimo Land that Good Pills hadn't breached. Now what I'd do with a hacked Toddler Tablet, I wasn't sure. But I'd do something with it. Because doing anything was better than doing nothing.

"Call Reggie," I said. "Ask him to bring lunch."

"You want to stop for lunch? At a time like this?"

"Lunch for the people stuck in the casino, Fantasy."

"I'm not calling Reggie and asking him to bring lunch for five hundred people."

"Would we rather Good Pills send food?"

She considered what Good Pills might send to the casino for lunch, and what it might mean for the people stuck there, and from the look on her face she was imagining them losing their pinkie fingers, or their hair, or their marbles, but landed on, "I'm still not calling Reggie."

"Okay." I poked through my contacts. "I will." Thirty seconds later, I said, "Are you busy, honey?"

"Honey?" Reggie said. "Why are you calling me honey?"

"Because Fantasy calls you honey."

"She absolutely does not call me honey," he said. "What is going on? Let me speak to my wife."

I passed her my phone. On a weary sigh, she asked him to stop watching ESPN for a minute—Sportswriter Reggie called watching ESPN all day working—and order pizza for five hundred because we had a lot going on and didn't want to deal with hangry orange people on top of all we were already dealing with. Order it in person. And deliver it in person to the valet office at the main casino entrance, but don't come in. Don't let anyone else touch the pizza and don't tell the people making the pizza what or who it was for.

"Are you for real, Fantasy? Do you have any idea how much pizza that is? You're asking for a thousand dollars' worth of pizza."

"It wasn't my idea to call you, Reggie."

I grabbed my phone back. "If we didn't need your help, we wouldn't bother you."

He hung up.

It was closing in on lunchtime. It was imperative we take what little control we could. Which meant feeding the half-naked orange people in the casino ourselves instead of waiting until Good Pills beat us to the lunch punch and caused even more mayhem than they had with the carotene-laced fake Starbucks. We had to assume no food inside the casino was safe to consume, and we had no operating food service outside of the casino. Fantasy and I weren't about to go to any of the kitchens of the mezzanine restaurants and try to cook for the five hundred people in their unmentionables. Neither she nor I exactly enjoyed cooking for our own families. We weren't about to cook for a casino full of half-naked orange people.

I shot off a text message to No Hair. *Sending pizza.*

He didn't respond.

Safe pizza. Reggie is bringing it.

Nothing.

Why are the carrot coffee people still in the casino?

No answer.

If it isn't pizza, don't eat it.

Crickets.

Are the Hazmats okay?

Not a peep. Which was troublesome.

Next, I dialed the maintenance department to ask them to turn up the heat in the casino. No answer. Five minutes later, still no answer. We'd have to stop by there on our way to my place.

Face shields and gloves nabbed from EMT suits we found in our undercover spy-wear closet donned, we made our way down the long basement hall and down one flight of stairs to the maintenance department in the sub-sub-basement, where we intended to find a warm body who could in turn manually warm the naked orange bodies in the casino, because with our system hacked and down, it wasn't going to happen electronically. When no one answered our repeated buzzes at the door, we disabled the keypad with the heel of Fantasy's Stuart Weitzman slide and waltzed right in.

Maintenance was dead.

Not a soul in sight.

Just the hums and clicks of equipment housed in metal boxes the size of guest bedrooms.

"What are we looking for?" Fantasy asked. "A thermostat?"

"I guess." Our voices and footfall echoed. "Wouldn't you think it'd be a big thermostat? I don't see anything that looks like a big thermostat."

"All I see past the metal boxes are greasy tools in cages."

"And water purification systems."

We turned a corner past a block of giant water purifiers and found a wall of thermostats three deep and ten wide.

"Are these thermostats?" Fantasy asked. "We have thirty floors and there are thirty dials."

"How old is our heat and air system that every floor has its own thermostat? Wouldn't an updated system with a master thermostat be more efficient?" I moved in for a closer look. "How could everyone in the casino be cold? These thermostats are set to a hundred and thirty-five degrees." I went down the row. "Every single one." I turned to Fantasy. "Who did this?"

"The same people who stole our system?" Fantasy reached for a dial. "Set all the way to blazing, I'd say the units are frozen. Will turning down the temperature on the thermostats thaw the units?"

"How would I know? Turn them down and let's see."

"To what? Seventy degrees? Seventy-two?"

"That's way too high," I said. "The slot machines put off heat. Let's go sixty."

"Sixty isn't exactly warm, Davis. Let's go sixty-eight."

We settled on sixty-four.

All dials set, our work there done, we took the service stairwell to the lobby. I was just about to ask Fantasy, considering we'd found all the heat in the building set to boiling, why we weren't sweating bullets, but before I could, my phone dinged in several text messages, one on top of the other.

Fantasy closed her eyes and pressed two fingers between her eyebrows to hold in the headache. "What now?"

"It's probably my mother." I pulled my phone from the back pocket of my jeans. I took a peek. "It is." I studied the garble for a long moment then translated. "She's back at the Bellissimo at the front door again with the rabbit but not my birth control pills or the girls. The school wouldn't release a prescription drug to someone it wasn't prescribed to, and they wouldn't release Bex and Quinn to her either. For one, the headmaster wants to speak to me and Bradley first. For two, because my mother isn't on the approved pickup list. And for three, even if she was on the list, she doesn't have proper booster seats installed in her car."

As we pushed through the service stairwell door, Fantasy said, "At least you got your rabbit back."

"Not my rabbit."

I texted Mother back to ask if anyone else was at the front door. She said yes, the woman with sprawling beasts was still there and she had a television man with her. I put out an arm to stop Fantasy on the first stairwell landing. "Starling is still at the front door."

"So?"

"With Prime Eight."

"That's not good."

"If we go to the front doors to get my mother, Prime Eight will film us."

"Prime Eight needs to go back to airing reruns of *Bewitched*," Fantasy said. "Any minute they're going to change the station name to Prime Sterling."

"Prime Starling."

"Prime Trash Television."

"What do we do, Fantasy?"

"Call Security. Tell them to tell Prime Eight and Sterling to go pound sand."

"Starling, Fantasy. Why can't you remember her name?"

"Because Sterling makes more sense. Her name should be Sterling."

"But it's not. And we need her."

"What for?"

"To get Baylor back for us."

She said, "Right. We need Baylor."

"And we need her laptop."

"How do we know she has a laptop?"

"Why wouldn't she have a laptop?"

"I don't have a laptop on me, Davis. You don't have a laptop on you. What makes you so sure Sterling does? And what is it you plan on doing with her laptop if she does have one?"

"After I go in the backdoor of our system and steal it back from Good Pills? A million things," I said. "Can you imagine the resources on a city-issued laptop?"

"Are we not trying to get to your house where you have ten laptops?"

"I have two and both are connected to the Bellissimo system. They won't do us any good. We're trying to get to my house to hack a preschool tablet that doesn't even have a keyboard."

"What good will that do us?"

"Exactly." I sent another text message to my mother. *What's she doing?*

Hoot?

The woman with the sprawling beasts.

HOOT?

The woman out there with you, Mother. She's probably wearing a halter top.

Sheets smacking cigars.

She's smoking a cigar?

Cigar its.

Cigarettes?

Yis! Kin U reed?

I'm doing my best, Mother. And I need to talk to her. I'm going to block my phone number, then call you, but I want to talk to HER. The woman with the sprawling beasts. When your phone rings in just a minute, answer it even though your phone won't say my name. It'll still be me. But I want to talk to Starling.

Whoot is startling%

The woman with the sprawling beasts.

There was a tiny bit more back and forth with Mother—her accusing me of not reading what I'd typed before sending because "sprawling beasts" made absolutely no sense, then a little interference from Fantasy, who said we were burning daylight—before I had Starling on the phone. By then, Fantasy and I, still standing on the stairwell landing, sat on a step. I put my phone between us and hit the speaker button.

She answered in her Dr. Phil voice. "Starling Halter. With whom am I sharing today?"

"Starling, this is Davis Way Cole."

We listened to her exhale smoke on a jagged breath. "Well, well, well." She dropped her therapy voice. "Cole as in Bradley Cole? President and Chief Executive Officer of the Bellissimo? You're Davis Way Cole, as in his wife? As in Bellissimo Security secret weapon?"

"Correct."

Fantasy stage whispered, *"How does she know all that?"*

Starling said, "We haven't talked since the first time I called. Months ago. Where have you been, Davis Way Cole?"

I stage-whispered to Fantasy, *"How does she know it was me on the phone that day? I didn't tell her my name."*

Starling said, "Yoo-hoo, Davis. Where have you been?"

I said, "Busy."

"You were rude to me."

"And you were full of headshrinker hot air, Starling."

"I have a job to do."

"For whom? Who do you work for?" I snapped. "Are you on the city's payroll? Are you on Bling-Bling's? Are you on Prime Eight's? Are you on all three?"

"Prime Eight?" Starling dug around for her therapy hat and plopped it back on her head. "I'll have you know I have not attempted to enlist the community's help in building a friendship bridge between you and your new neighbors a single time on Prime Eight without inviting a representative from the Bellissimo. That your casino doesn't want to engage in meaningful dialog via a public platform is not my problem. That you can't embrace the differences between your organization and Bling-Bling's in front of a live Biloxi audience is not my fault."

Fantasy mimed gagging.

"Starling," I said, "stop with the touchy-feely. I didn't buy it in the beginning and I'm not buying it now. You're a walking, talking Bling-Bling billboard who's launched a one-woman media campaign against the Bellissimo. I'm only asking what's in it for you."

"Davis," she said, "your jealousy of my newfound celebrity is nothing more than your overwhelming feelings of insecurity. You need to identify the cognitive contributions to your envious tendencies."

"That's it." Fantasy grabbed the phone, held it an inch from her nose, then proceeded to let Starling have it with our realities versus her delusional therapeutic denials. She started our side of the story—a well-rehearsed tale Fantasy and I shared with each other almost daily, in excruciating detail, in hopes of understanding it a little better, the retelling of which we'd never had a chance to unload on Starling until then—when her "newfound celebrity" resulted from a last-minute appearance on Biloxi's local cable channel, Prime Eight, during a half hour Community News segment no one watched. Either the station invited Starling to be a guest, she invited herself, or the Boy Scout Troop scheduled for that particular episode of Community News suddenly canceled. Prime Eight had nothing else to air mid-week at one in the morning, so they plugged in Starling.

Their market share rose seventy-two percent for the time slot.

It was the halter tops.

It had to be.

The station moved the show to primetime, kicking *Three's Company* to the curb, and began airing Starling introducing various Bling-Bling department heads to Biloxi. A Nielson sampling of twenty-five thousand households in Harrison County reported that more than ten thousand televisions were tuned in to the first interview featuring Starling and Bling-Bling's swarthy, black-suited Property Manager who told everyone watching, "In spite of what you might hear from our nosy neighbors, Bling-Bling's beautiful property is state-of-the-art and as solid as a rock." Three days later, more than fifteen thousand viewers met Bling-Bling's VP of Player Services, another sinister-looking man in a sinister-looking black suit who told viewers, "We will double any offer you bring us from the Bellissimo." Two days later, a reported fifty thousand people were glued to their screens as Prime Eight welcomed Starling and Bling-Bling's VP of Marketing, another snake-oil salesman in a black snake-oil salesman suit, who issued a Bling-Bling invitation of sorts when he mused, "Think about it before you go to another Biloxi casino, especially next door, and maybe don't go." Starling, who'd never defended us on air, not a single time, perched on a stool beside the snake-oil man wearing a shockingly sheer halter top, piped up with a little ditty. She actually broke into song. It wasn't twenty-four hours before the tune and its message had been recorded in a sound studio and was blasting across the Gulf. Turn on anything—television, radio, light switch—and the jingle Starling wrote for our infuriating competition whacked listeners in the ears. *"Don't go next door! Go to Bling-Bling! Bling-Bling! Bling-Bling-Bling-Bling!"* It was the most irritating five seconds of advertising garble ever put to music. I heard it night and day, caught myself humming it, and the worst, Bex and Quinn ran through the house singing the annoying little refrain with a clear message:

out with the decrepit Bellissimo and in with the bright shiny Bling-Bling. And if that wasn't enough, two nights later, Prime Eight welcomed Starling back with Bling-Bling's VP of Security. Tony Francesco. A small man with a raspy and decidedly un-Southern voice and beady little squirrel eyes. The on-air personality, a man named Spider Gibbins, who was also Prime Eight's station manager, feature producer, and backup cameraman, led with his usual: "We're so sorry a representative from the Bellissimo couldn't join us." Starling responded with, "Oh, me too!" Her hands flew to her heart, obscuring her huge breasts for a split second, a split second in which Spider Gibbons batted a hand at his knee, as in a stage direction that said, *move your arms so the audience can see your tatas,* which she quickly corrected, saying, "I begged them to come be part of the solution!" Then, when asked if Bling-Bling felt threatened in any way by the Bellissimo's successful crackerjack security, the squirrely man, wearing a slick black suit to match his slick black hair and his slick black pencil-thin moustache, staring straight down Starling's silk black halter top instead of at Spider, who'd asked the question, said he was well aware of the Bellissimo's outdated back-of-house security team, both in practice and people, at which point he finally looked up from Starling's breasts, straight into the camera directly at me and Fantasy, when he said in the smirkiest, raspiest, and squirreliest of ways, "We'd be happy to show you how it's done, Old Girls."

Old girls?

Us?

It was then and there I knew I'd done the right thing by sending Baylor on an undercover assignment at Bling-Bling. Because Baylor, the third and final member of my *not* outdated, in practice or in people, back-of-house security team, was as far away from an old girl as Fantasy and I were, maybe further, since he wasn't a girl at all. But that day on the stairwell step, the day our very existence on the Biloxi casino map was seriously in question and I was no longer sure I'd done the right thing by sending Baylor undercover at Bling-Bling, since they caught him and were threatening to not give him back, Fantasy took our shot at the woman we held largely responsible for creating the casino competition chaos that was surely a factor leading to the compromised position we found ourselves in that day.

The silence that followed her speech was absolute.

I whispered to Fantasy, "*Good job.*"

She whispered back, "*I feel better.*"

We stared at the phone, the timer logging the call still ticking away, so the line of communication was still open, but Starling hadn't said a word. She hadn't interrupted Fantasy a single time with therapy babble, psycho platitudes, or inane feel-good clichés. Thirty more seconds passed, then ten more, to the point of us wondering if Starling had abandoned my mother's phone and walked away, not hearing a word Fantasy had said, when Starling finally deadpanned, "Are you done?"

Fantasy sniffed. Sat up straighter. "Maybe."

"What a relief," Starling said. "Davis? Do you need an affirming trip down memory lane too?"

"Not so much," I said.

"Then tell me where you're hiding Baylor and why I no longer have access to him."

"No."

"Okay," she said, "tell me why your doors are locked."

"How about I let you in and tell you in person."

After a beat, she said, "That was easy enough."

"No Prime Eight."

"Spider just left," she said. "While your buddy was going on and on about nothing, I sent Spider to Panera to pick me up an arugula, Fuji apple, and rotisserie chicken salad."

"Bring my mother."

"The old woman with the rabbit is your mother?"

"She's not that old."

I heard my mother in the background. "I'm fifty-nine years young, thank you."

"What in the world is going on here, Davis?" Starling asked in far from a therapy voice. "Is this about you explaining where you're hiding Baylor and why the Bellissimo is closed, or is this about delivering your mother and her rodent to you?"

I argued the rodent part, telling her I thought rabbits were more mammal, to which she said she would not be dragging my mother's mammal in either unless she could interview Baylor. On the record. One-on-one. I wasn't invited. And that would be after I told her why the Bellissimo was closed. She added she would not touch the rabbit.

"What do you mean by on the record?" I asked.

"I'll need to record our interview," she answered.

"I thought you said Prime Eight was at Panera."

"I didn't say film our interview. I'm not camera ready. I said record it. I'll record the interview on my phone or my tablet."

I did a fist pump at the tablet part. "Okay," I lied.

Then she asked how she, my mother, and my mother's nasty rodent were supposed to get in when the Security suits, like guards at the Tower of London, wouldn't even look at her. "I don't know if you've noticed, Davis, but I'm hard to miss. And these guys won't even acknowledge my presence."

"Step left," I said, "away from the doors and out of their line of vision. Slide open the big Valet window and climb in."

"With an old woman and a rodent? No, thank you. And even if I wanted to, I can't, because that window is already open and stacked sky high with CiCi's pizza. It's like someone brought the buffet here. There must be five hundred pizza boxes in that window."

I dipped the phone down and asked Fantasy in a whisper, "Did you tell Reggie to bring five hundred pizzas?"

"No," she whispered back. "I told him to bring pizza for five hundred people."

Was the day going to get any worse? Back on the phone, I told Starling to scoot the pizza out of her way.

"I'll knock them out of my way but only if you'll tell me why Baylor only has one name. And why I can't find a birth certificate on him. And if he's married."

I didn't respond to any of it. Instead, I gave her directions to the service elevator behind Valet, told her to hug the wall quietly so the guards at the door wouldn't see her, or Mother, or the rabbit, then told her to meet me in the catering kitchen on the twenty-fifth floor. I said, "We'll talk then."

"Catering kitchen on the twenty-fifth floor? Why am I meeting you in a catering kitchen?"

"That's where Baylor is."

"What a renaissance man," she sang. "He's a chef too."

"Baylor can't cook toast, Starling."

She launched into a speech I only caught every fifth word of, starting with "you don't cook toast," followed by "hold on," then "Baylor," then "half a bar," then "Baylor," then "traipsing through the bushes," then "Baylor," then "can't get a signal," before finally finding a spot where I could hear her complain mightily about my mother's phone. She said she could feel herself irreversibly aging just holding Mother's antiquated phone and asked for my phone number, insisting any additional conversation between us be conducted on twenty-first-century phones. Another reason she wanted my personal phone number was because it all sounded both too bad and too good to be true to her. If I planned on not coming clean about why the Bellissimo was locked down or cheating her out of a one-on-one with Baylor, she'd at least come out of it with a direct line to me to call me all day every day to remind me I'd lied to her. Starling Halter was the last person I wanted to have my private phone number. I could easily have given it to her then changed my number, but that would be a pain, so I settled on giving it to her then blocking her. Problem solved. I shared my contact information with her. Immediately, her contact information dinged back.

Fantasy waved her hands in my face. "Get her to bring us a pizza."

Starling, I texted, *bring a pizza.*

"No bell peppers," Fantasy said.

Nothing with bell peppers.

"Or onion."

Or onion.

"But with black olives."

Black olives, please.

"And pepperoncini."

I texted Starling back about the pizza. Not the pepperoncini part, because I had sliced pepperoncini in my refrigerator if we ever made it to my house, but still about pizza. *Starling, the other 499 pizzas go to the casino doors.*

No way.

Please.

If you'll tell me Baylor's birthdate and where he was born.

Ask him yourself when you interview him.

Too personal.

Like his marital status isn't?

After ending the communication with a decisive click out of my message box, Fantasy and I finally left the service stairwell to make our way to the twenty-fifth-floor catering kitchen. Not wanting to use the hotel elevators, a mile from where we were, we caught the much closer service elevator to the fourth floor, the first floor of guest rooms, normally home to casino-junket guests who arrived in tour buses, currently home to the construction company repairing our pool, that would get us to an in-room dining elevator. We were expecting exactly no one, but the service elevator doors opened on the fourth floor to the pool crew foreman. The man named Dunk.

"Mr. Dunk," I said.

"Ma'ams," he growled, or graveled rather, tipping his hardhat.

We stood there until awkward. Dunk, because he was trying to enter the elevator but couldn't until we exited. Me, because I couldn't decide between chitchat, as if it was just another day at the Bellissimo, but only to feel him out to see if he already knew it wasn't just another day at the Bellissimo, or asking him why he or one of his people had let a fake Starbucks crew into our casino through the marina door. Fantasy stood there waiting for me or Dunk to make a move. Deciding we weren't going to, she did, grabbing my arm and pulling me out of the elevator. "Gotta scoot, Dunk."

We took off. When we heard the elevator doors close behind us, she said, "I feel like I need a shower."

"He's pretty creepy," I agreed.

"Is the rest of the pool crew as creepy as he is?"

"I have no idea."

"Who's in charge of the pool construction?"

"Grounds and Pools."

"That's two departments," she said. "There's Grounds and then there's Pools."

"Maybe they merged," I said.

"Well, maybe we should talk to them. Tell them how creepy the Grounds and Pools construction boss is."

"Right now?"

"Monday," she said. "Call them Monday."

"Be my guest."

Without passing another soul, creepy or otherwise, we turned another corner and caught the in-room dining service elevator that would take us to the twenty-fifth-floor catering kitchen where we'd meet Starling, her tablet, my mother, the rabbit, and the black olive pizza. From there, and one at a time because of space considerations, we'd catch the butler's pantry lift, large enough to hold a VIP dining cart, to Jay Leno's place on the twenty-ninth floor, the ten-thousand-square-foot celebrity suite next door to my home. The four-stateroom suite, first occupied by Jay Leno at the Bellissimo grand opening in the mid-nineties, thus the suite name, was currently occupied by no one. Going to Jay's place via the twenty-fifth-floor catering elevator would get me and my growing crew to my home without riding our private elevator which had surely been polluted by Good Pills. I was afraid if we stepped into it, we might never step out. At the very least, if they knew Fantasy and I were all that was left between them and total control of our resort, they'd trap us in the elevator.

With a loud rabbit.

And worse, Starling Halter.

And the very worst, my mother.

The in-room dining service elevator doors parted on the twenty-fifth floor to the VIP catering kitchen that served the VIP floors above it. Fantasy and I wove through stainless steel appliances and past service carts stacked with delicate bone china to the square door of the butler's pantry lift.

Fantasy pushed the call button.

"We need to wait on Mother and Starling."

"You need to wait on your mother and Sterling. I don't. I'll meet you at Jay's."

"Would you really leave me alone with them?"

She surely would have said something along the lines of, "You bet I would," had the butler's pantry lift door not creaked open just then. And it wasn't empty. We both drew our weapons and aimed them at the mad scientist who hadn't answered the door of his guest room on the fifteenth floor earlier. Dr. Winford Wurtz.

Friday, 12:00 P.M.

Dr. Wurtz's hands and feet were bound, he had a stretch of clear packing tape around his mouth and circling his head, his oversized and Coke-bottle-thick eyeglasses were dangling at an odd angle, and he wasn't happy to see us. In fact, he was terrified. His rubber-soled dress shoes squealed as he scrambled to fit himself into a corner of the small lift while whimpering noises escaped the packing tape. Musta been the firearms. I holstered my weapon, which was to say I tucked it into the waistband of my jeans, because my phone was buzzing away in my pocket with calls coming in, one on top of the other, and it was probably my mother.

It wasn't.

But it was Mother adjacent. My hometown of Pine Apple, Alabama, where my parents still lived, was home to four hundred and seventy-two souls. Hearing from anyone in Pine Apple would be Mother adjacent. It was Eugenia Winters Stone, President of the Pine Apple Historical Society, President of Pine Apple Ladies' Auxiliary, President of Pine Apple's Women's Quilting League, President of Friends of the Pine Apple Library, soprano soloist at both Pine Apple Baptist and next-door Pine Apple United Methodist churches, and newly elected City Council member. She'd left a message.

"My dear Davis," she began, *"I apologize for arriving unannounced. Your mother and I have had a terrible misunderstanding, and I find myself on your doorstep in hopes*

of enlisting your assistance in clearing up matters. Your father and I have known each other since he was in knickers and I in jumpers. Not once, not ever, has our friendship been anything more than one of mutual respect and a united mission to preserve the heritage and history of our beloved Pine Apple along with the occasional shared chuckle over lemonade when memories of bygone days strike our fancy. That I now find myself on Pine Apple's City Council obviously means I find myself in your father's company more often, and I'm afraid your mother has misinterpreted our very longstanding, civic-focused, and strictly platonic friendship. Which has led me to the front door of your magnificent residence unable to gain entry. I didn't realize gambling halls were closed on Fridays. Could you possibly accommodate me, uninvited and unannounced, for which I do apologize profusely, so that I may speak to you?"

One mystery solved: why my mother was leafing my farther.

While I'd mentally been in the middle of my parents' marriage, a place I wanted away from as quickly as possible, Fantasy had helped Dr. Wurtz from the butler's pantry lift. She'd unceremoniously ripped the packing tape from the poor man's walrus moustache and fuzzy white head. To me, she said, "Your mother?"

I couldn't even answer, so I cued the message again and passed her my phone. She listened, her face first registering boredom, followed by curiosity, replaced by astonishment, all wiped away by amusement. Her shoulders began shaking slightly and she dipped her head, turning it away from me. When she reached the end of Eugenia's recorded speech, still facing the wall, she held out my phone. I grabbed it, saying, "Wipe that smile off your face."

In a heavy German accent, Dr. Wurtz said, "Who are you vemon?"

Fantasy's head whipped back around. "Do you mean women?"

"That is what I said." Dr. Wurtz dusted his shoulders. Tugged at his lapels. Straightened his glasses on his nose. "Vemon."

I blinked hard at my phone, knowing Eugenia's message was on it, hoping it was meant for someone else. It wasn't. I scrolled through the transcribed text version of her message hoping it would have translated to something different. It hadn't. And all I could come up with was, "How did she get here?"

"How did who get here?" Fantasy asked.

"Eugenia."

"Your dad's girlfriend?"

"Cut that out."

"You have to admit it's pretty funny that your mother thinks your father is having an affair. Like that would ever happen." She thought about it. "Like that could ever happen. Isn't your dad, like, ninety years old?"

"There is zee emotional infidelitiez," Dr. Wurtz weighed in. "And there is most zertainly the pharmaceutical assistanze for the intimaciez."

Totally ignoring him, I said to her, "My father is barely sixty, thank you, and while I'm sure he's perfectly capable of having an affair—" I had to stop to shake the very idea out of my brain "—I'm just as sure he isn't. I'm not a bit worried about anyone having an affair with anyone else. I'm worried about how Eugenia got here."

"Let's assume she drove," Fantasy said.

"We can't assume that because she doesn't drive. She never has."

"Neither do I drive the automobilez," Dr. Wurtz said.

"You don't think your dad drove her, do you?" Fantasy asked. "Because we have enough to deal with without adding a love triangle."

"It is not a love triangle," I said. "Don't say that."

"Zee heart beatz only for zee one true love," Dr. Wurtz said.

Fantasy and I shared a glance in which we agreed his constant unsolicited commentary wasn't helping at all, so I swept an arm and pointed. "Back in the butler's lift, Dr Wurtz."

He blinked in surprise at the mention of his name. "Have we had zee pleasurez?"

I said, "You don't know us, but we know you."

Fantasy said, "And we need to talk to you about what you brought in your little black bag."

The old doc said, "Do you speak to my luggage?"

"No, I'm not speaking to your luggage, Doc," Fantasy said. "I'm speaking to you. About giving everyone in the casino hiccups."

"And orange skin," I added.

"And knocking out Surveillance with donuts."

Dr. Wurtz scratched his head. "I have no ideaz what you zay. Do you speak to my rezearch?"

"Get back in the lift," I said. "We'll speak to your luggage and your research upstairs."

"I do not wish to go back to zee upstairs everz againz."

I said, "Back to the upstairs? When were you to the upstairs?"

Fantasy, pushing past him, said, "I'll go first and check it out."

"What?" I wasn't sure who I didn't want to be alone with: Dr. Wurtz, my mother, Starling, a rabbit, or Eugenia Winters Stone. By then, Fantasy was gone. So I dialed Starling's number. She answered in her therapy voice again, that time, breathlessly.

"Starling Halter. If you feel it, I'll validate it. How may I help you, Davis—" she spat my name "—after your mother and I finish hauling your pizza to the casino doors while her rodent runs wild in your empty lobby?"

I asked her to turn around, look for a woman at the front entrance with a tower of silver hair, help her through the valet window, then bring her to the twenty-fifth floor too. She said not on my life and hung up. I texted her. *I have the door code to Baylor's condo.* She texted back. *He lives here?* I hit the thumbs-up response. She texted. *On my way with two old women, a rodent, and a pizza.*

When the butler's pantry lift returned, I could barely hear Fantasy when she yelled down the shaft, "Brace yourself, Davis." There was no bracing myself. I was too numb. I'd woken up that morning with all kinds of Friday energy. Ready for a short workday followed by a long weekend with my husband and daughters. And there I was, mere hours later, with more problems than one almost-red-headed woman could solve. It was as if bombs were detonating all over the building and I couldn't clear the debris from one before the next one exploded. I yelled up the shaft, "Brace myself for what?"

It sounded like she said a wild animal had destroyed Jay Leno's place. Upholstery shredded, lamps down, art destroyed, and hay everywhere.

Another mystery solved: where Bex and Quinn found a rabbit.

"What did the tall dark voman say?" Dr. Wurtz asked.

I gave him another little push. "Climb in, Doc."

The slow door of the pantry lift began closing just as the speedy door of the service elevator across the catering kitchen shot open, and the perfect timing allowed Dr. Wurtz a glimpse of my mother bolting out with a rabbit in her arms. As the lift took off, the good doc yelled at the top of his lungs, "Villhelmina!"

And yet another mystery solved: who the rabbit belonged to.

I knew exactly what was coming. My mother, marching across the kitchen floor with a ten-pound floppy-eared caramel-colored bunny in her arms that looked way more cocker spaniel than rabbit to me, and way too big for the backpack it had supposedly ridden in to Willow School for Exceptional Children, held me one hundred percent responsible for Eugenia Stone's presence and one hundred and fifty percent responsible for having to ride in a service elevator with my father's "concubine."

Starling Halter was against the back wall of the elevator with the pizza. On top of the pizza, her tablet. She announced, "Women's relationships are so complicated."

Under other circumstances, I might have told Starling that all my mother's relationships were complicated had my mother and Eugenia, who was right on Mother's Easy Spirit slip-on heels, not started speaking all over each other at me. All I could make out were the tones and nuances of Mother's rage and of Eugenia's impeccable manners. The butler's pantry lift opened, empty, I told them we'd sort it out upstairs, then helped my mother and the rabbit in. I sent them on their way. When the lift returned, I did the same with Eugenia, who pulled a monogrammed linen and lace handkerchief from inside the sleeve of her twinset cardigan to swipe at the floor of the lift before squeezing herself in. She couldn't find a way to enter delicately, so she backed in, bottom first, then sat with her legs bent beside her with a stiff spine and one shoulder thrust forward like she was modeling a 1940s swimsuit. The top of her bouffant hair grazed the lift ceiling. I sent her on her way too, at which point it was just me, Starling, the pizza, and her tablet. I took ten steps, breezing past her, to a stainless-steel prep table in the middle of the catering kitchen. I pulled out a stainless-steel barstool, sat on it, landed my elbows on the cold table, then dropped my head into my hands. Starling followed, pulling out her own barstool and sitting opposite me. She slid her phone between my elbows and engaged the recording function. I lifted my weary head. "Really?"

"Where is Baylor?" she demanded. "You said he was here."

"He had to step out. He'll be right back."

"I don't believe you."

One of the faucets at one of the sinks along the back wall of the catering kitchen dripped.

"Why are all the Bellissimo doors locked?" she asked. "What's wrong in the casino? A heist?"

I disengaged her microphone with a tap to the screen, keeping my face blank and my voice flat when I said, "You're not here to interview me. You're here to interview Baylor."

"I fully intend to just as soon as you produce him. And you fully agreed to tell me why the doors are locked."

The woman was insufferable.

"Spill," she said. She engaged the microphone again. "Has there been a death by natural causes in the casino? Unnatural causes?" She leaned in. "*Murder*?"

"No." I disconnected the microphone again, then crossed my arms and attempted to sit back menacingly, forgetting I was on a barstool. I grabbed for the edge of the stainless-steel table and tried to regain my equilibrium, but not before I caught her quick chirp of laughter, as if me almost falling off a barstool was entertaining, when it was really me losing the upper hand in the standoff between us that had amused her. I cleared my throat. "I want to know when the city knew Bling-Bling wasn't a performance venue, Starling."

"And I want to know if the people locked in the casino are hostages of a mad gunman or if this is nothing more than the

Bellissimo desperately trying to pull media attention away from Bling-Bling."

"You are the single source of Bling-Bling's media attention," I said, "and in a million years, nothing we are dealing with today has been manufactured in hopes of stealing your attention away from them."

She studied her nails.

"Starling, why are you so intent on causing problems between us and the casino next door? Is that not the polar opposite of what you were sent here to do? Why are you so dead set on stirring up more trouble than there already is between us and our new neighbors?"

She pretended to yawn.

"Who are you, anyway?" It was the first time I'd shared personal space with her, and it was a bit of a shock. Images of her as she traipsed about town, and especially when she was on television torturing us, made her appear to be in her late twenties, maybe early thirties, but a closer look told the truth. She had a few miles on her. She, like me, might have a shorter distance to forty than thirty. Her tawny-hued hair was straight from a bottle, and that day, behind her head in a loose bun secured with a #2 pencil instead of the stiff salon beach curls that usually fell in her face, partially obscured it, then spilled over her shoulders. Without the big hair, the tiny lines at the corners of her gray eyes, minus the heavy makeup that was her television standard, were obvious. And indicated she'd seen more than she let on. Everyone missed it, including me, because all eyes, including mine, were continually drawn to her halter-top cleavage. I realized it was by design. Part of her program. She didn't want anyone looking anywhere else and seeing the hard set of her jaw, the dark intent in her eyes, the more serious Starling I was a slab of stainless steel away from. A slab of stainless steel I tapped, to get her attention. "Who are you?"

"I am enough," she said.

"What?"

"I create peace, power, and confidence of mind and heart within myself. I am enough."

"That is total and complete nonsense, Starling, and I don't believe *you* believe a single word you're saying. I ran a background check on you when we first heard the city would be assigning a liaison. What'd I find? Nothing. Whoever's in charge of dual identities at the Police Resource Center in Milwaukee, if that part is even true, didn't go deep enough."

"I can neither confirm nor deny."

"They didn't go deep enough with your Psych 101 prep either," I said. "Your advice is drivel. It's like you've memorized a script of therapy responses."

"Denial is a defense mechanism."

"See?" I said. "Like that. And I'm not buying the Baylor business either. You have no more of a personal interest in Baylor than you have in the man on the moon. What's your professional interest in him?"

She didn't answer.

We listened to the intermittent drip from the sink faucet. Ten drips later, I took a deep breath, caught and locked eyes with her, then mustered all the sincerity I could to pose a serious question hoping for a truthful answer. I quietly asked, "Do you work for Bling-Bling? Is it Bling-Bling that's so interested in Baylor? Just tell me."

Twenty drips later, she answered with what felt like candor when she said, "I work for the government."

I leaned in. "Does the government know what Bling-Bling has planned for today that's causing all the chaos here?"

"Take responsibility for your own drama, Davis."

And with that, I gave it a rest. I stood. I was getting nowhere with her, and I needed to be somewhere. Four floors up, trying to restore the Bellissimo system and checking on my boss, No Hair, stuck in the casino, who I hadn't had any contact with in more than an hour. I needed to be upstairs spending five minutes with my mother explaining that I didn't have another minute to spare, and that she and Eugenia were going to have to work it out without me. Mostly, I needed Starling upstairs, trapped in my safe space, so I could take another stab at her. Or if I'd gone too far bad cop on her, let Fantasy have a turn at good cop. Because Starling was still our best chance at getting Baylor back. And I needed to accomplish everything before three o'clock so I could pick up my daughters at Willow Academy for Exceptional Children. With all that in mind, I made my way to the butler's pantry lift in the catering kitchen. Over my shoulder, I said, "Are you coming?" She retrieved the pizza and her tablet from the prep table and joined me just as a Security alert hit my phone. *Hotel guests sheltering in place are reporting no hot water. Calls have come from every floor of the hotel. No hot water.*

How could that be? The first thought that popped into my brain as I poked the butler's lift call button was to do what I'd normally do, call Maintenance and ask what happened to the hot water in the hotel, until the second thought that popped into my brain overrode the first. Maintenance had left the building. Just then, Fantasy and I were everything, including Maintenance, which was when a third thought smacked me. Had Fantasy and I turned down thirty floors of hot water heaters when we thought we were turning down thirty floors of heat and air units? Including in my home? And the floor above me, the Penthouse, where the owner of the Bellissimo and his wife lived?

"Hey!" I could barely hear Fantasy's voice through the butler's lift door that still hadn't opened. "Davis!"

I yelled at the door hoping my voice would carry up the shaft. "What?"

She yelled down, "I can't hear you."

I yelled up again, but that time at the top of my lungs. "I can't hear you either. Call me."

Beside me, Starling said, "Sheesh."

A second later, my phone rang. Fantasy led with, "Are you on your way?"

"I'm trying," I said. "I sat down for two seconds."

"You'll need to sit down again when I tell you what I found up here."

"Up here where?" I asked. "My house or Jay's place?"

"I'll start with your house," she said. "There's a note on your front door from July."

"July?"

I must have said it like I'd never heard her name before. Because Fantasy said, "July. As in Baylor and July. As in Little Dude's mother."

"I know who July is, Fantasy."

"I don't." It was Starling. "Are you talking about July the month or a person named July?"

I held up a wait-a-minute finger to Starling, but it was really a none-of-your-business finger. I asked Fantasy what the note said.

"It says she and the baby will be at her parents' until further notice, and don't call her, she'll call you when she's ready."

I turned to Starling. "What'd you do?"

"Me?" Starling said. "Nothing. What are you talking about?"

"How hard have you been stalking Baylor?"

"No more than usual." She looked perfectly innocent. "Why? What happened? What's wrong with him? Is this about his dentist?"

"His dentist?" I demanded. "What about his dentist?"

"Nothing." She shifted her stance. "Nothing."

"Davis!" Fantasy said into my ear. "We don't have time to worry about July or the dentist. Climb in the lift and get to Jay's place. Immediately."

To Starling, I said, "We'll talk about the dentist later." To Fantasy, I said, "Send the lift back down."

Starling said, "If you have dental phobias, don't project them onto me, Davis," just as Fantasy said, "The lift isn't here."

"It isn't here either."

I looked up. For divine guidance. I told Fantasy we'd take the service stairs.

"Take the service stairs to where?" Starling asked. "Baylor's condo?"

"Hurry," Fantasy said.

"Why?" I asked her. "Just tell me."

"I'll start with the good news."

"I could use some good news."

"The doc turned one of the staterooms into a chemistry lab," she said. "You should see it."

"That's good news?"

"It's better than the other news."

"Tell me, Fantasy. Get it over with."

"The ponytailed woman with the poisoned twenty-dollar bills?"

"What about her?"

"She's here."

"At Jay's place?"

"Yes," Fantasy said, "and she's dead."

From the corner of my twitching eye, I watched Starling, realizing whatever Fantasy was telling me was at the bare minimum juicy news, slide her hand into her pocket. Going for her phone. She either wanted an open line so someone could listen in, or she intended to record my side of the conversation. So I lifted the back of my shirt and showed her the Ruger in the waistband of my jeans, because I intended to control the situation. Starling raised her empty hand in the air with a *you-win* look on her face.

"She was bound like Dr. Wurtz was," Fantasy said. "Hands and feet, packing tape across her mouth."

"He had packing tape around his entire head."

"I know," she said. "I'm the one who yanked it off."

"And she just has packing tape on her mouth?"

"Davis, did you hear the dead part? Does it matter?"

It didn't matter, that I could put my finger on, so I moved on to a subject that did.

"Where's my mother?"

"I parked everyone at the kitchen table at your house, then went back to Jay's place to look for a rabbit cage because the rabbit is crazy and your dogs are losing their minds. That's when I found the science lab and the dead ponytailed woman."

What I meant to do was lean on the nearest solid object for support. What I didn't mean to do was tip over a cart piled high with delicate bone china dinner plates.

Friday, 12:30 P.M.

Fantasy and I stood in double doors of the master suite, Jay's room, staring at the lifeless body of the ponytailed woman on the bed. Starling was behind and between us breathing down our necks. Having tossed our face shields and gloves somewhere way back, Fantasy and I had our hands clapped over our mouths and noses so that anything nefarious on Ponytail wouldn't jump on us. Starling—monkey see, monkey do—also had her hand over her mouth and nose.

"Did you check her for a pulse?" I asked.

"I didn't touch her," Fantasy said.

"Then how do we know she's dead?"

"Look at her."

From between her fingers, Starling said, "She looks dead to me."

Ponytail did have a look of finality about her.

"Do we leave her here or move her and disturb the crime scene?" Fantasy asked.

"How do we know this is the crime scene?"

"Because, Davis, she's dead."

"But there's no blood," I said. "I don't see a weapon."

"Strangulation," Starling said from behind her hand. "Or maybe asphyxiation."

We ignored her.

"With a pillow," she added.

We continued to ignore her.

I asked Fantasy from behind my hand, "Are you suggesting we move her to my house?"

Fantasy answered from behind her own hand, "I'm suggesting we put her on ice."

"Do you have that much ice?" Starling asked.

"It's an expression," I said.

"I meant it literally," Fantasy said. "The walk-in cooler in the catering kitchen would be the perfect place to stash her body until we can get to her."

I blinked at her. "Until we can get to her?"

"She's already dead, Davis. We have plenty of people who are still alive to worry about."

"What the hell is going on here?" Starling asked.

"Do you want to be stuffed in the pantry lift with her dead body then drag it to the walk-in cooler, Fantasy?" I asked. "Because I know I don't."

Starling added, "Neither do I."

Fantasy said, "The pantry lift is already stuck. Somewhere between here and there. And no one asked you to, Sterling."

"Starling," she corrected. "Rhymes with darling."

"What we need to do is go to my house." I was about to say so I could go into the Bellissimo system and re-key Jay's place to keep whoever had access from running in and out, possibly including my own daughters, when I remembered I was the one without access. To the Bellissimo system. And even if I did, re-keying the electronic lock would only slow them down, not stop them. "For now," I started over, "let's leave her here." Not only did I want the comforts of home, I needed to make sure Mother and Eugenia weren't pulling each other's gray hair out, I had to find a way to check on No Hair and the five hundred people in the casino with him, and more than anything else just then, I needed Baylor. "We'll go to my house, sit down, calm down, and talk this through step by step starting with the first hiccup this morning. Surely somewhere in there we'll figure out what to do with her body."

With a touch to my elbow, Fantasy led me farther into the bedroom, closer to the dead ponytailed woman, to whisper, "We're officially in over our heads, Davis. I think it's time to call in the police, the FBI, Roadside Assistance, the PTA, the National Guard, the Humane Society, somebody, anybody, and let them figure it out."

"Figure what out?" Starling was right behind us again. She'd dropped her hand from her mouth and slid it into her pocket.

I held my hand out, palm up.

She said, "What?"

"Give me your phone."

"Never," she said. "Not happening."

"What's on it you don't want me to see?" I was just about to accuse her of having Bling-Bling electronic deposit notifications up and down her inbox or thousands of pictures of Baylor on her phone when the dead ponytailed woman under the blanket moaned.

Starling, closest to Ponytail, dove out of the way. Unfortunately, she hit her head on the corner of a side table on the way down.

"What a lightweight," Fantasy said.

I took two steps back, checked Starling's pulse, made sure she was breathing normally, and looked at her head where it caught the table. She was fine. She'd have a headache when she woke, but she'd be fine. Then I reached into her pocket and helped myself to her phone just as mine buzzed in my own pocket. It was a Security alert. *Hotel guests sheltering in place want to know when room service will resume. They've emptied their minibars.*

When we'd ordered pizza for the casino, we'd forgotten about the twelve hundred guests stuck in their rooms. Security alerted our phones again. *Is anyone in the casino awake enough to authorize distributing the pizza stacked at the doors to our hotel guests?*

Fantasy and I looked up from our phones and at each other. We said it on the same beat, a long-standing habit of ours when we reached the same conclusion at the same time after hearing the same impossible news. "Awake?"

I said, "No Hair didn't text me back earlier because he's asleep. Everyone in the casino is asleep."

"And this one's asleep too." Fantasy pointed at the ponytailed woman under the blanket.

"It must be the same deep, deep sleep Surveillance slept earlier."

Fantasy craned her head to see Ponytail from a different angle. "She reminds me of someone."

"I thought that when we had her up on the big screen in our office earlier," I said.

"It's her hairline and her forehead," Fantasy said. "I wonder whose forehead that is."

"I wonder if she got a dose of her own medicine." I sidestepped Starling, still out cold, and crept closer to Ponytail. "And I'm wondering why Good Pills wanted everyone asleep in the middle of the day." I held my breath, tugged my shirt sleeve down until it covered my hand, then gave her a quick push. There was her crossbody bag. Still crossbodied. I stepped aside so Fantasy could see it too. "Do you want her head or her feet?"

"Where are we going with her?"

"To my house. Before she wakes up."

"You just said you didn't want to move her."

"I said I didn't want to drag her dead body to a walk-in cooler. She's alive," I said, "and we need to talk to her. Too, when she wakes up, we'll know the casino is waking up. Whatever happens to her after that, we'll know it's also happening in the casino."

"Davis, if we touch her, we'll get whatever she has."

Good point.

We checked Starling again, still out like a light, then rummaged around Jay's master bath. We left with Bellissimo hair towel turbans wound around our heads and faces leaving nothing exposed but our eyeballs with moisturizing spa gloves on our hands. First, we yanked the folded duvet out from under her feet. She didn't notice. Then we wrangled her Michael Kors crossbody bag off her body, which wasn't easy because the slick moisturizer inside the gloves was very moisturizing. Neither of us wanted to carry the crossbody bag, so we dropped it on Ponytail's stomach for the ride next door. We spread out the duvet beside her, rolled her and her crossbody bag onto it, then lifted the whole cocoon, Fantasy at her head and me at her feet.

"These gloves have got to go." Fantasy hadn't finished saying it through the thick terrycloth turban covering her mouth before the slippery gloves on her hands slid off taking the blanket she'd had bunched between them along for the ride.

Ponytail's head hit the floor with a decisive thud.

She didn't seem to notice that either.

"She's probably dead now." I lowered my end.

We traipsed back to Jay's master bath, that time around the pile of Starling instead of over her because we had no peripheral vision past our towel turbans and didn't want to trip over her, then washed the greasy lotion off our hands and rinsed the rest of the moisturizer from inside the gloves. After all that, it was back to Ponytail. We tried again. We hoisted our blanket stretcher, hauled her out Jay's front door, then through mine. It was harder than it sounded, in spite of the fact that it sounded plenty hard to begin with.

"What do we do with her now?" Fantasy looked right and left in my foyer.

"Over there," I panted, nodding at a settee under a massive oil painting of nothing that matched everything. "She can finish her nap."

"Shouldn't we put her on one of your porches, so our eyebrows don't fall off?"

"Good idea." I gave the towel on my head a nod in the direction of the guest wing thinking we'd tuck her away on the lanai between guest rooms, but remembering my mother, Eugenia Winters Stone, not to mention Dr. Winford Wurtz and his rabbit were there too, and not knowing who of that group might need to stay overnight (hopefully none), I almost gave myself whiplash swinging the towel on my head in the opposite direction. The family room. "We'll have to put her on the front patio."

"Then what?"

"Then I don't know what, Fantasy. One step at a time."

We lugged the blanket full of Ponytail through the quiet family room—no Mother, no Eugenia, no Dr. Wurtz, and no rabbit. I had to rest my end of Ponytail on the floor to free my hands enough so I could slide open half of the patio door. I picked up the lower end of her again, we stepped onto the patio, wove around the outdoor fire table, then landed her on a cushy sofa in the shade. I peeled back the blanket to reach for the crossbody bag. Ponytail, still asleep, pulled against what her unconscious brain must have registered as restraints, then flipped herself over the wrong way. We barely caught her before she hit the stone floor. We rolled her the other way, tucking her into the deep pocket where seat cushion met back cushion. She settled in.

I gently eased the crossbody bag away, tossing and landing it on a wicker table between two loungers on the other side of the fire table, then gently pulled the packing tape from her mouth. She scared us to absolute death when she immediately sucked in a huge gulp of fresh air. Fantasy and I could have easily jumped out of our skin, but instead we jumped back as far as we could.

"Now what?" Fantasy asked, far enough away to feel safe pulling the turban off her head.

"We go back for Starling, drag her here, then we go through Ponytail's purse." I landed my turban on top of hers.

"And who keeps an eye on Ponytail while we do all that?"

I stuck my head through the open patio door. "Cotton! Candy!"

Like an elephant on the wild tundra headed our way, my one-hundred-sixty-pound sheepdog, Cotton, barreled through the house. Solo. Without Candy. Which was odd. Even odder, instead of charging through the open side of the sliding glass door to get to me, Cotton chose the closed side. The impact shook the thick glass and bounced him back ten feet. He landed with four huge paws clawing air.

Fantasy craned her neck. "Is he okay?"

"He's fine." And just to prove it, Cotton popped up, righting himself, dog smiling from ear to ear, circulating the air with his wagging tail, a tail so large and powerful he'd inadvertently sent Bexley and Quinn sailing through the air way too many times, with an all-around *you-rang?* presence about him. "There's surprisingly little dog under all the fur. His fur absorbs all the shock when he runs into walls and doors. I don't think he can feel a thing through it."

"Have you had his eyes checked?"

"I have."

"Can he see?"

"Yes," I said, "but he has depth-perception issues."

Fantasy said, "Dear Lord."

I said, "Cotton, come." He came. "Where's your sister? Where's Candy?"

"Does he talk too?"

I ignored Fantasy and kept my attention on Cotton, sitting in front of me awaiting further instruction. I said, "Cotton, this is yours." I pulled my shirt over my mouth and nose, eased toward Ponytail, and reached to pat her leg with my gloved hand. He gave her a good sniff. Then I said, "Cotton, watch it." Cotton, in some ways the smartest dog in the world, in other ways quite the opposite, and in all ways the clumsiest, would guard anything I asked him to. I discovered it quickly after he joined our family. Realizing all was quiet on the home front, too quiet with Cotton in residence, I went on a Cotton hunt. I found him guarding two pieces of a broken red Crayon in the girls' playroom. I asked Bex and Quinn how long they'd had Cotton guarding the Crayon. They said they asked him to watch it before breakfast. It was lunchtime. I knew with Cotton on guard duty, Ponytail wasn't going anywhere until I released him. Cotton would sit on her if he had to. Ponytail problem temporarily solved.

"Does he have any other tricks?" Fantasy asked.

"No, but Candy finds things," I said. "Give her the scent and she can find anything."

"Like what?"

"Like anything."

"Well, send her to find Starling," Fantasy said.

"Candy isn't here."

"Where is she?"

"I don't know." I stuck my head in the door. "Candy? Mother? Eugenia? Albert Einstein doctor?"

Nothing.

"You know they're here somewhere," Fantasy said.

I peeled off my gloves. "Maybe they're all in Bex and Quinn's outdoor playground and can't hear us. Let's go get Starling, bring her here, slap an ice pack on her head, then we'll find everyone else. And when we do, we're locking the front door. After that, no one in or out until we get control of this situation."

"Control of which of our situations?"

"Let's start with our Baylor situation."

We sailed through my front door and took a left for Jay's.

"Didn't we leave the door open?" I asked.

"We did," she answered. "We had our arms full of Ponytail."

"Then why is it closed?"

We busted through the keypad with Fantasy's Stuart Weitzman just like we'd busted into Maintenance and went straight to Jay's bedroom.

Starling and her tablet were gone.

She must have thought her phone flew out of her pocket when she went down, because Jay's room was a mess. Side tables were upturned, pillows and cushions had been tossed, and the bed was stripped down to the mattress. The room's balcony doors were open, the patio having been tossed too, all in her efforts to locate her phone I'd swiped. I made a mental note of the fact that with the furniture in disarray, I could see Bex and Quinn's outdoor playroom landscaping from Jay's balcony, which I found odd, because you couldn't see Jay's balcony from Bex and Quinn's outdoor playroom, and that could possibly be where they'd found a rabbit, who'd sneaked through, or how they'd obtained the rabbit, by sneaking through themselves, and might have taken five minutes to investigate had it not occurred to me there was another item on my to-be-investigated list that needed me more. "Where's the lab?"

Fantasy led the way.

We crossed the vast living room to reach the guest wing of the suite, and as soon as we took a left down the hall, I saw an open padlock dangling from an industrial hasp clumsily mounted to the exterior of the first door. In a suite designed and furnished by the same New York firm responsible for Vegas' Bellagio's elegant interior, the hardware store-issued lock looked more than out of place. I proceeded with caution to see what had been held captive in the room against its will. I stopped at the doorway, hesitant to step in, and tried to make sense of it all. The bedroom furniture had been replaced with two oversized banquet tables. The table to my right brimmed with bottles, jars, vials, flasks, beakers, scales, droppers, disposable gloves, masks, eye goggles, and a stack of molded plastic tubs that looked perfect for soaking twenty-dollar bills, all around a one-gallon stainless steel spray container. A handheld wand snaked up from the bottom and hooked onto the rim. The silver container was labeled *EDIBLES*. Scattered throughout the chemical menagerie were at least ten disposable coffee cups abandoned in various stages of consumption. The table to my left held four freestanding drying racks. They were white, plastic, and standing on the table in inverted Vs with five long thin rows on both sides. Some were edge-to-edge full of twenty-dollar bills, others sparse with only one or two twenties, and still others completely empty. I pulled my shirt over my mouth and nose to step in to see what was below the racks. Taped to the table in front of the first drying rack was an index card that read, *100%*, and below that, *Pinbe,* and what was probably Pinbe's chemical symbol, *Pb*. The index card in front of the second drying rack read, *50%*. Below that, *Belusen, Bl*. The third read, *35%*, below that, *Zimec, Zc,* and the fourth, *10%, Requelime, Rq*. I was no chemist, but even to my untrained eye it looked as if there were a mix-and-match element to the synthetic nerve agent recipe, as if some combinations of the ingredients produced corrupted twenties that granted the receiver different symptoms at different strength than other contaminated twenties. But it was what I saw against the back wall that was the most disturbing. Between the two tables was a thin blanket and a flat pillow where someone had slept the night before, probably after working tirelessly to spray food and taint twenty-dollar bills with various degrees and different combinations of chaos.

Having seen enough, we returned to the living room where Fantasy took a right for Jay's side of the suite instead of following my left for the front door. "Where are you going?"

"I'm looking for the pizza."

Friday, 1:00 P.M.

If Starling Halter had a lick of sense, she'd have wiped her phone immediately when she couldn't find it. Although not wanting to lose her contacts, history, or pictures of her parakeet, if she had one, she might choose to purchase a new phone, activate it, retrieve her phone data from her tablet, which was a tedious process in and of itself, then download it to the new phone. It was just as complicated as it sounded. And unless it was something you did all day every day, say from behind the tech desk at a cellular service provider, it took a minimum of thirty minutes. Which gave me twenty-nine minutes to dump and clone her phone and finally be assured of a little anonymity with which to communicate with the outside world.

Not like I had twenty-nine minutes to spare.

While Fantasy searched high and low for my mother and crew, I went straight to my home office behind my kitchen, activated a new phone from my bottom-desk-drawer stash—I was hard on phones; I kept a supply handy—then hacked into Bling-Bling's Wi-Fi next door instead of what might or might not be left of the Bellissimo's internet that Good Pills had control of. After jailbreaking Starling's phone and installing an application that bypassed her security, because I didn't have time to run it through a password cracker, I disabled her Where's My Phone? feature, then downloaded SpiPhone on the new phone before transferring every single bit of data from Starling's lost phone, including the phone's identifiers—so illegal—to my new one. I didn't wipe her old phone clean afterward. Starling would be ten steps behind me downloading to a new phone, and if there was nothing to download, she'd know I had her data. I dusted off my digital fingerprints, including reinstalling her security features, as if it really was under a chair cushion in Jay's bedroom and not in my hot little hands.

As soon as the transfer finished, the identical phones began ringing. The caller ID said BELLISSIMO RESORT AND CASINO. So Starling was still somewhere on our property and still looking for her phone.

Fantasy appeared in the doorway, waving half a slice of pizza. Her mouth full of the other half, she said, "Ham and pineapple. A pizza travesty. And your mother isn't here."

I tossed Starling's old phone in my middle desk drawer, pocketed my own phone in one back pocket and her cloned phone in the other, then pushed away from my desk. "What about Eugenia? The doctor? The rabbit? My other dog?"

Fantasy shook her head. "Not here."

"They have to be here. Where else would they be?"

"I've looked everywhere." She shooed pizza crust crumbs from her top. "They're not here."

"We have ten thousand square feet," I said. "You haven't had time to look everywhere."

"I found your mother's and your dad's girlfriend's big old woman purses, Davis, but I didn't find any old women. Or an old German doctor. Or any animals. They must be roaming the halls."

"The last thing we need is for them to be roaming the halls. We don't have time to roam the halls looking for them."

"Are we late for something?"

I stood. "Watching television and playing golf."

She grabbed another slice of pizza travesty and followed me out of the kitchen. "Am I watching television or playing golf?"

In the foyer, I opened a hidden closet door, then reached into my husband's golf bag and blindly grabbed. I passed Fantasy a club. "What am I supposed to do with this?"

"You're going to poke through Ponytail's crossbody bag while I poke through Starling's phone."

Back in the living room, Fantasy peered out the patio door. "Where'd we leave her crossbody bag?"

From Bling-Bling's Wi-Fi again, I screenshared Starling's phone with my smart television. "On the table between the loungers."

"The only thing left on the table between the loungers is the strap," she said. "Not the purse."

"Maybe the wind blew it off the table and all you can see is the strap." I opened and closed the shallow drawers of the cabinet under the television looking for the wireless keyboard and mouse I kept there.

"Nope," she said, still in the doorway.

I found my wireless mouse under a unicorn sticker book. "You're going to have to step out there, Fantasy." I found my wireless keyboard under a box of My First Alphabet flashcards. "It's fresh air." I connected the hardware. "You'll be fine." I clicked on Starling's internet browser. "Just stay away from Ponytail." As Google opened, I checked the time. Eighteen minutes. I'd cloned a phone and used it to create a makeshift computer on my television in just under eighteen minutes.

From one foot out on the porch, Fantasy said, "I can't find the purse."

"You're not looking hard enough. I know we left it out there." Every bit of me wanted to nose around Starling's email inbox, or her browsing history, or any recent calls from Baylor's dentist—what in the world was that about?—looking for any hint as to why July might have taken the baby and left for her parents' in a huff, because Baylor was going to freak when he learned his girl and his baby weren't waiting for him at the end of the day if Bling-Bling didn't kill him first, but I was too worried about No Hair and the people in the casino to take the time. I stayed in the web browser, entering the Bellissimo's 32-bit IP address, and just like that, I tiptoed in through the backdoor of the Bellissimo's system. "What's Ponytail doing?"

"She looks like she's asleep," Fantasy said, "but she's wiggling."

"Wiggling?" I nosed around the Bellissimo system for surveillance cameras. "Is she waking up?"

"Ponytail?" Fantasy called out. "Are you waking up?"

No answer.

Her head inside the door again, Fantasy said, "You know, Davis? You drive like a ninety-year-old woman with your nose on the windshield, white knuckling the steering wheel at ten and two, and at half the posted speed limit. But you can turn a television into a computer from a stolen phone." I didn't take the time to protest yet another complaint about my driving skills—I'd been a police officer for six years, which had been six years of extremely defensive driving—to explain again that I wasn't a bad driver, just a rusty driver, because it'd been a minute since I last drove and I hadn't had time to joyride around town long enough to work out the kinks. I scrolled through the Bellissimo's closed-circuit camera IDs, a list of more than a thousand individual numbers, long strings of numbers, trying to locate a large block with digits close to each other, only one or two off, because those would be the casino cameras. I selected twenty camera IDs with digits close enough to be kissing cousins and hit enter. Thumbnail shots of the casino started populating on the television screen.

Fantasy said, "I found Ponytail's crossbody bag."

I finally looked away from the television and over my shoulder. Fantasy was still on the porch. The shreds of what used to be Ponytail's crossbody bag were in the living room. Between the two, a golf club. Cotton had eaten most, but not all, of the crossbody bag. Cotton would, and did, eat rocks when he was in the mood.

Cotton!

I'd forgotten about Cotton!

"Fantasy?" I could hear the hesitation in my voice. "Where's my dog?"

"He's between the loungers," she said, "and out like a light."

I shot straight up from my seat on the rug in front of the television, where the last of the casino images were filling the screen. I ran to the patio, straight to Cotton, who was snoring away. Between the snores, all hundred and sixty pounds of him bucked.

Hiccups.

Not only was Cotton asleep, he had the hiccups.

"Your dog dosed himself," Fantasy said.

"He has the hiccups and he's asleep at the same time, Fantasy. He double dosed himself." I lifted his eyelids to check his pupils, looked at his gums to make sure they were pink, and held my hand to his heart to see if it was racing—all the things his vet had me do on the way to the doggie ER the times Cotton had eaten socks, a ten-pound bag of potatoes, too many toys to count, eight bars of soap in one sitting, a hanging basket of begonias, a two-pound box of long-grain jasmine rice—until Fantasy's legs distracted me when they came into view as she took a seat on one of the loungers.

"Davis, it's time to face facts."

"Face what facts, Fantasy? That I asked my dog to guard a poison purse and he ate it?"

"You asked your dog to guard Ponytail. Big difference. He took it upon himself to eat her poison purse. The fact we need to face is that we've been exposed." She slapped her knees. "You're all up in your dog's face after we just poked around a mad scientist's lab and we're ten feet from Ponytail without any protection. At this point, we've exposed ourselves to everything. We might as well get a pillow and a blanket and lay down, because we'll be asleep any minute. And when we wake up, we'll probably have horns sticking out of our heads."

I sat back on my heels. "We've been dosed."

She pointed through the open patio door to the television. "And we've been robbed."

I whipped my head around to look at the screen. Five hundred people, including the Hazmats, were stretched out, curled up, and piled on top of each other up and down the main aisle of the casino seemingly sleeping as hard as Ponytail and Cotton were. As hard as the surveillance techs had. Behind them, in front of them, on all sides, and as far as we could see, slot machine doors were wide open, their cash boxes gone. And that was why Good Pills put everyone in the casino to sleep. So they could rob us blind. The hiccups were to encourage us to lock our casino doors. It worked. Disabling our surveillance department was so there'd be no recorded evidence. Again, success for Good Pills. The hearing loss was to provide cover for the forty-five hundred slot machine alerts sounding all at once as the machine doors were electronically unlocked. So far, so good for Good Pills. The point of the carotene-laced fake Starbucks must have been to usher in the fake Starbucks crew who would gather the cash boxes after everyone fell into a deep sleep, and the fake Starbucks truck at the marina entrance was to whisk away the crew and money after the deed. My guess was they successfully checked that item off their list too. All in all, a perfect casino heist, but not much of one if they only took the cash boxes from the slot machines on the casino floor.

My phone buzzed. I ignored it, because I was busy mentally estimating the total of what might have been taken from the machines, somewhere in the three-million-dollar range, and almost hoping the fake Starbucks crew took the time to breach the casino cage, where the real money was, or our vault, where the real-real money was, because that would mean the nightmare was over, until my phone buzzed for what felt like the tenth time in a row. Then again. I pulled it from my pocket. The caller ID said Victoria Elise Fabré. Fantasy, still sitting on the lounger with me still on the ground beside my hiccupping and sleeping dog, stared at my phone too. "Why is a steamy romance author calling you?"

"I don't know, but it can't be good."

"Don't Bex and Quinn go to school with her daughter?"

"That's why it can't be good."

Our heads whipped around when the scuffle of Ponytail trying to right herself on the outdoor sofa demanded our attention. She managed it by first sitting up, then swinging out her legs and landing her bound feet on the stone floor. She held her loosely taped hands out. "What is this?" She stomped her feet held together at the ankles with packing tape. "What's going on?" Confusion poured over her. "Where am I? Who are you? What did you do to that dog?"

Friday, 1:30 P.M.

She had amnesia. She had a form of amnesia. Ponytail could recite the periodic table, sing a song of states and capitals, alphabetically, and knew the books of the Bible, in order, but she couldn't tell us her name. She said she didn't remember ever being in a casino in her life, she didn't know the clothes she was wearing, she had no idea what might have been in the crossbody bag before Cotton ate it, and she'd never heard of Good Pills Biopharmaceuticals. "Do they make Hello Happy gummies? My mother eats those by the handful. My mother!" Her face lit up. She shook her closed fists in excitement. "I have a mother!" Her face fell. Her hands went back to her lap. "I don't know her name."

"How can you remember that Olympia is the capital of Washington and not remember your mother's name?" Fantasy asked. "Or your own, for that matter?"

"I can see her in my brain, but that's it."

"Well, in your brain," I said, "what's she doing?"

"Eating Hello Happy gummies."

I poked around Safari on Starling's cloned phone looking for a plausible diagnosis. "It's either retrograde, anterograde, or transient global amnesia," I announced. "Maybe. The good news is they're all temporary."

"How does that help us?" Fantasy asked.

"I don't know that it does," I said.

"How temporary?" Ponytail asked.

"I don't know that either."

Nothing about Ponytail felt threatening. She was pleasant, cooperative, and polite. But we kept our guard up just the same. We introduced ourselves from a safe distance on the porch and explained where she was, who we were, how we'd found her, and gave her a bare-bones rundown of our predicament. Then we gently told her the role we believed she might have played in it.

Her face was blank. And pale. She shook her head slowly. "I didn't do any of that." She followed up with, "At least I don't remember doing any of that." Then, "Why would I do that?" Finally, "If I did any of that, I am *so* sorry."

Clearly, we were up against a monster.

We just didn't know who or what the monster was.

It didn't appear to be Ponytail.

Fantasy and I untangled her from the packing tape and ushered her inside. She chose water over coffee, gulping down two glasses. While she splashed water on her face and tightened her ponytail, from which long strands of hair the color of honey had slipped loose, she yelled through the open powder room door, "I recognize my face in the mirror, but I still don't know who I am!"

We recognized her face too—the almond-shaped hazel eyes, the small sharp nose, the full lips—but didn't know who she was either.

After quickly poking through what was left of the contents of her purse with two kabob skewers from my kitchen, not finding ID or any indication that she was a guest at the Bellissimo, just a Bobbi Brown Bare Pink lip balm, a very smart watch Cotton had snacked on, and fifty or more mangled and tainted twenty-dollar bills, Fantasy and I lugged my dog inside. As we passed the powder room's open door, I told Ponytail, "Your watch is on the porch. My dog might have played with it. Can you grab it and see if there's an inscription on the back?"

Fantasy yelled, "Look for any scars or tattoos that jog your memory." Then to me, huffing and puffing, she said, "Your dog weighs more than my husband."

"Oh, really?" I was out of breath myself. "How often do you haul Reggie around?"

Ponytail stepped back into the living room strapping her watch to her wrist just as we were settling Cotton in. "My pockets are empty, and if I have any scars or tattoos, I can't find them. That's a really cute dog. I hope he's okay."

I straightened my achy spine. "He got a dose of whatever you did," I said, "so if you're okay, it stands to reason he'll be okay."

"Are you okay?" Fantasy asked her. "Feeling like yourself yet?"

"I feel fine." She patted her face, shrugged, then quickly shimmied the rest of the way down, just to make sure. "But I still don't know myself." She held out her ringless left hand. "I think I'm single." She'd shaken most of the cobwebs and no longer had an air of sheer terror about her, but she didn't know what day of the week it was.

"Where are we?" She looked through the patio doors, past where she'd napped, and studied the city skyline marked by casinos. "It looks festive," she said, "and it's warm."

"Biloxi, Mississippi," I told her.

"How close are we to New Orleans?" Her voice was animated, as if all the puzzle pieces might have fallen into place at the mention of The Big Easy, but those hopes were dashed when she said, "I've always wanted to vacation in New Orleans." Then, "I think I've always wanted to vacation in New Orleans. I might have landed at their airport a few times on my way to somewhere else, but I can't remember." Then, "Wait. Are we on the beach? New Orleans is in the Gulf and Biloxi's close to New Orleans, so we're in the Gulf, right? Are we close to the beach?"

I pointed the other way, opposite of the city, south of my home. "The beach is out there."

"If you're that excited about the beach, you must not live near one," Fantasy said.

"I might live around water," she said, "because that feels familiar, but not the beach."

"We'll show you the beach in a minute," I said.

She clapped her hands in a small way. In a goody-goody way. Then said, "I don't mean to be rude, or an inconvenience, but I'm hungry."

Fantasy said, "Do you like pineapple pizza?"

Ponytail's eyes rolled up, searching her brain. "I don't know."

Fantasy stood. "Let's find out."

Ten minutes earlier, while Fantasy had quizzed her, enjoying the periodic table recital, I'd been electronically nosing around the Bellissimo on the television. For one, scanning surveillance video of my front door to catch my mother and company exiting, which I didn't, because Fantasy was right; they weren't there. For two, I'd been preparing a slideshow for Ponytail. I told her I'd like her to look at a few photographs, to see if any faces rang any bells. She settled in on the sofa. I started the slideshow. "If you recognize anyone, tell me. As it hits your brain. Anything that comes to mind."

Her ponytail bobbed.

First, my television screen filled with a photo of Dr. Winford Wurtz.

Her ponytail shook a no.

"Are you sure?" I asked.

"I'm sure."

"You didn't see him cooking up mayhem in the lab next door?" I wanted to ask, but didn't, instead moving on to Colleen Ricci, President and CEO of Good Pills Biopharmaceuticals.

Ponytail shook her head. "I've never seen that woman."

Then a man named Brian Mancini, Human Resources Director, another photo I'd pulled from my two-minute peek at Good Pills' website.

"I don't know him," Ponytail said.

"Are you positive? If you work for Good Pills, he would have hired you."

She shook her head again. Cotton, between us, stretched in his sleep, then yawned. Ponytail jumped. Because Cotton yawning was like the belly of a 747 grazing the roof. He gave it his all. "He's vocal." I reached over and tried to shake him awake. No luck. "And very dramatic." I directed her attention back to the television and showed her Good Pills Head of Security. Lucas Romano. And after reading his name aloud for her, I realized there was a very good chance the buffet was Italian at the Good Pills Christmas luncheon. Ricci, Mancini, and Romano. Spaghetti, tiramisu, and red vino.

"No," she said.

Ponytail and I heard the pizzeria ding of the microwave in the kitchen. Before she had time to turn her attention to the noise behind her from the television in front of her, Starling Halter's Casino Liaison photo filled my television screen. Ponytail barely reacted, but react she did. She inhaled quickly, her dark eyes flashed, and her jaw clenched. All appearing and disappearing in the split second before she said, "No."

Fantasy, who'd stepped into the living room and was in the process of setting down a slice of pizza travesty beside her saw it too. She said, "Are you sure?"

She shook her ponytail no. A little too adamantly. "I don't know her."

Maybe Ponytail didn't know Starling, but she recognized her. At least subconsciously. I'd have written it off as seeing her on television had I not just witnessed Starling take a dive when

Ponytail began waking at Jay's place. Was that so Ponytail wouldn't recognize her? Did the two women have a connection? A history? Was there a story there? "Look again, Ponytail."

Her head scanned the room. "Who is Ponytail?"

All our heads swiveled the other way when we heard my front door blow open hard enough to slam into the wall behind it—that would leave a mark—ushering in the Bellissimo owner's wife, Bianca Casimiro Sanders, who yelled what she believed to be my name. "DAVID!"

(It's Davis.)

We listened with sheer dread as Bianca Sanders marched through my foyer and down the hall. She appeared in the doorway to the living room wearing only a white chiffon robe over the barest slips and strings of white undergarments underneath that left nothing to the imagination. On her feet, Manolo Blahnik white satin mules with three-inch heels. On her face she wore a thick crocodile green mud mask that stretched from her hairline to her collar bones. It left us nowhere to fix our gazes. Except maybe her eyeballs in the sea of near nakedness and pickle green. She inhaled sharply, squared her shoulders, then announced, "I have no hot water in my home, David. My dermal esthetician, Jules, needs to remove my anti-aging mask and there's nary a drop of hot water in my home. How, David, do you expect her to remove my anti-aging mask when there is no hot water? What have you done to the hot water?"

For once in our long history, Bianca had accused me of something for which I was actually guilty.

Fantasy's head tipped back, gearing up for a good laugh at Bianca, but when her head came down, a hiccup escaped. She clapped her hands over her mouth. Through her fingers, she said, "Unrelated. Random. Just a—" She hiccupped again.

I was right behind her.

I checked the time, hiccupping a second time.

We had an hour before we lost our hearing and two additional hours before we fell asleep. In that time, I had to help No Hair in the casino, find my mother, Eugenia Stone, Dr. Wurtz, and the rabbit, free Baylor of his Bling-Bling shackles, retrieve my daughters from Willow Academy for Exceptional Children, then somehow record it or relay it to someone or write it all down in case when I woke up, I, like Ponytail, had amnesia. Mid-hiccup, my eyes rose to meet those of the only person in the world who I could count on for help just then, but she was busy examining the lengths of her outstretched arms as if it was the first time she'd ever seen them, waiting for them to turn orange.

"We won't turn orange, Fantasy."

"Davis," she almost cried, but maybe it was just that she said my name mid-hiccup, "I'm already turning orange!"

"How?" I hiccupped. "Where's the—" (hiccup) "—fake Starbucks truck?"

Her face went blank as she gave me the point, then she hiccupped.

"David!" (Hiccup.) (It was Bianca.) (Still almost naked below her pea soup face.) "I demand to know—" (hiccup) "—exactly what is happening."

I couldn't answer for two reasons. One, I didn't know. Two, Fantasy and I were at my kitchen sink hiccupping through a cold-water scouring with Dawn dishwashing detergent—it worked for baby ducks, maybe it would work for us—scrubbing our hands all the way to our elbows, our faces, and every other inch of exposed skin we could find.

Friday, 2:00 P.M.

One single thing was going my way, and that was Security, a testament to our boss, No Hair, who hired the best, raised them right, and was quick to reward the well-oiled machine that was Bellissimo Security for jobs well done. At present, they were being rewarded somewhere near the top of the astrophysicist salary scale. After wiggling into internal communications on my makeshift television computer, I issued a security alert, hiccupping the entire time. *Status report from front entrance, casino entrance, and all guards posted on guest floors in the hotel.* They immediately responded from their assigned stations, no one mentioning hiccups, chocolate donuts, hearing loss, discolored skin, or severe mood swings. And they obviously weren't asleep or they wouldn't be piling on the bad news faster than I could read it. The front entrance was secure but crowded on the other side of the locked doors with local authorities, television news crews, plus guests with confirmed reservations arriving and demanding entry. The casino was secure, Security there reporting no activity and no attempts from anyone inside to communicate with anyone outside. Which seemed odd, because with Ponytail awake, the casino should have been awake by then too. But if they were, surely they'd let it be known by barreling through the locked casino doors. Where they'd run straight into pizza. The reports from the hotel floors were more alarming. Many guests were ignoring shelter-in-place orders and trying to storm out. Others were irate about lack of room service, casino access, and hot water. And all were threatening to call their attorneys, demanding to know what was wrong, and using hotspot internet access to broadcast live to every social media platform out there about being held prisoner by the Bellissimo. Which was probably why the security guards at the front doors were reporting authorities and news crews congregating.

Through hiccups so strong she resorted to half speech and half charades, Fantasy communicated that she would be in the kitchen watching the live news coverage at our entrance to see—she used her hands as binoculars circling her eyes—what they were saying. She used her hands, snapping her closed fingers quickly against her thumbs to indicate chit-chat. I used limited speech and extensive charades to communicate back that I would be looking—binocular eyes—for my mother again. For the word "mother," I cradled and rocked an imaginary baby. Fantasy said, "Are you—" hiccup "—trying to—" hiccup "—tell me—" hiccup "—you're pregnant?" One thing I think we both realized, but didn't have the energy to convey to each other, was that we had the hiccups harder and faster than anything we'd seen in the casino that morning.

Like Cotton, we might have been double dosed.

Which cut our timeline in half.

I didn't have three hours.

At that point, I had less than two hours before I fell asleep.

Bianca Sanders, who had the hiccups at a higher rate and stronger velocity than even Fantasy and I did, refused to go back to her home and get dressed. Which I crazy dance requested through my hiccups several times by pointing upstairs—a no-brainer, because there was nothing above us but the penthouse, where she lived—then pantomiming myself pulling an imaginary shirt over my head and stepping into imaginary pants. All for nothing. After ten minutes of protesting at the top of her lungs between hiccups and demanding I do something, which was after she refused to Dawn dishwash herself, because she'd use an abrasive household detergent meant for cutlery on her alabaster skin "exactly never," she gave up, settling herself in a side chair in my living room assuming an unnecessarily dignified pose factoring in her Wicked-Witch-of-the-West face that was drying, cracking, and flaking off onto her sheer chiffon robe. Throughout it all, her chest bucked with hiccups to the tick of the second hand on a clock.

"We—" hiccup "—gotta—" hiccup "—do—" hiccup "—something—" hiccup "—about—" hiccup "—her," Fantasy sort of said. Then hiccuped.

"We—" hiccup "—need—" hiccup "—her—" hiccup "—meds," I sort of said back.

Then hiccuped.

Ponytail sat quietly. Watching the show and scratching her ponytail.

Cotton slept on.

All alone. Which, in the middle of everything else, reminded me my other dog was missing. Where was everyone? Where was my mother? Where was Eugenia Winters Stone? Where was Dr. Winford Wurtz? Where was the rabbit? Where was my goldendoodle, Candy? I caught Fantasy's eye and tried to ask through my raging hiccups if she'd seen Candy sleeping anywhere. I did it with a flat hand on my brow, surveying the imaginary horizon, then puppy dog pants, with paw hands and tongue lolling, then my hands pressed together against my cheek, indicating sleep. Fantasy held up quizzical hands. She had no idea what I was trying to say. I licked an air sucker. In my mind, it was a multi-colored swirl sucker as big as a saucer, the kind of sucker I associated with carnivals, trying to convey the word "candy," almost to no avail, until Ponytail, who didn't have the hiccups and could string two words together, tried to interpret. "She wants you to lick the dog!"

I threw my hands up in defeat.

Then Ponytail brilliantly suggested we write notes.

A novel idea.

I turned for the computer that was my television, poked around Starling's screenshared phone until I found her Notes application, then typed. "Did you see Candy sleeping anywhere when you were looking for my mother?" flashed across the television in huge letters.

All that just for Fantasy to shake her head no, then lift a wait-a-second finger, run for the kitchen, and return with the pizza travesty box and a Sharpie from my desk.

She scribbled, then passed the pizza travesty box to me. *How can you be so concerned about your dog when your MOTHER is missing?*

I grabbed the Sharpie from her and turned the box over. *Because my dog is probably with my mother.*

She opened the pizza travesty box to write on the inside. *Ask Security. They might not notice or remember seeing your mother, but they'd notice a dog.* After I read it, agreeing, and turned for my makeshift television computer, she scribbled again, then passed me the pizza travesty box. *Ask if they've seen your rabbit. Now that, they'd really remember.*

I grabbed the travesty box and scribbled back, *NOT. MY. RABBIT.*

I sent a second Security alert. *Has anyone seen a Goldendoodle? Her name is Candy. She's Mr. Cole's dog.*

Every response filling the screen was the same. No. Where in the world was my dog? Because my mother was surely with my dog. Who was with Dr. Winford Wurtz. Along with Eugenia Winters Stone. And the dadgum rabbit. But where?

I felt utterly defeated.

Fantasy and I had gone as far down the road as we could go alone.

It was time to interrupt the closed-door session of the Gaming Commission meeting. My husband had said don't do it again unless it was a true emergency, and I was smack dab in the middle of quite a few true emergencies. From Starling's cloned phone, I texted him. *Bradley, it's Davis, and I'll explain the phone situation later. S.O.S. And I mean it this time. Almost everyone at the Bellissimo—employees, guests, Fantasy and me—has been exposed to synthetic nerve agents. Nothing lethal, just irritating. Good Pills has control of all Bellissimo cyber operations. The cash boxes inside all the slot machines have been swiped. They're probably rolling down the street in a fake Starbucks truck. You absolutely HAVE to leave the Gaming Commission meeting, fly back to Biloxi fast, then pick up Bexley and Quinn. I won't be able to and there's no one I can call to pick the girls up short of the police, which would make Mrs. Wellesley's head explode. Not to mention scare the girls. You have to pick them up. But you probably shouldn't bring them here.*

He texted back immediately, in spite of the fact that it wasn't three o'clock, the time he said I'd hear from him next. Which said to me something had gone wrong at the Gaming Commission meeting. *How do I know it's really you?*

10.22.

I need something more secure than our wedding date.

Cotton ate a woman's purse, and I'm with Bianca who is half-naked.

That works. WHERE IS YOUR PHONE?

I patted my back pocket knowing I'd put it there. I looked around. Where was my phone? It had been in my back pocket until Fantasy and I picked up Cotton to wrangle him inside. At which point, I remembered, I'd dropped it. I left it there for two reasons. One, Good Pills was probably watching my phone activity. Two, Victoria Elise Fabré wouldn't stop calling. But not having my phone meant I hadn't been on the receiving end of calls or messages.

I hiccuped to the patio door.

No phone that I could see.

I couldn't take the time to toss outdoor furniture cushions.

I turned around and caught Ponytail's eye. I held phone fingers against my head then poked my chest. Back and forth. Repeatedly.

"Your phone?" She scooted to the edge of her seat. "You want me to find your phone?"

I nodded vigorously.

"Where do I look?"

I pointed at the patio. She rushed past me as I rushed back to Starling's cloned phone. *When will you be back, Bradley?*

Find your phone. Catch up.

CAN YOU LEAVE SO YOU CAN PICK UP BEX AND QUINN?

Find your phone, Davis. Catch up.

It took Ponytail several minutes, but she stepped into the living room from the porch phone first. I grabbed it out of her hand. I'd missed forty-three voicemails, one hundred and forty-three text messages, and one thousand and forty-three calls. The first message was from my mother.

Tavis, your farther's trampoline has the pickups. We R going to the lice doctor's hotel womb for a pure.

They had the hiccups. They went to the doctor's room for a cure. He had a cure? In which room? The old doc had a guest room on the fifteenth floor and a terrifying lab next door at Jay's place. I'd get to both just as soon as I finished with whatever it was Bradley wanted me to catch up with, but on my way to him, I read a message from Cricket at Willow Academy for

Exceptional Children. And it wasn't a message so much as it was a single photograph. No explanation needed. It was a picture of my darling daughters, each holding a perfect long dark braid with tiny red satin bows at the tips. The braids belonged to the little girl between Bex and Quinn who had the worst haircut I'd ever seen in my life. I knew the little dark-headed girl with the bad cut. She was Victoria Elise Fabré's daughter. Eliza Fabré. The only child of the bestselling bodice-ripper romance author famous for, among other things, her long, thick, dark mane of hair she wore only one way, in a loose Regency-era braid, just like the heroines on the covers of her bestselling books, and just like her mini me, her daughter Eliza. Bex and Quinn's classmate. Except Eliza wore her hair in two dark braids. In a loose kiddie Regency-era way. I guess that would be formerly in a kiddie Regency-era way.

In the photograph, Bex and Quinn were grinning from ear to ear.

Eliza was not.

I dropped my phone on a side table and fell into the chair opposite hiccupping and angry Bianca. Because I was too lightheaded to stand. Before she could open her mouth to demand I produce a hiccup specialist that very minute, I stopped her with, "No." In no uncertain terms. Just as Fantasy, from the kitchen door, said, "Davis. You're going to want to see this."

I was staring at the floor. "I don't want to see anything, Fantasy. Ever again."

"You need to."

"What?" I asked the floor.

"The news. In the kitchen."

"What?" I asked the floor again.

"It's Victoria Elise Fabré. She's at the front entrance giving a live interview to Spiderman from Prime Eight. She's accusing Bex and Quinn of playing beauty shop with her daughter, Elsa."

"Eliza."

"Like they'd ever do that," Fantasy said.

Then Ponytail spoke up. "Your hiccups are gone."

She was right. Our hiccups only lasted a half hour to the casino's hour. I stole a glance at Bianca to see if she still had the hiccups. She did. She still had the hiccups and she had helped herself to my phone on the table between us. I grabbed it from her just before she reached her husband's name as she scrolled through my contacts. The last thing I needed was for Richard Sanders, the owner of the Bellissimo, on safari with his sons on the other side of the globe, to hear it from Bianca.

Friday, 2:30 P.M.

I took care of Bianca first, even before I checked the messages from Bradley that would catch me up, because nothing else would be accomplished until I did. Fantasy and I cleared the top shelf of my medicine cabinet—the empty space reminding me my birth control pills were still in the wild—finding nothing stronger than Motrin. We dumped my mother's purse on the floor and didn't find anything close to medicinal, unless Winterfresh chewing gum, which certainly smelled like medicine, counted. We dumped Eugenia Winters Stone's purse and hit the jackpot. I presented the amber pill container for Bianca's inspection. She popped off the lid and helped herself to two Valium. She swallowed them dry. When her hiccups subsided, she barely noticed. And it wasn't much longer until she absolutely didn't notice, or care, that she wasn't dressed or that she looked like a chemistry experiment with half her jungle-green mask on her face the other half in her lap. She stopped accusing me of trying to ruin her life. She stopped telling me the atrocities I'd heaped on her that day were worthy of a firing squad. She stopped demanding I march myself upstairs to her penthouse home and boil enough water to fill her two-hundred-gallon soaking tub so that she might drown her anxiety. She kicked her Manolo Blahniks through the air, almost nailing poor Ponytail, and stopped everything to admire her pedicure, slumped low into the deep seat of her armchair, bare legs waving, crisscrossing, and even bicycling in the air, humming to herself, and occasionally belting out lines of arias from operas in languages no one spoke.

Settle Bianca down? Check.

Fantasy and I tried to calculate how long we had before we fell asleep. If we'd received a double dose of whatever was floating around, therefore double-timing it with the effects, we only had a symptom-free hour left. Our hearing was fine, so we were right when we guessed that whatever caused hearing loss in the casino had been piped through the speakers. We wouldn't turn orange either, because there wasn't a fake Starbucks truck anywhere nearby. And we'd be fully clothed when we went down for our naps, because there were no Hazmats to ask us to undress. Based on our calculations, we would sleep for at least an hour, and that based on everyone in the casino sleeping for the two hours it took Good Pills to rob us blind. It was knowing how much I had to do before I fell asleep, and that when I woke I wouldn't know what day of the week it was, that had me worried. First, it was Ponytail, who still couldn't tell us her name. Then the casino.

While Bianca gave it her *Madama Butterfly* all behind us, and just as I was reaching for my phone to catch up, my makeshift computer television stopped me. I joined Fantasy and Ponytail, glued to it, watching the casino wake. Even without audio, which I couldn't access from Starling's duped phone, it was clear we were watching five hundred people who didn't know who they were, who anyone else was, why they were in a casino, and mostly, why they weren't wearing clothes. What might have been, probably should have been, a tension-filled atmosphere didn't appear to be. While we could see signs of modesty—hiding behind open slot machine doors, blackjack tables, and one man behind a directional sign he'd ripped from the wall—ladies this way, gentlemen that—there was no indication of frustration, anger, or anything else bordering on negative, as if everyone woke up on the right side of the bed, or casino floor, as it were.

It took no time at all for someone to dump the contents of a Hazmat canvas bag. The other seven bags followed until there was an apparel mountain in the middle of the casino floor. Five hundred people began digging through, but no one knew what they were looking for. They didn't know their own clothes. They held various garments against themselves, checking for fit, trading with each other, then either tired of waiting their turn to dig through the clothes pile or feeling uncomfortable in a casino full of half-naked total strangers, they gave up and began grabbing and pulling on whatever they could lay their hands on with no regard to size. Or appropriateness. Or fashion dos and don'ts.

Fantasy whispered, "This is like watching some kind of weird native robing ritual."

I whispered back, "Where's No Hair?" when I realized I still hadn't checked my phone, but just as I tore my eyes away from the computer-television to reach for my phone, Cotton popped up from his nap. Ponytail had amnesia, five hundred people in the casino had amnesia, and Cotton had amnesia.

He yawned deeply. He stood and shook it off. Then he saw me. "Hey, good boy."

He didn't tackle me, his only greeting. In fact, he backed away.

"What's that noise?" Fantasy asked.

"I don't know." I patted the rug beside me. "Cotton, come."

We heard the low rumble of an outboard engine again. It was coming from Cotton. Somewhere deep in his throat.

"He's growling," Ponytail said.

He was. I'd never heard him growl. I didn't know he could growl. And he was growling at me. The person who fed him fifteen times a day, because he was that hungry. The person who carved out an hour of her life every three days to brush him, because that was what it took for an Old English sheepdog. The person who weighed considerably less than him yet lobbed him into the backseat of my new car—front half, then back half—where he squeezed himself between Bex and Quinn's booster seats, because he refused to jump in or out of anything, including the car, yet loved riding in it.

He didn't remember me.

And I might have spoken too soon on the hearing loss business, because Cotton began slowly advancing, barking at me with the volume on high, and with gusto, a forceful bark I'd never heard from him, and he was loud. He barked at me as if I were the dog catcher with a tranquilizer gun, or the vet tech with a huge syringe, or the world's most hateful cat. If he kept it up, we would all have permanent hearing loss.

Ponytail yelled over the barking. "Where's the pineapple pizza?"

Fantasy pointed across the room to our pizza travesty message box.

Four slices later, Ponytail was Cotton's new best friend. He still wouldn't look at me without growling, explored the living room as if he'd never set paw in it, and decided he was a one-woman dog, that woman not me. Also forgetting he wasn't a lap dog, he settled himself on Ponytail. We could see nothing but her legs. The rest of her was behind or under Cotton.

Fantasy said, "Your dog has a few screws loose, Davis, and that means for sure we're going to lose our memory."

I was going to lose my mind was what I was going to lose.

"Keep watching the screen until you find No Hair, Fantasy. Let me finish checking my phone."

I made my way to the second message I'd missed, behind the photographic evidence of Eliza Fabré's missing braids. It was from BRILAP, in other letters, FBI. BRILAP was the Bribery of Labor Crime Investigation Unit in New Orleans, which was another way of saying the Mob Squad. The team that tracked organized crime for the Gulf region. They needed to speak to me. Immediately.

Too bad.

I wasn't about to stop what I was doing to call them back. Mostly because there wasn't a doubt in my mind that they called for the same reason they always called—someone suspected of having crime family ties was rumored to be passing through Biloxi and would we keep an eye out. After trying my hardest to hand them an entire organized crime empire on a silver platter and getting nowhere, I wasn't in the mood to do BRILAP any favors. So I would not be keeping an eye out. My eyes were so sore from watching underweared casino guests and employees on my television, not to mention Eliza Fabré's haircut, I could barely see at all. And I certainly couldn't waste what little vision I had left on BRILAP, so I kept going. The next ten messages after BRILAP's were from my husband. Including, *"Where are you?"* And several, *"Why aren't you answering your phone?"* Plus, *"Davis, why is the switchboard closed? Why is the casino closed? Why are reporters broadcasting live from our lawn? DAVIS, WHAT THE HELL IS GOING ON?"* Then I listened to his final message. It lacked the force, volume, and urgency of the ones before. He spoke slowly. And incredulously. As if he didn't believe himself. And as if he felt utterly defeated. *"Davis, I'm on my way back because a woman who writes romance books is threatening both you and our daughters on national television. She intends to shave our daughters' heads. And yours too, by the way. Why? I can't imagine. And I can't get you or anyone else to answer your phones. I'm waiting on a NetJet. The Bellissimo jet I arrived in has compromised landing gear. Goodbye."*

That stopped my heart for several beats.

Landing gear on pristinely maintained aircraft didn't compromise itself.

That would require assistance.

When I could breathe again, I moved on to the next message I'd missed. A cryptic text from July. It said, *Davis, the baby and I are in New Orleans with my parents. I'm not sure when we'll be back or even if we'll be back. Which isn't why I'm calling. I think I was followed here. To my parents' home. Why do I think that? Because ten minutes after I arrived, a black limo pulled up. The driver left a large thick envelope on the doorstep labeled Urgent and To Be Opened by Addressee Only. It's to Baylor. He's the addressee. What has Baylor gotten himself into that someone would follow me and the baby to my parents' house with something this important for him? Call me back when you have a chance so I can make arrangements to get it to him, and don't bother telling him you heard from me.* I gave a second's thought to calling her. Not to get in the middle of their relationship drama I absolutely didn't have time for. And not to suggest Baylor's paranoia about the baby's safety might be rubbing off on her, because black limos were everywhere in Biloxi, New Orleans, and all points between. I sincerely doubted she was followed. But I couldn't call her or Bradley before I reached the final two voicemails that had parked on my phone. And they were the absolute worst news in the virtual universe of horrible news so far that day, so far in my whole *life*—because the voicemails were about my daughters, but from my ex-ex-husband. Eddie Crawford. Who I hadn't spoken to in almost a year. And I didn't want to break my winning streak then. It was bad enough listening to messages from him. More like listening to poorly written and badly recorded audiobooks of catastrophe novellas.

"*Hey, Davis. It's me. Eddie. Eddie Crawford. Your old husband two times. Big news, your dad is banging Eugenia*

Stone. Sick, huh? Turns out your ma is so pissed about your dad having a girlfriend she stopped cooking Sunday pot roast, and my ma, Bea, Bea Crawford, your old mother-in-law two times, is pissed about no Sunday pot roast. So Ma planned a big pot roast interference meeting for everybody today, but your mom took off for your place. My ma talked old Eugenia into chasing after her because it's Friday and she wants this deal done before Sunday. Ma couldn't drive her because she has a nasty ingrown toe fungus and can't wear shoes, so she made me drive old Eugenia. My feet are fine. Ma says to tell you to have the interference meeting and fix everything, which is funny because me and you both know you can't even fix breakfast, so that's a stupid plan. But I was hungover and didn't feel like duking it out with Ma, so I drove old Eugenia down here. Thing is, I let her out at the front door, then had to hit the little boys' room, then I went across the street and had two pork chops and three fried eggs at the Waffle House because I was hungry, then I parked my car, and by the time I did all that I couldn't find old Eugenia, and I couldn't get in the door of your place. So I went to the new casino next to you. Blang-Blang. COOL PLACE. Since it was my first time here, they GAVE me a room in the hotel. Free. Except I have to gamble or it won't be free. So I hit up the ATM and got thirty-four dollars, and I was playing the quarter slot machines with dragons on it when your sissy husband called and asked me to pick up your kids. He couldn't get you or anybody else or even the police on the phone, so he called your dad to see if he'd heard from you and your dad told him about me driving old Eugenia down here. That's why your sissy husband called me and asked me to get your kids from school. I asked him what was in it for me. He said if I picked your kids up and got them home safe before some book writer lady scalped them, he'd let me live ten more minutes and that was all that was in it for me.

I was like, DUDE. That's a brutal way to talk to someone who you are asking to do you a favor. Then I told him I'd go get your kids, but they'd have to ride in the trunk. I'm in the flea market business now and I took out the backseat of my car because I needed the space. Mostly I sell hubcaps. Your sissy husband said I could have your car. Told me the code to get it going without the key. COOLEST CAR I EVER DROVE. So I went and got your kids at their school in my new car. The school people didn't even ask who I was. They threw your kids in the backseat and told me to get them gone. They were real glad to see me, yelling, "Hey, Uncle Eddie!" real loud and wanted to know if we could go to the water park. I told them we were going to Blang-Blang and they could swim in the big fountain in the lobby. They were way cool with that until they got busted by the Blang-Blang people, but they fished me out about eighteen dollars in change before they got kicked out, so it's all good. Now we're in my free hotel room while your kids dry out. Man, I'm tired of talking to you already. I'm locked up in the head leaving you this message while your kids watch a slasher movie in the bedroom with the sound all the way up, and I don't want to yell over it. Call me back. I can't take much more of your kids and need to know how to get them to stop jumping on the bed, because they are getting it wet with their wet clothes and because they won't stop asking me for food when I already ordered them room service once, which I'll need the money back on, but they keep telling me they are still hungry. I think they're lying. They already had enough French fries and ice cream and Cokes to put them in a coma. I told them no way they're getting more food, except maybe later we'll get some hot wings. This place has good fries and ice cream, so they probably have good wings too, and your kids can sure suck down the Coke. Later."

Across the room, responding to Ponytail's increasing apprehension as she peeked farther and farther past the wall of Cotton in her lap for a better view when my legs gave way and I fell into a chair, then as the blood drained from my face, all the while repeatedly gasping in utter horror and maybe mumbling I'll kill him, kill him dead, Fantasy quietly explained to Ponytail that I'd grown up in a very small town and accidentally married and divorced the same stupid jerk twice. She told her I'd been young. I hadn't known better. That it was long ago, water under my bridge, but every once in a while, the beast of my ugly past reared its idiot head.

All true.

And that beastly idiot had my daughters.

At Bling-Bling.

I braced myself to listen to the second message from my ex-ex-husband that had logged in thirty-two minutes after the first. I checked the time. He'd left the second message seven minutes earlier.

"Hey, Davis, it's me again. Eddie. Eddie Crawford. I am on my way to your place with these yard apes you call kids. While I was in the little boys' room leaving you that nice message, your kids ordered spaghetti from room service. How do your kids even know about room service? Do you take them to hotels all the time? It's like you raised them in a hotel. Kids should not know about room service, because room service costs big money, and you'd better find some because you owe Blang-Blang a truckload. Your brats ordered enough spaghetti for a hot dog eating contest. They said they were starving to death and that was why they ordered all that spaghetti, but for sure they were lying because they ate enough gummy bears and candy corn and smashed Oreos on their ice cream to not be hungry for a week. You know why they ordered all that spaghetti? For a FOOD FIGHT. After I left you that nice

message thanking you for my new car, I opened the bathroom door and got smacked in the face with a meatball. They said they were having a snowball fight. With MEATBALLS instead of SNOWBALLS. I sent them to the bathroom to get rid of all the evidence, and everybody in the world except your dingbat kids knows what that means, while I tried to rub all the sauce off the walls with shampoo, which didn't even work, especially on the curtains, because they are white, and instead of doing what I told them to do, which was flush all those meatballs, your brats tried to stomp the meatballs down the tub drain. When they wouldn't go down, your little animals turned on the water because they thought meatball SOUP would go down. How dumb is that? Well, here comes the law, the casino law anyway, because the tub overflowed and the lady underneath us got hit with meatball soup and started bitching about it, then I GOT KICKED OUT OF BLANG-BLANG BECAUSE OF YOUR BRATS. Thanks a lot, Davis, for trying to push these total hell-raisers off on me. That ain't happening. I'm giving them back. You and your sissy husband with his sissy job and those sissy suits he wears can work it out yourselves and leave me alone. I'm done with these little beasts. The casino law who kicked me out made us go out the back way because they didn't want anybody seeing your kids looking like they do. They said it would scare people. Wait till you see these little thugs of yours, because it will scare you too. One of them has meatball stuck in its ear. So two things. GET ME A FREE ROOM AT YOUR PLACE, because you owe me, and then round up some money to pay Blang-Blang for all this hell your kids raised in my room and also for the lady downstairs who got hit by meatball soup, her room too, plus all the room service ice cream and French fries and Coke and spaghetti, plus your kids watching TWO slasher movies, one on the TV by the bed and a different one on the TV by the couch, at the same time, but different movies, plus the curtains that are totally TRASHED, which is not my fault because I tried to clean them, and meet me out back at your place to pick up these kids of yours that only look like kids but are really little devils. And if you don't come get them, I'm strapping them in my new car and going home so my mother can take care of them, because they have worn my ass out. She's always saying she wishes she had grandbabies. Here's her chance. That might be four things instead of two. And you better believe I am dunking them in your big pool to get the rest of the spaghetti off before I put them in my new car. I am glad I didn't have kids with you. You are worse at kids than you are at being married."

I slowly pulled my phone from my head only to see I'd received a text message from a blocked number while listening to Eddie the Barbarian's atrocities. *And now I have your mother,* the text said. *Will trade her for Blake Russo.*

Friday, 2:45 P.M.

I dropped my offensive phone like it would explode if I held it one more second.

I ran.

I ran past Bianca, who'd switched to showtunes, slumped sideways in her chair with her head resting on one upholstered arm and her legs slung over the other, animatedly alternating between snips of songs from *Hamilton* and *Grease*, with chair choreography from *Chorus Line*. I ran past Cotton, who flashed his dark eyes at me, still all the way across Ponytail, pinning her to the sofa, barely registering that she was poking her half-eaten watch which must have been an extremely smart watch to have survived Cotton, probably livestreaming the Victoria Elise Fabré show on our front lawn. And after tripping on one of Bianca's shoes, I ran past Fantasy, who yelled, "Go with or stay here?"

"Neither!" I picked up my pace in the hallway with no human, canine, furniture, or footwear obstacles. Over my shoulder, I yelled back, "Find someone named Blake Russo! Bling-Bling has my mother and wants to trade her for someone named Blake Russo!" She yelled back, "Who is Blake Russo? I don't know anyone named Blake Russo!" At the front door, I yelled loud enough to wake the dead, "OBVIOUSLY SOMEONE RELATED TO TICK-TOCK RUSSO! FIND HIM!" I barely heard her yelling, "I've got this, Davis! You get Bex and Quinn! I'll get your mother!" Then with enough adrenaline pouring through me to likely launch me over the deep-sleep-nap hurdle I probably had coming, I made my way downstairs to what Eddie the Idiot referred to as the back of the Bellissimo. There was only one thing behind the Bellissimo, and it was a construction site. Not a pool for him to dunk my daughters in before he strapped them in what he believed was his new car to deliver them to—of all people—his mother, Bea Crawford, who needed a podiatrist. I didn't want my daughters wandering a dangerous construction site unsupervised while waiting for me, and Eddie the Idiot wasn't capable of supervising a clock ticking, or grass growing, or paint drying, so I ran as hard and fast as I could.

I made it to the lobby in record time where I exited one bank of elevators and sprinted for a second set that led to what used to be the Bellissimo's award-winning pool, but with the pool closed, so were the lobby elevators leading to it. With apologetic instructions to check back soon. All public entrances to the pool were closed. I'd have to find an alternate route. I rounded the next corner, spilling into the west end of the main lobby, where I stopped dead in my tracks. Between where I was at one end and a football field away at the other, there were people. Lots of people. Some in groups, some alone, all wandering aimlessly admiring the lobby as if they were first-time guests, and all dressed in mismatched and ill-fitting clothing.

The casino hostages had escaped.

With amnesia.

So if there was a Blake Russo in the mix, he probably wouldn't know his own name.

I immediately backtracked, but not before I heard a man in the middle of the pack who sounded suspiciously like No Hair yell, "PICKLE! PICKLE! *PICKLE!*" I was so disoriented I didn't even try to make sense of a man who sounded like No Hair yelling the word "pickle" three times at top volume. I didn't have time to investigate, even mentally, a man who sounded like No

Hair yelling the word "pickle" three times as loud as he could, although I was forced to slow down because I wasn't entirely sure which way to go. Using the wall I was hiding behind for support, I bent over, hands to knees, and caught my breath, trying to determine which service area of what used to be our pool deck I could access that might spill me out on the west side of our building, the Bling-Bling side, the direction my ex-ex-husband and daughters would be coming from. Or might have already arrived. Surely when he found himself at a five-acre construction site that, last I heard, still had a bottomless pit of questionable water possibly filled with baby octopi, he'd try to get in the building. But if I was having trouble finding a way out, he'd never find a way in. He'd give up. Then my spaghetti-covered daughters would be on their way to his mother in Pine Apple, Alabama, with *him* at the wheel of *my* car. If he bothered to ask the pool construction workers at the site, they'd point him to the casino service entrance they used. Which would give Eddie the Atrocious two choices: the service hall or the casino. He'd go for the casino. And I didn't want my children in the compromised casino any more than I wanted them at a dangerous construction site. No one at the site would know to tell Eddie the Barbarian the only safe access into the hotel would be through the closed kitchen of Splash, formerly the poolside restaurant on the east side of the hotel. Or around the pebble path behind what used to be our stretch of private cabanas in the middle of the pool deck. Or the manhole down to and the stairwell up from the pool pump room on the west side.

The pool pump room!

On the west side!

As I was routing a mental map from where I stood to the pool pump room leading to the pool deck where I could intercept Eddie the Raging Idiot, I heard the man who sounded like No Hair again. Closer that time, and more urgent. "RAISIN! RAISIN! *RAISIN*!"

I had to be imagining it. My name wasn't Raisin any more than it was Pickle. I broke into a sprint to get away from him one second too late, because I could hear shoes pounding marble behind me. I didn't turn to look when he spotted me again yelling, "CAMEL! CAMEL! *CAMEL*!"

I wasn't imagining it. The man who sounded like No Hair was chasing me. So instead of taking a right for the parking garage exit, the quickest way around the building to the pool pump room, I took a left and blew through a set of swinging doors marked Staff Only, hoping if the man continued to pursue me, I'd lose him in the maze of the first-floor inventory area. I wove through countless pallets of merchandise—packaged snacks and sundries, carton after carton of Bellissimo bathrobes and t-shirts, crates of items emblazoned with the Bellissimo logo—then through a section of surplus food service furniture and equipment for the lobby eateries, then finally through a casino catch-all graveyard, dodging retired slot machines and broken blackjack stools slated for recycling, to exit the main building through a bay door. Panting, frantic, and terrified for my daughters and my mother, then suddenly blinded by the sun, I stopped dead in my tracks. I was expecting a fenced-in loading dock. An empty fenced-in loading dock. To my utter bewilderment, I was met by concrete trucks. Four of them. Filling the fenced-in loading dock. Four huge concrete trucks. It took me a second I didn't have to process why they might be there until I remembered that the construction crew was pouring the footings for our new pool that day. Which had nothing to do with my daughters, so I wove between them on my way to the pool pump room praying the door wasn't locked.

It was.

I opened it the only way I knew how right then and right there, with a shot from my Ruger, a split-second after I heard the man who sounded like No Hair yell, "SCATTER THE CAMERA! SCATTER THE CAMERA! *SCATTER THE CAMERA!*"

There was no mistaking the man yelling the drivel and chasing me didn't just sound like No Hair. Standing in the open door I'd just blasted through, I realized the man yelling drivel and chasing me *was* No Hair. He had to be. There weren't twenty people on the Bellissimo payroll who knew the lobby-level inventory room well enough to have made it to the loading dock in the short amount of time he had. No Hair and I were two of them. The other eighteen worked there. I yelled over the recycling bins. "NO HAIR?"

He yelled back, "WEATHER! WEATHER! WEATHER!" Which hit my ears the same way "WAIT! WAIT! WAIT!" would have, so with my Ruger still ready to fire, I ducked behind a concrete truck and waited the thirty seconds it took him to make his way to me. And there he was. Wearing a hazmat suit ten sizes too small, two feet too short, and a fake Starbucks apron looped around his neck covering his chest.

We put everything on hold to throw our arms around each other in a bear hug of relief. On my part that his memory was intact. He obviously knew who I was. The relief on his part might have been about being free of the casino chaos. Both of us would have been even more relieved had he been wearing people clothes. And speaking English.

I pulled away from him at the same time I reached for his hand to pull him through the pool maintenance door I'd shot my way through and into the dark stairwell beyond. "Come on, No Hair."

He tried to pull me the other way. "Fluttering spicy typewriter," he pleaded, his head nodding back to the main building. "Winter wheel!"

I shook my head in disbelief. "I can't understand a word you're saying!"

To which he responded, every word dripping in extreme annoyance, his face blood red, his hands flailing in frustration, "Copper monkey floor with the tree steak!"

Gibberish.

Not one word out of his mouth made sense.

"Bex and Quinn!" I tried again. "Please come with me, No Hair! Eddie Crawford has Bex and Quinn at the pool!" I pointed two or three different ways, so disoriented as to not be entirely sure which way the pool was. "I need to go through the pump room to get to the pool deck. Help me, No Hair! Help me get my daughters!"

His eyes cut right and left, then he shooed me on. As in let's go. We were halfway down the dark narrow stairsteps by the light of the open door I'd talked him through when we stopped cold at the sound of a loud engine starting. Then we heard what sounded suspiciously like a concrete truck on the move. We turned to run up the steps we'd just run down, but we didn't get there before we heard the jarring sound of the maintenance stair door slamming shut. Thanks to a concrete truck. The door was so closed and blocked by the huge truck, not even a sliver of daylight was detectible at any juncture, leaving us no choice but to continue down the stairs to the pool pump room. Then dodging equipment and exposed overhead plumbing, we made our way to the other side of the pump room to a ladder of iron bars leading to a manhole. Past the manhole was the pool deck. It was the route I'd intended to take all along. But couldn't. Because the manhole had been soldered shut from above. We tried it separately and, dangling off both sides of the iron ladder bars, we tried it together. Not once did the manhole budge even a millimeter. The rounds left in my Ruger wouldn't help. If they didn't ricochet off the iron plate and put our eyes out, they wouldn't make a dent.

No Hair and I were trapped in the pool pump room.

Friday, 3:00 P.M.

The fates of my daughters and my mother were temporarily out of my hands unless we could find another exit, so that was our next course of action. Neither of us were exactly familiar with the pool pump room, so we searched high and low carefully. The room was deeper than it was wide, maybe eighteen by ten, with very little space to navigate around the equipment. The walls were made of cinder block, so we wouldn't be beating on them crying, "Help! We're locked in here!" Or in No Hair's case, beating on them crying, "Meatloaf! Jingle glue!"

There were no windows.

I wondered how much air we had and how long we'd have it.

The air we did have was thick. It smelled like stagnant water and stale chemicals. The atmosphere in the pool pump room was equally dank. One side of the room held overhead plumbing, so clearance was low, no more than six feet in places, and the only lighting was on the opposite side. It was dim, sporadic, and flickering. The equipment we dodged wasn't in operation, so the room itself wasn't loud, but being a cavernous space, the sound of our movements as we explored our new prison were amplified. Mostly our ragged breath as we gasped our way to accepting our new totally unacceptable predicament.

"Who do you think locked us in here, No Hair?"

We ducked, even me, a foot and a half shorter than No Hair, to clear two feet of a rectangularly shaped steel box dropping down from the ceiling and running the full width of the room effectively splitting it in half. It was held in place with U-shaped PVC piping on both ends.

"Neighborhood pigeon sprout," he said.

"Good Pills?" I looked over my shoulder to see his face, looking for his reaction, either confirmation or denial, because I knew it wouldn't be in his words.

"Ignite the tree siege."

We shared a frustrated nonverbal exchange where I sighed and he huffed, then, with nothing else meaningful to say to each other, we continued our exploration of the pool pump room looking for an alternate exit.

In one dark corner, we spotted a shutoff switch for the intake and output pumps. A metal supply cabinet missing one of its doors was to the right of the red emergency lever. A first aid kit mounted to the wall was on the left. The most interesting piece of equipment we found was a clear polycarbonate cylindrical filter too large in circumference for me to wrap my arms around. At first glance, I spotted a hundred-dollar poker chip, a bikini top, and a charm bracelet among the more unsavory petrified items swimmers had lost to our pool before Bling-Bling destroyed it. Between sterilization tanks and recirculation blowers we found the vented metal shell of a large piece of equipment wearing a steel name tag declaring it to be a MegaWarm 15,000 BTU Commercial Pool Heater. Everything, including the heater, and with the exception of the PVC pipe holding the steel box to the ceiling, which had somehow escaped decay, had several layers of corrosion and an overall air of abandonment. I was certain my first visit to a resort pool pump room would also be my last. And we didn't find an alternate exit.

We settled on the MegaWarm.

Side by side.

In all our years of working together, I'd never seen No Hair's calves. But there they were, muscular and sinewy, below the hems of the hazmat suit legs that barely covered his knees and above the man socks and dress shoes still on his feet. All under his fake Starbucks apron shirt. When he spoke, his voice was soft. And tired. "Leather curtains preserve scissor pears."

I said, "I hear you, No Hair," then asked, "Can you understand me?"

He nodded.

"Do you understand yourself?"

He looked at me quizzically.

"When you speak," I explained. "Are you trying to say one thing, but the words come out another?"

He growled, which I took as agreeing with my assessment of his latest synthetic-nerve-agent predicament.

"Do you know how long you've been talking this way?"

He said, "Volleyball bomb?" Which I think was, "Say again?"

"When you woke in the casino, did you have amnesia?"

He displayed his lovely attire as affirmative evidence. No Hair was a snappy and meticulous dresser. Had he woken up with a single memory of undressing, he'd be wearing the tailored suit he'd worn to work that morning instead of a hazmat jumpsuit stretched far beyond its limits. And a fake Starbucks apron.

I asked how long it took for his memory to return.

He held up a finger.

"One hour?" I asked.

He nodded.

"Was that when you started talking crazy? When your memory returned?"

His answer was slow in coming and even slower in presentation. "Toothpaste roof vivacious mail." He kept going.

Angrier. "Seashore thumb to puzzle clatter table." Which I think meant, "When I find the people who did this, I'm going to rip them apart with my bare hands."

"I'm no longer entirely positive who did this, No Hair, so I'm not sure who you should kill. All signs leading up to this have pointed to Good Pills, but now there's a new player at the table. Blake Russo. Do you know who Blake Russo is?"

He shook his head no.

"Have you ever heard of him?"

No again.

"We knew Jimmy 'Tick-Tock' Russo had a daughter. Did you know he had a son?"

Another no.

"Well, let's hope Fantasy can find him."

He said, "Short video beans for bears?" Which was probably, "What does Blake Russo have to do with anything?"

"Bling-Bling has my mother," I said. "They say they'll trade her for Blake Russo."

To which he spat, "Butterfly crates upset pastels." Which was probably, "I thought you were looking for your daughters."

"I am."

He said, "Stubborn valley party tubs."

I had no idea what he meant by that. Or why those words carried so much weight. So I switched gears to say, "I think you got a massive dose of whatever was on the twenty-dollar bills."

He said, "Falling cobwebs?" It sounded an awful lot like, "Says who?"

"Says me," I said. "Because in the very beginning, you were holding a handful of the twenties. Remember?"

He said, "Skip toast." I think he meant, "I remember."

"You're like a Patient Zero with the synthetic nerve agent."

He said nothing.

"I was dosed too."

His eyebrows drew in on each other.

"Fantasy and I both took a hit," I said, "but I don't think we took a direct hit like you."

He said, "Sticky feather fences," which sounded a lot like, "You have no idea what you're talking about."

"Yes," I said, "I think I do." I didn't go so far as to tell him I'd found four different synthetic nerve agents at four different concentrations, plus an additional edible synthetic nerve agent, and everything I found with them indicated they could be tweaked to produce different results in different combinations depending on how they were delivered. Instead, I said, "We were directly exposed like you were. Doesn't it stand to reason that indirect exposure wouldn't pack the same hard punch? At first we thought we'd been double dosed, but I'm wondering if maybe we weren't half-dosed. For instance, we only had the hiccups for a half hour. Not an hour."

He immediately went to his left wrist. Where his Montblanc watch wasn't. Which meant in addition to the casino cash haul, the fake Starbucks crew had relieved our guests of their personal possessions while they were sleeping. No Hair continued to look at his bare wrist. He held it out for me to see, saying, "Fire." I think he meant, "Look."

"I know." I patted his hazmat knee. "It's awful. We'll get your watch back. In the meantime, guess."

"Bacon tax?" I think he meant, "Guess what?"

"Guess how long it's been since your memory returned and you started talking crazy."

He said, "Doorknob?" And I think he meant, "Why?"

"Because all the side effects from the synthetic nerve agent have lasted an hour for you."

"Banana?" I think he meant, "So?"

"Let's say you started talking this way a half hour ago," I said. "That would mean the Tower of Babel business will be over in another half hour."

He scratched his bald head.

"Until then," I said, "I'll do all the talking. How's that?"

He agreed, nodding along, "Magnificent brushes resemble ketchup."

"Okay." I patted his hazmat knee again. "Okay, No Hair."

We sat quietly. Quietly enough to hear the sounds of muffled movement above and around us. Both human and mechanical. We were a thick slab of concrete away from making out distinct voices or anything else specific other than a repetitive muted clack somewhere above our heads, maybe closer, possibly somewhere deep inside the pool pump room, but nothing else.

"My children are up there." I pointed. "Bex and Quinn. At the construction site."

His eyebrows, which with him being cue-ball bald were on the expressive side anyway, shot up asking why.

"It's such a long story, No Hair. I don't know where to start."

He placed a comforting hazmat arm around my shoulders and pulled me in.

"The girls needed to be picked up from school because of Victoria Elise Fabré, the romance author, who threatened to cut their hair."

He said, "Lumpy zebra!" It sounded very much like he was trying to say, "That's horrible!"

"I know!" I said. "Right?"

He said, "Arch engine false elastic?" Which I took as, "Would you please explain?"

I took a refortifying breath of stale pool-pump-room air and happily complied. "Long story short, because there are so many blanks I can't fill in until I can talk to him, Bradley asked Eddie the Idiot to pick up Bex and Quinn." I looked up to meet No Hair's eyes in an effort to put as much emphasis on my next words as possible. "That's how desperate today has been. That's how far it's gone to hell and back. Eddie was the only person Bradley could find to pick up our daughters." Then I rushed out the rest of the story: Bling-Bling's fountain, meatball soup, compromised landing gear, and that I was supposed to meet Eddie and the twins out back. "And here I am. Trying to meet them out back."

He said, "Possible market?"

Which I think meant, "Where is he?"

To which I said, "He, who? Bradley or Eddie the Neanderthal?"

No Hair said, "Album."

Which I think meant, "Bradley."

"He's trying to get back from the Gaming Commission meeting in Jackson. I can only hope and pray he's well on his way or already here. Safely."

No Hair gave my shoulders a reassuring squeeze. He said, "Thirsty giant cactus receipt." I'm sure he meant, "He probably is. No doubt saving the day. And he'll find us. In the meantime, you have to remain calm, Davis. You can't fix everything at once. You can only do what you can do. And you're locked in a pool pump room, so you can't do much. Bradley will know what to do. Your mother will irritate whoever has her so much they'll let her go. They'll say, 'Here. Take her back.' And stop worrying about Bex and Quinn when there's nothing you can do about them either until we get out of here. They're smart little girls, Davis. Smarter, by far, than Eddie. And they live here. They know their way around. They'll find their way to safety."

To which I said, "I hope you're right, No Hair. I really hope you're right."

Then he said, "Delivery pause with privacy soup." Which I think meant, "You're not alone in this, Davis. Settle down."

To which I said, "I can't settle down, No Hair. With us stuck down here, it leaves Fantasy is handling everyone else."

He said, "Itchy brass clogs?" which I'm sure was, "Everyone else who?"

"The doctor who looks like Albert Einstein," I said. "And Eugenia Winters Stone. And Starling—" I filled with frustration at the very mention of her name, even though I was the one who'd mentioned it. "You can't imagine what Starling Halter has put me through today. And Ponytail. And the rabbit. Do not get me going on the rabbit. And poor Fantasy. Alone."

He said, "Waylay the jittery bread?" Which I'm sure was, "Why is Fantasy alone? Where is Baylor?" To which I said, "Huh?"

Because I didn't want to tell him.

No Hair closed his eyes and shook his overloaded head.

We sat quietly for a brief moment, until he used his free hand to make walking fingers up.

"I know," I said. "We need out."

He held telephone fingers up to the side of his head, his face a question mark.

"Do I have a phone?" I slid off the heater to land on my feet. "Why didn't I think of that?" I patted my pockets all around and found my phone. I shook it in the air. "We're saved!" I powered up the phone and my hopes were immediately dashed. "No service in this bunker. And it isn't even my phone." I'd dropped mine like a hot potato after reading the messages from my imbecile ex-ex-husband. And with no signal, I couldn't even call 9-1-1 or Bellissimo Security from Starling's cloned phone. I couldn't call my husband. I couldn't call the idiot I'd married twice before I'd married my real husband to demand he walk my daughters straight to my front door, get them in safely, drop off the face of the earth, and don't even look at my new car again.

No Hair pointed at the phone. "Crooked juicy never ray?" And by that, I think he meant, "Whose phone is it?"

"It's Starling Halter's," I said. "Actually, it's a clone of Starling Halter's. And not only do we not have service to call for help, it only has ten percent battery. It's a new phone." I shook it. "I didn't have time to fully charge it."

I slid the phone back in my pocket and took my seat beside No Hair. Then was as good a time as any. I turned to face him. I took a deep breath. "No Hair, I've had Baylor undercover at Bling-Bling since the day they opened."

He narrowed his eyes at me. "Boiling trains melt pineapples." By that, combined with his disapproving furrowed brow, I believe he was saying, "I knew that already."

My eyes popped open. "Does Bradley know too?"

He nodded.

So much for my stealthy skills. Or more likely, Baylor let it slip, which meant my super-spy skills were intact. "They're sitting on dead bodies and they're laundering dirty money."

He disagreed. In tone, timbre, and eyebrows. "Workable yellow dwell woozy." His next words and eyebrow gyrations were a reprimand. "Invincible calculating weather."

"I know," I said. "No one believes me, and you told me to leave it alone. Bradley told me to leave it alone. Legal told me to leave it alone." I put a have-mercy-on-me hand on his hazmat arm. "I wish I had. Maybe none of this would have happened. Or maybe it would have happened anyway, because nothing that's happened to us so far has had anything to do with Bling-Bling."

No Hair said, "Polite appointments sweep funny cucumbers."

It sounded so much like he was saying, "Unless you've been right all along, and it has everything to do with Bling-Bling."

"The only way Bling-Bling is behind this is if they paid off forty BRILAP agents in New Orleans. And even though they've been absolutely no help to us lately, they do operate by the book."

He said, "Chubby fugitives?" Which was, I'm sure, "They who?"

"The BRILAP guys. And I'm glad you brought them up."

He scowled, as if to say he hadn't brought them up.

"They called earlier."

One of his eyebrows shot up.

"I didn't catch the call," I told him. "I'd left my phone on the porch where Ponytail was sleeping it off."

His other eyebrow shot up.

"Cotton was watching her."

He shook his head quickly, as in, "*What? Who?*"

"Cotton," I said. "My dog. You know Cotton."

He rolled his eyes. No Hair was way more a cat person. Or maybe he hadn't been asking about Cotton at all. I think I was right, because when he said, "Ladderback?" I had the feeling he meant, "Ponytail?"

"Ponytail?"

He blinked yes.

I thought he blinked yes, anyway.

"She started it," I said, "this morning. Which, with all that's happened, feels like a month ago. She's the one who went through the casino dropping twenty-dollar bills that were laced with synthetic nerve agents invented by the Albert Einstein doctor that gave everyone hiccups, but she doesn't remember a thing." I grabbed his arm. "Did you see her?"

He threw both arms in the air as if to say, "*Did I see who?*"

There really wasn't any way to explain Ponytail. For one, the clanks and grindings outside of the pool pump room were picking up, as if everyone was suddenly in a big hurry, and I wasn't sure I had the energy to start and stop the story between what began reverberating through the room like drilling above our heads might, combined with the fact that our one-and-a-half-way as opposed to two-way conversation wasn't really getting us anywhere except for me clearing my conscience about Baylor, and not wanting to clear it any further, as in telling him Bling-Bling was actually holding Baylor hostage, I was happy to move on to the subject of Ponytail. But it wasn't any easier to talk to him about Ponytail than it was talking to him about anything else. I tried to tell him I found Ponytail in Jay Leno's suite, and she'd either dosed herself with synthetic nerve agents or someone else had dosed her, but probably not the man who'd invented everything, Dr. Winford Wurtz, who looked like Albert Einstein, who didn't strike me as being particularly complicit, other than inventing everything, because like Ponytail in Jay Leno's bedroom, I'd found him gagged and bound in a butler's pantry lift—how complicit was that?—not to mention I believed he'd been held against his will and forced to use his inventions nefariously, at which point No Hair stopped me by yelling, "TOOTHBRUSH!"

I think he was saying, "STOP TALKING!"

It was a lot of information.

It would be easier if I had a photo of Ponytail, and for that matter, Dr. Wurtz too, if for no other reason than that of seeing No Hair's reaction. He might recognize one or both, then he'd know who I was talking about. But I didn't have pictures. Which was when I remembered I actually did have pictures. A picture of Dr. Wurtz, anyway. I had the slideshow I'd prepared for Ponytail on Starling Halter's phone. It was a start. Too, I could show him the rest of the Good Pills' photos I'd shown Ponytail, because for all I knew, No Hair might have pertinent information I didn't about someone on the Good Pills organizational chart, and that could lead us in a productive direction.

Not that he'd be able to relay any pertinent information.

I pulled Starling's phone from my pocket again, powered it up to see it was down to nine percent battery, and knew I needed to hurry. I opened her inbox where I'd parked the Good Pills management headshots before sending them to my television earlier to see that several emails had downloaded between the time I was on her cloned phone in my living room and losing internet service in the pool pump room. And that was when I learned Starling Halter wasn't a casino liaison at all. Starling's inbox had four new emails. Three from the Department of Justice, Organized Crime Division addressed to Agent S. Halter, Criminal Investigator, Anti-Money Laundering Unit, Chicago Division of the Federal Bureau of Investigation.

Starling Halter was a fed.

A fed from Chicago.

At first, I didn't believe it. It was incomprehensible to me that Starling's superiors, presumedly trained, skilled, and trusted employees of our federal government, had allowed her to operate at the level of unprofessionalism I'd witnessed. Denial led to shock. Had everything we'd lived through going back a solid year been orchestrated to take down Bling-Bling by sacrificing the Bellissimo—innocent bystanders who played by the rules—for the federal government's purposes? If so, who sanctioned it? Our governor? Vernon Rider Wilson? Why would he do that? Finally, I was personally offended. How hurt were the feds' feelings when they couldn't find evidence against Jimmy "Tick-Tock" Russo that they didn't stop to consider Biloxi's when they decided to let a Chicago operative named Starling Halter tear our city apart just to make their stupid case? But as shock stepped aside to give logic a chance, I had to acknowledge it was the first piece of information I'd learned about the enigma that was Starling that actually fit. Made sense. And Starling the enigma federal agent had written me an email. The fourth and most recent email to download before her cloned phone lost service was to *me*. Meant for me. It was written from her email address and sent to her email address with the subject line, CUTE TRICK WITH MY PHONE, DAVIS WAY COLE. And with it, comprehension continued to creep my way, the frustrating pieces of the whole Bling-Bling puzzle began gathering, and while far from in place, they were at least lining up to present themselves clearly so I could put them where they belonged.

I hesitantly opened the email, clicking with caution, as if whatever Starling had to say to me might start another firestorm. Or detonate a bomb. Or blow up our pool deck again with No Hair and I trapped below.

I tried to tell you, Davis. The first time we spoke, I asked you to meet me at the coffee shop in your lobby. I had every intention of reading you in. How about we let bygones be bygones and skip to present day. There are three things you need to know. One, get out and stay out of my way or you'll be looking at multiple obstruction charges. Two, the woman you call Ponytail is Jimmy "Tick-Tock" Russo's daughter. Could you not see the resemblance? Her name is Blake. She owns Good Pills Biopharmaceuticals. Her mission is to protect what she believes to be her rightful inheritance. The third and final item, directly related to the second, is the most important. Leave Baylor right where he is. At the moment, he's safer at Bling-Bling than he is at the Bellissimo. He needs to be as far away from her as possible. When it's time to spring him, I'LL do the honors. And that will be after I secure his wife, if he has one—thanks a lot for not answering the simplest of questions in all this time—and his son. They're in your ponytailed woman's crosshairs too, at this juncture maybe even more so than Baylor, and if they're harmed, it'll be on you.

I found Blake Russo.

Who wasn't Jimmy Russo's son at all.

And at present, in my *home.*

With my partner. And with Bianca Casimiro Sanders.

With four percent battery left on the phone and not a drop of blood left in my face, I passed the phone to No Hair. "Read it fast."

I watched his eyes dart up and down the screen for no more than ten seconds before three things happened at once. One, the phone died. Two, No Hair asked, "What does she mean leave Baylor where he is? Where exactly is Baylor, Davis?" And three, upon saying my name at the end of his follow-up question, the one I didn't want to answer, his right arm shot up, elbow first, as if it were on an automatic power hinge, and met my left eye. It was almost ten minutes later, which felt more like ten hours later, and only after we accepted the fact that No Hair was not only a danger to me but to himself as well because of his sudden onset total loss of muscle control, and it was just as I had him somewhat secured in the safest place I could find under the drop-down metal box attached to the ceiling and between four bulbous water filters wrapped in a wide swaths of padded insulation where he could flail away without killing either of us, I realized his gift of speech had returned. By that time, my left eye was raw, and my nose was so tender I was afraid it was broken. I'd also taken a hard kick to my right shin, the whole time, No Hair, inadvertently kicking air and throwing punches right and left, his head jerking, one of his eyes twitching like mad, couldn't stop apologizing. "I'm sorry, Davis! I'm so sorry!"

"It's not your fault, No Hair. It's the synthetic nerve agent's fault."

"Is this—" his upper right lip was curling in a snarly Elvis way so rapidly he was having trouble speaking "—about the ponytail again?"

"This is about me being so relieved you're finally speaking The King's English."

Between his arms shooting up in the air like a two-hundred-and-fifty-pound bald hazmat cheerleader, then both arms slamming down like a two-hundred-and-fifty-pound bald hazmat gate closing, he managed to say, "What. About. That." Then his right leg shot through the air as if he were attempting a field goal. His foot connected and dislodged one of the overhead PVC pipes holding the steel box to the ceiling. The end of the steel box he was under broke away and slammed down to the pool pump room floor. With limited and unpredictable motor skills, No Hair somehow managed to escape decapitation when the raw edge of the steel box was on its way down by rolling right and flattening himself between the two water tanks an inch from the jagged steel. Then money began landing on his back. Banded stacks of money wrapped in cellophane dropped from the ceiling. Every three or four seconds, another money brick either fell from the sky or rolled down the ramp he'd created when he kicked the steel box.

I crept that way, No Hair somehow managed to slide far enough from the crash site to sit up, and we watched money pile up. It quickly grew into a money mountain of banded and cellophane-wrapped stacks of small-, medium-, and large-denomination bills. I carefully made my way to the other end of the steel box still connected to the ceiling and found a two-foot-wide conveyor belt above our heads, which would have put it just below ground level, easing the money along from Bling-Bling to us. It was only as I stared into the abyss long enough for my eyes to adjust that I realized the conveyor belt went both ways. Not only was Bling-Bling sending money to our house, but we were returning it. They weren't laundering two decades of Chicago mob money in their casino. They were tunneling it to the Bellissimo where we were laundering it for them. Then sending it back as clean as a whistle. Destroying our pool hadn't been a construction accident. It had been deliberate. To provide money-laundering cover. That was when I yawned. I yawned as deeply as I'd ever yawned in my life. I stared at the money mountain, and all I wanted to do was curl up on it and sleep.

Friday, 3:30 P.M.

My groggy brain knew it wouldn't be long before the receiving end of the dirty money realized that the incoming cash had stopped. They'd investigate. They'd find the break in the supply chain, and when they did, they'd find us. They being the pool construction crew that wasn't a pool construction crew at all. They were a Bling-Bling money-laundering team facilitating the underground transportation of ill-gotten gains from Bling-Bling's house to ours, where we'd been unknowingly circulating it through our casino. How had casino accounting missed it? How had our bank missed it? For that matter, how had we missed what had been happening under the construction tent in our own backyard? We'd missed it by design. The plan all along had been to distract us. The entire day had been manufactured by Blake Russo to distract us. Why that day? I had no idea. But it was just like Bradley said, I'd been looking up when I should have been looking down. I'd looked left when I should have been looking right. I'd looked over when I should have been looking under. Under the tent in our own backyard. None of which I could fully process, or put a stop to, or even begin to process or help put a stop to, because I couldn't stay awake long enough to process a full thought or do anything but stop dead in my own tracks. I couldn't stay awake enough to listen to No Hair, who I thought might be asking if I could climb the ramp and crawl through the opening in the ceiling from which the money continued to steadily drop. He didn't have enough muscle control to climb a single stairstep. Much less up the flimsy ramp created by one end of an unstable steel box. I only caught a word or two of him pleading with me to fight through the fog and stay awake. And snips of him hammering me with questions about the Ponytail story I'd told him trying to flesh out more detail, asking if she'd given any hint as to how to interrupt the effects of the synthetic nerve agent so he could keep me awake long enough to be of some, any, assistance. I could barely see him because I couldn't keep my right eye open. There was no keeping my left eye open. It had swollen shut and was probably already discoloring, losing the tender red it would have turned after the initial blow on its way to black and blue. Not that I had a mirror or any reflective surface at all in the pool pump room to see the damage, or that I could move my sleepy limbs enough to get to it if there was one, and not that I cared about it at all just then, or could stay awake long enough to care about it, but something was keeping me from giving all the way in to sleep. It wasn't No Hair trying desperately to keep me awake so much as it was bits and pieces of realization dawning and flashes of my life knocking on my consciousness door keeping my lights from going all the way out. My daughters. Where were they? My husband. Was he safely back at the Bellissimo? Had he secured our girls and moved on to looking for me? My mother. Had Fantasy accomplished enough alone to make the Blake Russo-Ponytail connection and trade her for my mother? All of which led to thoughts of Baylor. Our Baylor. Our sweet, sometimes clueless, always faithful Baylor. From Baylor, my foggy brain skipped to July. Then to the baby. From the baby, my mind jumped straight to the mayor. Our new mayor. It was the thought of Celeste Reed that almost broke all the way through the haze of sleep trying to take me down, because it dawned on me that she was a fed too.

She had to be.

Because Baylor and July.

They met four years earlier at the Bellissimo's Scary Rich slot tournament. It was love at first sight. They'd been trying to marry ever since. After four failed attempts at marriage—one wedding canceled because of a snowstorm, the next because of a hurricane, a third because of killer tomatoes, and, most recently, when Fantasy and I were abducted by a crazy golfer—it was the thought of their fifth failed attempt at marriage that kept me awake.

"The mayor..." I could hear myself slurring words.

"What?" No Hair sounded breathless. "Davis, wake up!"

I could barely hear him, but through my half-closed left eye, I caught the blur of movement. His hands shooting out on both sides of his body, his head following his lead hand, flattened and palm down, the other hand, behind him, palm up. To my drowsy right eye, it didn't look so much like his previous out-of-control action as much as it looked like he was walking. Like an Egyptian. There were no Bangles singing "Walk Like an Egyptian," yet No Hair was doing the dance. I fought through the haze to ask, "Are you an...Egyptian dancer?"

"WAKE UP, DAVIS!"

Was he trying to wake me up by dancing like an Egyptian and yelling at me while I was trying to talk to him about Baylor and July's fifth attempt at getting married? It was a year earlier, almost exactly a year earlier, that they'd applied for a marriage license to be quickly and quietly married the same day at the Biloxi courthouse only to have their license denied by our newly appointed mayor of one week, Celeste Reed, who said skipping four weddings was quite enough, and she wouldn't waste city resources issuing a fifth license to a couple who clearly couldn't make up their minds. She hadn't been in town long enough to unpack, much less know anything about Baylor and July's four previous marriage licenses, none of which were applied for in

Biloxi. She couldn't have known without an army of private investigators or access to a database as large as the FBI's. And since when did city mayors weigh in on marriage licenses? Since never. What purpose did keeping Baylor and July from marrying in Biloxi serve the new mayor when they could have easily hopped one city, county, or state line over and married the same day? Obviously, it became clear, as clear as things could possibly be just before consciousness left me, I realized our new mayor was in on it. Celeste Reed, like Starling Halter, was a federal agent too. They'd followed Tick-Tock Russo's operation to Biloxi, and Baylor, our Baylor, had been on their radar from the beginning. And just before my lights went all the way out, I connected the final dots of Starling's email meant for me. If Starling was trying to protect Baylor, July, and Little Dude from Ponytail, who, as it turned out, was Jimmy "Tick-Tock" Russo's daughter, Blake, who wanted to secure her inheritance, it could only mean one thing: Ponytail was in fear of losing her inheritance to Baylor. The only way that was possible was if Baylor was Jimmy "Tick-Tock" Russo's biological son.

All of this was about Baylor?

Our Baylor?

I tried to tell No Hair but couldn't. Although it did register in my sleepy brain that he'd traded "Walk Like an Egyptian" for the YMCA dance.

Stomping all over the money.

Friday, 3:45 P.M.

I woke up in a vat of ammonia wearing a ten-pound ice hat after No Hair Texas-Two-Stepped his way to the first aid box dangling off the south wall of the pool pump room. Maybe it was the north wall. And maybe it wasn't a vat of ammonia so much as it was a strong whiff from a pouch of something gelatinous called AQUA SLAMSHOCK and a five-by-five-inch cold pack called Instant Ice Therapy strapped to my left eye with the sleeve of a hazmat suit. No Hair helped me sit up. "Do you know me?" I nodded, my busted eye leading the way. "Do you know who you are?" I nodded again. "Do you know where we are?"

I was too groggy to say anything more than, "Bex Quinn."

"Right." He stood. He backed up. Then he landed his arms straight out, one at a time, then flipped his palms over. One at a time. "We're in the pool pump room because you're looking for Bex and Quinn on the pool deck." He crossed his arms in an X over his chest to cup his opposite shoulders, the bare one and the sleeved one.

"No Hair, what are you *doing*?"

"I think it's the Macarena." He landed his hands behind his ears, one at a time, while gyrating his hips, and there was nothing natural about his execution. Every step was forced and every move unnatural. And to say he was displeased about the dancing program was to say the desert was dry.

"You need to stop," I said. "You're giving me a headache." Which might have been more about the SLAMSHOCK than his dancing. Or it might have been my black eye. Or it might have been because I hadn't eaten a bite of food since two frosted strawberry Pop-Tarts for breakfast. And was in desperate need of water. Hot caffeinated water. A bucketful. A bucketful of hot caffeinated water. With a splash of cream. That I could hold with both hands and guzzle down.

"Don't you think I want to stop?" He angrily jumped ninety degrees to his left. "If you ever tell anyone about this, you're fired." He jumped ninety degrees to his left again, his back to me. "That old doctor is going to prison." He jumped again. "Do you hear me? Prison."

"He invented the nerve agent, No Hair. I think he administered it under duress." And with that, the threats and dangers that had fallen asleep with me woke up too. They eyed each other—including my daughters, my mother, and the rabbit—then all but Ponytail backed away, leaving her standing alone as the single obstacle for me to overcome before I could tackle the others. What it all meant for Baylor woke me up the rest of the way. I struggled to sit up straighter and stretch my legs, the cold pack slipping from under the slick material of my hazmat sleeve headband and landing in my lap, knowing I had to wake up enough to relay it all to No Hair. I wasn't there yet and needed to get there quickly. "How long was I asleep?"

"Fifteen or twenty minutes." His arms shot out one at a time, starting the Macarena all over again.

"How long have you been dancing?"

"Too long," he said. "You slept through The Hustle."

"I've never heard of it."

"It was before your time."

"Surely you're close to the end."

"The end of what?"

"The dancing."

"You think?" His hands were behind his ears again. "Then what? Will my head start spinning around on my neck? Will I grow fangs? Will I start seeing unicorns?"

I reached for the pouch of AQUA SLAMSHOCK beside me. I held it out. "Try this," I said. "Take a whiff."

"I did," he said, "when I opened it. It's straight ammonia. I couldn't help but take a whiff." He started the jumping thing again. Ninety degrees left. "Read the back. It says it restores consciousness to the unconscious. I'm not unconscious. It didn't work." He jumped again. "Here's the thing, Davis." I stared at the backside of his hazmat suit. "I think you were right. I got a full dose. A much stronger dose than whatever got ahold of you." He jumped around for the last time and was facing me again. Breathlessly facing me again, because cardio wasn't necessarily No Hair's thing, and the dancing was wearing him out. "Whatever's in my system is going to play itself out no matter what I sniff."

The Macarena ended.

He stopped moving.

I didn't want to point it out and somehow accidentally start up the dance recital again, but he noticed it too. With relief. Which gave me an opening, combined with the fact that I was close enough to shaking off the cobwebs of sleep to relay the information about Ponytail, Baylor, July, and Little Dude he needed to know. Until he started dancing what might have been the Mambo. Either the Mambo or the Salsa. I can't repeat what he said. To me, to the concrete walls, to the money mountain, to the world at large. And I think he'd have gone on lamenting in the same outraged way had I not noticed the room around his anger was still, other than the dancing, and interrupted. "The money stopped."

Then the cursing stopped.

The Mambo didn't.

He pivoted to Mambo right, tilted his head up for a better look at the motionless conveyor belt, then uttered one last swear. "I'll be damned."

To which I responded, "No Hair. We need to talk."

And maybe we would've had the conveyor belt not jerked alive again.

Our eyes locked.

Not exactly.

Both his eyes bounced, factoring in the Mambo, and I only had one eye open enough with which to engage, but with the limited vision we had, our eyes agreed we'd been caught. The receiving end of the money had communicated the lack of incoming funds to the supply end, and they'd stopped the money train to find the break.

We were about to be caught.

"We have to get out." I struggled to standing with MegaWarm's help. I gave myself a moment for equilibrium's sake. I tested my feet. They worked. "Let's try the stairwell door again."

"Or let's meet them head on." He Mamboed sideways.

"Meet who head on?"

"Whoever is coming." He danced. "They'll be trying to repair a conveyor belt. Not looking for us." He danced. "We'll have the element of surprise."

"And how do we surprise them? With the waltz?"

"You're packing, right?"

He was right. I slapped my back and landed on my faithful Ruger.

"How many rounds?"

I checked the clip. "Five."

"Climb, Davis." He Mamboed sideways again. The other side.

"Climb what?"

"Into the tunnel."

"I won't fit in the tunnel, No Hair."

"Sure you will. The conveyor belt is at least two feet wide."

"With what looks like one foot of clearance around the two-foot-wide belt."

"It may be larger once you're inside," he said.

"And it may not be."

"You're small."

"I'm not that small."

"You're plenty small."

I stepped around him, avoiding his Mambo arms that didn't match his Mambo feet, and examined the dark abyss. "How is me climbing into the tunnel and crawling along the conveyor belt going to help us?"

"Do you have a better idea?"

I didn't. With one foot, I tested the steel-box ramp leading to the conveyor belt. It would probably hold my weight. Which didn't mean the conveyor belt would. "Let's say it works."

"It will work."

"Once I get on the conveyor belt, which way do you suggest I crawl?"

He rolled his Mambo eyes. "Do you want to crawl a thousand yards down a dark tunnel to Bling-Bling or ten yards down a dark tunnel home?"

Right. The shortest distance to death by pool crew would be the best.

But that was when the conveyor belt whirred to a jerky start again.

"There you go," No Hair said. "A ride. Hop up there and ride the conveyor belt to freedom. Then send Baylor to get me out."

My mouth was open to say one thing, probably a verbal last will and testament before I was mangled to death by a woman-eating conveyor belt, but when I spoke, it was, "Baylor?"

"Yes, Davis. You can find your daughters and send Baylor at the same time."

It didn't feel like the right time to explain the Baylor situation, such as it was, and if his idea worked and I escaped the pool pump room via conveyor belt, I could secure Baylor, July, Little Dude, and my mother just as soon as I secured Bex and Quinn, which would make explaining everything just then a waste of valuable time, so I might as well wait and explain later. But that was when a thud echoed from deep within the Bling-Bling side of the tunnel.

No Hair heard it too.

We held our breath. Well, I held my breath. No Hair was dancing too hard to hold his. "Could that have been the conveyor belt stopping and starting again but going the other way?" I speculated. "Returning money from our casino to theirs?"

"Can you not see which way it's going?"

"Everything's black, No Hair. There's no light in the tunnel."

"To my knowledge—" he was standing still "—there's no money left in our casino to return."

Right again.

I'd momentarily forgotten we'd been robbed. I was smack-dab in the middle of wondering why Bling-Bling would be sending dirty money to our casino when our casino was closed, which they had to know, along with the fact that a closed casino couldn't launder money, when No Hair said, "Get up there and look."

Weapon in hand, and having no other choice, I got up there to look. I started my ascent up the ramp again wishing Starling

Halter's cloned phone had enough battery to light my way to freedom when we heard the thud again. And closer to us that time.

"What is it?" Mambo King asked.

By then, I was at the top of the ramp. I stuck my head into the black hole. I immediately pulled my head out and didn't climb down the ramp so much as I tumbled off the side of it as fast as I could, then said, "I don't know, but it's big."

Friday, 4:00 P.M.

With something large headed our way from the Bling-Bling end of the tunnel, I demanded a Plan B. Regardless of exactly what it was clunking down the pike, by virtue of the fact that it was large enough to announce itself meant I had no intention of riding the conveyor belt with it. What if it picked up speed and crushed me? What if it was a bomb that exploded with me in the tunnel? "What if it's a fire-breathing dragon and I'm incinerated?"

"That's ridiculous," No Hair said. "How do you come up with this stuff?"

"It's a metaphor for the unknown being flammable," I said, "and shooting a fireball down the conveyor belt straight at me."

"First of all, I'm not sure you know what a metaphor is, and second of all, again, Davis, it's ridiculous."

"What do you expect, No Hair? This entire day has been beyond ridiculous. All the way to unimaginable."

He couldn't argue with that, but he could present his case. Which he did. Most likely, he thought, it was more dirty money, but bulk wrapped that time. Taking up all the space. Maybe teetering from side to side. Which was what we were hearing. And besides, I'd be riding the conveyor belt a very short distance the other way.

"Let me get this straight, No Hair. What you're saying is if I'm right, and whatever's up there kills me, you're willing to stand in front of my husband and explain what happened to the mother of his children while wearing a one-sleeved hazmat jumpsuit that doesn't fit and a fake Starbucks apron."

I guess he wasn't willing to because it was only with the thought of explaining my grueling death to Bradley that he agreed to discuss a Plan B. We were in the process of formulating it, along the lines of gathering combustibles from the old stash of pool chemicals and building a fire-breathing metaphor of our own that would blast through the manhole at the top of the iron step ladder leading to freedom, when two things happened at once. First, we realized No Hair wasn't dancing, and second, the giant surprise in the tunnel hit a snag. And none too gently. First we heard a loud clunk, followed by the conveyor belt whining and wheezing, then coming to an abrupt halt.

"It's stuck, No Hair."

He was on one side of the steel-box ramp. I was on the other. I watched the conveyor belt jump as whatever it was attempted to free itself with no luck. He peered into the black hole.

"Climb up the ramp again," he said. "Maybe it's close enough to see."

"You're not going to rest until you get me in that tunnel," I said. "Why don't you climb up the ramp and see?"

"I'm not about to climb up the ramp when I have you here to do it for me."

My head tilted his way. "What did you say?"

"I'm sorry," he said. "I don't know what got into me. What I meant was I don't have to get in the tunnel because I have you here to get in it for me. Get in."

"No Hair!"

"What I meant was don't be a crybaby sissy girl and get your ass in the tunnel."

I blinked. Stunned. Well, my right eye blinked. Because it was stunned. "Can you hear yourself?"

"Davis, I'm sorry," he said, and he sounded like he meant it, quickly followed by, "but I've had enough of your insubordination."

He meant that too.

I sat down on a pile of money. "What are you talking about?"

"When I give you a direct order, it isn't to hear myself talk."

"Since when do you give me direct orders?"

"Since right now." He stomped a foot. "I'm sick of you. I'm sick of Fantasy too. In fact, I'm sick of both of you—" his eyes narrowed "—I was going to say I was sick of you and Fantasy arguing with me and bullying Baylor, bossing him around like he's your own personal property, but you know what?" He took a menacing step forward, as menacing as it could get with a steel ramp between us. "I'm sick of you and Fantasy, period."

"No Hair, you should stop."

"I think it's high time you two stopped. Split up." He was stabbing a finger in the air, as if his words needed any accompaniment for emphasis. "Neither one of you hit a lick," he spat, "you play. You show up for work at nine or ten, long after you're supposed to be there—" he waved frolicking hands in the air "— then drink fancy coffee for the next hour, her saying, 'Oh, Davis! I missed you so much since I saw you yesterday!'" He raised his voice another octave on his way to poorly imitating me. "'Oh, me too, Fantasy! Let's talk about pocketbooks and lip makeup until lunch!' Just last week I looked for you two everywhere. You weren't in your office, you weren't answering your phones, and come to find out you and Fantasy took a spa day to have your eyelashes waxed, then had the nerve to tell me you'd been looking for spy cameras in the massage rooms."

"We did look for spy cameras."

"You're lying again!"

"No Hair, stop."

"You know what I'm going to stop? Putting up with you two. When we get out of here, Davis, you're a beat cop." He nodded, agreeing mightily with himself. "You're going into a blue jacket and walking the casino floor. You're going to help little old ladies who get turned around in the penny slots find their way to the buffet and call Yubers to take drunks home." He liked his idea. "And Fantasy? She's going straight to property management detail. She's going to learn how to sleep standing up, because she's going to be guarding a parking garage door forty hours a week. I'm done with you two. Baylor and I will handle it. I'm disbanding your team."

"No Hair, you're going to regret every word you're saying."

"You know what I regret, Davis? I regret that I've let you run wild for so long. I've given you too much rope. And you know why? Because your husband is my boss. It's nepotism. And I'm sick of it. I'm sick of him too. 'Oh, let's all calm down. It'll be fine—'"

"Nope." I stood. I tried to gauge how long it would be until the mean as a striped snake spin on the synthetic nerve agent worked through his system, and, knowing I could suffer through fifty-five more minutes of him berating me, especially since I was the one with the loaded gun, I knew with just as much certainty that I wouldn't make it through fifty-five minutes of him letting my husband have it. "Stop. Go back to dancing."

"Don't tell me what to do. It's the other way around. I tell you what to do."

I switched my channel to the soothing station. "This isn't your fault. It's the nerve agent. You don't mean a word you're saying—"

"You're wrong, Davis. I mean every word."

I changed channels again to the redirect station. "The football man who retired should have stayed retired."

His head whipped around. His cheeks flamed. "Brady?"

I nodded. Sure.

It worked. No Hair went off on an NFL rant that would probably lead to our immediate rescue. He was that loud. I let him go on and on, the whole time searching my brain for a path forward in the event he tired of football until I landed on traffic. No Hair's complaints about every driver behind the wheel of every vehicle on the road who didn't meet his strict driving standards would eat up at least fifteen additional minutes, and while he was going off on people who simply wanted to switch lanes while he happened to be on the road, I'd find another of his hot buttons to get us through without destroying our relationship. The service industry. That's where we'd go. One of No Hair's biggest pet peeves was anyone in the service industry who couldn't talk and work at the same time. From there, we'd go to personal services, how they were impossible to come by for Biloxi residents. Tourists? Yes. Residents? No. What worried me, as No Hair continued down the NFL path, going back decades—bad trades, stupid flags thrown, crazed fans—I realized that by the time the hissy fit chapter of the nerve agent book turned the page, we'd have been trapped in the pool pump room for more than two hours. I had to intervene.

I couldn't shoot him.

Maybe I could, but somewhere innocuous.

Like a leg.

I quickly discarded the idea. The aftermath of his nerve agent verbal attack on me would fade quickly. The aftermath of a bullet in his leg wouldn't.

I gave the short end of the conveyor belt a hard look and a second thought. He was right about one thing: it led home. Plus, I wouldn't have to listen to him rail away for fifty more minutes.

And more than anything else, we needed out of the pool pump room. I wasn't in as much danger with the large object on the way stuck in the other end of the tunnel as I would be if it were still moving, but the conveyor belt not moving meant I couldn't ride it home. I'd have to crawl. If it didn't kill me, it would lead me home. Just as I worked up the nerve and was trying to figure out how to get six feet in the air to the home side of the tunnel, No Hair going on and on about someone named Joe Judge who could have been the NFL's greatest head coach in history, and still could, if anyone would listen to him (I was trying my best not to listen), my attention was torn from the Bellissimo side of the conveyor belt when the large package on its way from the Bling-Bling side that had snagged on something unsnagged. The conveyor belt whirred to life and a dead body wrapped in clear tarp dropped down to rest on the ramp between us.

That shut No Hair up.

Friday, 4:15 P.M.

For all of sixty seconds.

I ripped the other sleeve from No Hair's hazmat jumpsuit and stuffed it in his mouth. At his request and with his permission. We were no more than fifteen minutes into his soapbox hour with the nerve agent, and like every other aspect of the physiological and emotional rollercoaster that had been forced upon him that day, he was fully aware of what was happening, yet unable to stop it. With me as his only target. After pausing in the middle of a loud sermon about everything wrong with the NFL draft when the dead body joined us to demand I explain why I'd killed a man, then mummified his body in a cocoon of thick opaque tarp and used black nylon rope to tie him up like a rib roast, then buried him, only to dig up his skeleton a decade later so I could send him down a conveyor belt and let him drop at No Hair's feet just to ruin his day, I stopped rolling the dead man burrito to the wall so we wouldn't step on him long enough to look up and say, "For real, No Hair? You think I killed this man?"

He clapped a hand over his mouth to keep himself from accusing me of murder a second time and mumble-yelled it at me into the palm of his hand. Then his eyes darted around the room.

"What are you looking for?" I asked. "My gun? So you can shoot me?"

His hand dropped. "Something to help me keep my mouth shut."

That was when we went for the other sleeve of his hazmat jumpsuit, stuffed some in his big trap, split what was left into two long strips, then tied it tight around his head. He continued to yell into it while he helped me roll the body the rest of the way to the wall. Just in time for our heads to whip around when we heard another screech from deep inside the Bling-Bling end of the tunnel. Having found a new resting place for our first dead guy on the east side of the room, maybe it was the west, near the stairwell, we sat on the bottom step to wait for what would surely be the second.

"You know what this means?" I asked.

He probably said something offensive and accusatory into the hazmat sleeve, but I'm sure what he wanted to say was, "I know exactly what this means, Davis. You were right all along. Not only has Bling-Bling laundered money, and through our casino no less, but they shipped all their dead body evidence here too. Just like you said."

"Right," I agreed, as two more wrapped skeletons dropped—thud, thud—from the hole in the ceiling. One rolled one way, one the other, and they both ran into dirty money.

No Hair mumble-yelled no telling what into his hazmat gag again. No doubt what he meant to say was, "And while I'm at it, I didn't mean a word of what I said earlier. I hope you can find a way to forgive me." To which I replied, "There was a grain of truth in everything you said except getting our eyelashes waxed when we said we were looking for hidden cameras at the spa. It was our eyebrows. No one waxes their eyelashes, No Hair. But you were right to say Fantasy and I treat work as an extension of our friendship. We do. What you didn't say was that it helps us more than it hurts us. And that there's never been a time when it really mattered that we didn't come through. But you're right that we need to be more productive on a day-to-day basis between big jobs. We do. You were also right when you said we pick on Baylor. Point well taken. He's a grown man with grown man responsibilities and we need to treat him like one. Now when it comes to my husband—" No Hair yelled into his hazmat gag again "—yes, he is the calm in the storm. You're exactly right. But that's what it takes to run a billion-dollar corporation. A level head. And maybe he cuts me some slack when it comes to my job, but he cuts everyone else slack too. Starting with you."

I might have gone on and on defending my husband had the bodies not started dropping again and kept coming for ten long minutes. Seventeen more wrapped and decomposed corpses arrived. We watched them silently from our seat on the bottom step until they stopped, and it was a good thing, because the pool pump room was packed. Just in time for us to hear an engine to start above us. The cement trucks. The mercenary construction crew at the Bellissimo end of the conveyor must not have known yet that there'd been a break in the supply chain and were waiting on the dead bodies to fall into the black hole that should have been our pool. Where they intended to bury them in cement.

I grabbed No Hair's arm as we heard the engine turn on a second cement truck. "We can get out."

His eyebrows shot up.

"They're moving the cement trucks. Maybe they'll move the one blocking the door."

By then, his hazmat sleeve gag had loosened enough for him to talk over it. "That's the stupidest thing I've ever heard."

It caught me by surprise until I remembered. "Turn your head around." He grudgingly complied. I tightened the shreds of hazmat sleeve. "Let's go."

We took two steps on our way to escape when I thought I heard a live body hail us from the Bling-Bling end of the tunnel. "*Hey!*"

I grabbed No Hair's arm. "Did you hear that?"

He mumbled something awful into his hazmat gag until the voice echoed through the tunnel again, and closer that time. "*Hey!*"

We froze on the dark step.

"Did you hear it that time?"

No Hair nodded.

We picked up our pace and made it up five more steps on our way out the door before we heard it for a third time. Closer. And with more urgency. "*HEY! Is someone there?*"

It turned me around.

I ran down the steps and was looking for a path through the bodies, No Hair at my back yelling atrocities into his hazmat gag the whole time. In my haste, I tripped over one body and landed on another. I could see clunky red women's pumps through the cloudy plastic body tube. Only to forget all about sharing such close quarters with a dead woman and her red pumps when I looked up to see Baylor's face—covered in grit and grime, his dark hair matted to his head, panting like a dog—in the tunnel opening. "Davis." He smiled, his teeth stark white against the rest of him. "You're never going to believe who busted me out of Bling-Bling lockup." He seemed so pleasantly surprised to see me, as if we unexpectantly pulled up beside each other at a red light. "You'll never believe it. Guess. Just guess."

"I don't want to guess."

"Guess!"

"Starling Halter."

The smile slid from his face. Disappointment took its place. "Well, guess what else."

"No, Baylor. I don't want to guess."

"Guess. Just guess. It's about her."

"Starling is a federal agent."

Once again, I'd burst his balloon.

"Okay, smart ass. Guess what else."

"No, Baylor. We don't have time for guessing games."

"Guess."

"You're Jimmy 'Tick-Tock' Russo's son."

That he knew nothing about.

Friday, 4:30 P.M.

After talking Baylor off the ledge, or out of the tunnel as it were, and on with the crisis at hand whether he was or wasn't Tick-Tock Russo's son, considering there was nothing he could do to confirm or deny it in the pool pump room, then promising I'd tell him exactly why I'd say something so "ugly and twisted" at the very first opportunity, we were three strong. Maybe two and a half strong, considering No Hair, who still couldn't filter anything between his overwhelmingly negative thoughts and irate speech, ripped out his hazmat gag and welcomed Baylor by firing him twice and exiling him to the most remote corner of the Galapagos Islands with nothing but the filthy shirt on his back, then went on to wish him a slow death by starvation and/or suffocation by boa constrictor. All because he didn't have a phone. (Which, first of all, wouldn't have done us any good, and second of all, wasn't Baylor's fault. His phone, along with his sidearm, had been confiscated somewhere in the middle of his third omelet at the Goody-Goody Café that morning. The black suits had surrounded his table. "Breakfast is over, Pretty Boy. We're too busy for your spying today.") Upon finishing his welcome speech, No Hair reached behind his own head and indignantly tied his gag on again, making us almost three strong, which meant we might succeed, because everything big in my life had come in threes. I had three daughters. There were my twins, Bexley Anne and Caroline Quinn, named after their maternal and paternal grandparents, and there was my firstborn daughter, Emmeline, named by the couple in Tennessee who adopted her when she was an hour old. The mistakes I made after learning I was pregnant led to my initial marriage to Eddie the Airhead. I probably wasn't the first teenager to ever misstep into a doomed marriage to protect the innocent baby she was carrying, but I might have been the only young adult woman to marry the same lowlife again years later in a misguided attempt to right the wrong. And he wasn't even the baby's father. Either time I married him. But new to the police force with unlimited cyber resources at my fingertips, I desperately wanted to locate the daughter I'd given up and thought "happily married and gainfully employed" would help me win her back only to discover Emmeline living a life I could never give her with parents she adored who cherished her. I couldn't do it. Nor could I stay married to the village idiot. And before it was over, I lost my job on the police force too. But had I not married and divorced Eddie the Imbecile twice, I'd have never met Bradley, who I loved without exception, and who I sincerely hoped to grow old with. If I ever made it out of the pool pump room. And as late afternoon dug in on the day I found myself trapped with Mean Motormouth, overwhelmed and dirt-caked Baylor, twenty dead bodies, and tens of thousands of dollars of ill-gotten gains, I was faced with three choices. Three paths forward. I could tell Baylor he might have a sister who meant him harm, possibly great harm, and that he, July, and Little Dude were in imminent danger. Another way might be to dig information out of him. He'd escaped his Bling-Bling captors—something he probably could have done with or without Starling's help—and found his way back to the Bellissimo. In the process of accomplishing all that, he might be sitting on critical intel. Like where my mother was and how she was being treated. He might have information I desperately needed and wouldn't know unless I took five minutes to dig it out of him. Or I could shelve both of those ideas for the time being and, with Baylor's help, escape. Because neither path one nor two could be resolved until three was accomplished. And I'd have started down that road had he not beat me to the punch asking how we'd ended up in the pool pump room. I told him about Bex and Quinn. After I scraped my heart off the concrete floor, put it back in my chest, and my blood began pumping again, I asked him the same question: how had he wound up in the pool pump room? The short version of his long answer was he'd followed the money and bodies. Starling Halter sprang him from Bling-Bling's drunk tank and passed him a guest room key, telling him to take the stairs straight to the room, barricade himself in it, and stay until she got there. Thinking July wouldn't like that plan at all, he waited until Starling was out of sight and chose door number two. He found himself in a long dark hall.

"Guess what was at the end of the hall, Davis. Just guess."

"Not this again."

"A hospital room."

Instead of describing the room my imagination flew to, filled with hundreds of sterile beds lined up to accommodate desperately ill synthetic nerve agent patients, and casting a horrified glance at No Hair, wondering if a hospital was in his future, Baylor described a much smaller room full of medical equipment, machines, and a single hospital bed.

A single empty bed.

At which point I wished we had a defibrillator handy.

If we had, and knowing who'd most likely been in the hospital bed, I might have used it on myself.

"Guess what was next door to the hospital room, Davis. Just guess."

"No." My head was in my hands.

It was Bling-Bling's private high-stakes gaming room. That wasn't a private high-stakes gaming room at all. It was a cold storage and count room with an underground tunnel behind a sliding door on the wall. From the shadows, he watched and waited until the last dollar and body were loaded, waited for the last black suit to leave the room, then slid the door open, found the tunnel, and followed the money and the bodies.

I asked him what possessed him to take that kind of risk.

He said he knew the tunnel led home.

The word "home" seemed to echo off the concrete walls.

Baylor stopped it with, "What happened to your eye?"

"I ran into No Hair's elbow," I said. "It was an accident."

He turned to No Hair. "What happened to you?"

I answered for him. "The biopharmaceutical convention, Baylor. They brought a nerve agent with them. No Hair is practically Patient Zero." I quickly ran through the list: hiccups, hearing loss, spiked coffee, deep sleep, amnesia, the waltz, and angry outbursts.

"How?" he asked.

Instead of bringing Ponytail into the conversation just then, I said, "We'll figure that out later."

"Why?" he asked. "Why would someone do that to our guests?"

No Hair yelled something horrible into his hazmat gag.

"To distract us from this." I spread my arms wide. "So we'd be too busy to notice their final destruction of the mobbed-up missing evidence."

"That makes sense," Baylor said.

"How? None of this makes sense, Baylor."

"Bling-Bling is changing hands at midnight tonight, Davis. It makes sense that they'd clean house before."

I wanted so much to ask how he knew their casino was changing hands and which Russo hands were involved in the exchange but bit my tongue to stop myself. It was, for Baylor, a matter to be dealt with after we escaped the pool pump room and secured our families. And family was where he went, with, "We need out of here as soon as possible, Davis. Something's up with July. If something's up with July, then something's up with Little Dude."

I chose my words carefully. "What makes you say that?"

"She won't answer her phone."

"July and the baby are at her parents' in New Orleans, Baylor."

He processed the information quietly. Then stood to make his final departure from the steel-box ramp, probably thinking he was on his way to New Orleans. "Let's go."

"We can't," I said, "we're trapped. And they know we're down here."

Baylor, still surveying the cramped and airless room full of long-dead bodies and copious amounts of money, asked, "They, who? Who knows we're down here?"

"The pool crew," I said, "that isn't a pool crew at all."

No Hair's head continued to bounce back and forth between mine and Baylor's, following the conversation, contributing often, or more like contradicting and chastising often, but thankfully, we couldn't understand him.

"What about the manhole?" Baylor pointed over the bodies.

"Soldered from above."

He looked up the stairwell. "Why can't we walk out the door?"

"Because there's a cement truck parked against it," I said.

He continued to study the carnage he'd just followed through the tunnel, then looked in the direction of where the cement trucks were parked, then to the Bellissimo end of the tunnel. That led to our pool. Or, rather, the hole that would be our new pool. Brilliantly, he said, "I get it." Then, explaining it to himself, "These bodies are supposed to go to the bottom of our pool." Then, giving himself the final detail, "Under the cement."

He took a step in the direction of the stairwell. "I'm never swimming in a pool again, and you were right the whole time."

"Where are you going?" I asked his back.

"I'm leaving."

"I just told you the door was blocked. There were four trucks on the loading dock nowhere near the maintenance door. The minute No Hair and I stepped in someone drove one to the door to block our exit."

"It can't be that blocked."

"If it weren't, Baylor, we wouldn't be here."

"You couldn't get around it?"

"I didn't even try. The cement truck is way bigger than the door."

"You couldn't crawl over it?"

"The trucks are fifteen feet tall. With huge bucket things at the top."

"The hopper," he said.

"The whatever," I said.

"And you couldn't crawl under?"

"How?" I asked. "How was I supposed to crawl under a cement truck?"

"There should have been enough clearance for you to crawl between the tires."

"No, I didn't crawl between the tires. The middle was—" I used my hands to demonstrate, spreading them wide, then cupping them, then rocking them back and forth "—moving."

"That's what cement trucks do when they're parked," he said. "If wet cement isn't constantly turned, it turns into dry cement. It hardens."

No Hair screamed into his hazmat gag.

"He's right," I said.

"How do you know what he said?" Baylor asked.

"I don't. But if I had to guess, I'd say he was reminding me that just before you dropped out of the tunnel, we heard one of the truck engines start. Then another. Maybe they moved the cement truck from the door."

"Let's go." Baylor cleared a stack of bodies in one leap to land at the bottom of the stairs he took two at a time. No Hair and I sounded like a herd of buffaloes behind him, slipping, sliding, and stepping all over dead people, until it occurred to me, we didn't know who or what might be on the other side of the stairwell door. I grabbed at what I could, which turned out to be the left leg of No Hair's hazmat jumpsuit, and unfortunately came away with a long strip of personal protective fabric before I whisper-shouted, "Stop!"

We were ten steps from freedom.

No Hair and Baylor turned.

"Let's not barge out the door." I had a tight hold on the iron handrail with one hand while the other was full of hazmat material. "Whoever locked us in here knows we're still here and by now there could be a firing squad waiting."

"Or not," Baylor panted.

"We only heard two truck engines start," I said. "There were four trucks, Baylor. The door is probably still blocked."

No Hair, trying to look over his shoulder and peeking under his fake Starbucks apron to see how much coverage he might or might not have lost beneath it while alternately staring at the length of hazmat scarf in my hand, seemed to be wondering what new state of undress he was in just then more than anything else.

"What are you suggesting?" Baylor asked.

"I'm suggesting we think before we make a move."

"What is it we need to think about?" Baylor tugged at the tail of his t-shirt and used it to smear tunnel dirt around his forehead. "If the manhole is soldered shut, that leaves three ways out. Through the tunnel to Bling-Bling, through the tunnel to the Bellissimo, or out the door." He pointed. "I'm not going back through the tunnel. No one in their right mind would go through the tunnel if they didn't have to."

No Hair yelled into his hazmat gag.

"You're too big, No Hair," Baylor said. "You'd get stuck."

I said, "I don't think that's what he said."

"Okay, mind reader. What'd he say?"

No Hair stabbed a finger at me.

"Ah. He wants you to go through the tunnel," Baylor said. "And he's right. You won't get stuck."

"But I'm in my right mind," I said.

"What's that supposed to mean?" Baylor asked.

"You said no one in their right mind would go through the tunnel. I'm in my right mind."

He rubbed the back of his neck. His eyes darted left, then right, then in the direction of the Bling-Bling end of the tunnel. "I didn't mean it."

"Yes, you did. Is it full of snakes?"

"No snakes," he said.

"Then what?"

"Let's just say the tunnel is temporary."

"What do you mean by that?"

"The tunnel is made of dirt, Davis. Everything around the conveyor belt is dirt."

"And?"

"The bodies coming through didn't help. The tunnel could collapse. Any minute it will."

"That's encouraging." I pushed between them and took another step up.

"Where are you going?" Baylor asked my back.

"To meet the firing squad," I said. "I'd rather be shot than buried alive."

No Hair yelled into his hazmat gag, the message for both of us, because his angry eyes bounced back and forth between us.

"What's he saying?" Baylor asked.

"He's saying I need to go through the Bellissimo end. Which probably hasn't been compromised by all the dead bodies. And is way shorter."

Baylor said, "There you go."

I said, "There I don't go. What's at the end of the Bellissimo tunnel, Baylor?"

"The pool." I let him think about it. "The hole that's supposed to be a pool."

"Exactly. What am I supposed to do when I get through the tunnel to the hole? Fly?"

Baylor rolled his eyes, then pushed past me and trudged up the remaining steps in a bring-on-the-firing-squad way.

"Wait!" I pulled my Ruger from my waistband.

He took it, checked the clip, flipped down the thumb safety, and flattened himself beside the door. No Hair and I hit the opposite wall. So to speak. We got out of the line of incoming fire should there be any was what we did. Baylor reached a long arm out to the doorknob, then flung it open. And there was a concrete truck. Right where we'd left it. Still blocking us in.

"Climb over it," I said.

"I can't climb over it," he said back.

"Climb under it."

"I can't climb under it."

"Climb through it."

No Hair spit out his hazmat gag. "Shut up. Both of you."

We retreated to the bottom step and squeezed in three across with No Hair in the middle. We did nothing but listen to each other breathe until the dead bodies were louder than we were. I had to break the spell. I leaned past No Hair to ask Baylor, "What about my mother?"

"What about your mother?"

"She's at Bling-Bling."

"What would your mother be doing at Bling-Bling?"

"That's what I want to know," I said. "A text from a blocked number said Bling-Bling had my mother. I'm asking you if you saw her."

"I didn't see your mother."

Between us, No Hair grunted into his hazmat mask and stuck a scuffed and dusty shoe out to land it on a brick of hundred-dollar bills. He worked his jaw enough to be heard through the hazmat fabric as he dragged the money our way to say, "Reach down and get that, Davis." With absolutely nothing better to do, I bent over to pick up ten thousand dollars of mob money. I passed it to No Hair as if he'd asked me to pass the salt. For whatever reason, his and his alone, he tucked it under the fake Starbucks apron and into his hazmat jumpsuit.

I leaned past him to ask Baylor, "Where'd they put you?"

"In the drunk tank."

"For how long?"

"Two naps."

"Were you interrogated?"

"Not really."

"What did you do when you weren't napping?"

"Mostly trying to get out."

"Baylor," I said, "this is like pulling teeth. Tell me what happened. Start at the beginning and don't leave anything out."

He started at the very beginning. Little Dude's first bottle before sunrise. July making him breakfast tacos, his favorite, which was sweet, because July hadn't made breakfast tacos since before Little Dude was born, but he told her he couldn't have breakfast tacos because he had to eat omelets all day, and that was probably why she was mad and hauled off to New Orleans, but who gets that mad about tacos? He was about to tell me about stepping into the shower and getting dressed in his restaurant critic clothes until I interrupted. "The beginning of your workday, Baylor. I don't need to hear about you tying your shoes."

His head dropped to look at his shoes. Drowning in dirt. Like the rest of him.

"Start with the omelet café," I said.

"Right," he said. "The omelet café. I was on my third omelet, the worst one, not that the other two were any good, but not as bad as the third one because the third one had a vegetable I hate in it, but it might have been because by then all I wanted for breakfast was breakfast tacos—"

"Baylor." I leaned past No Hair. "I don't care about what you did or didn't have for breakfast."

"You just said start with the omelets."

"Can you reach that?" No Hair, who'd worked out of his hazmat mask, pointed past me at the money brick he had his eye on. "Could you get it?"

I leaned way left and grabbed a brick of money. "We'll need this for evidence—"

"If we ever get out of here," Baylor added.

"—but I can't see that now's the time to gather it, No Hair."

"It's twenties." No Hair sailed the brick of money through the air. It landed with a thud on a body. "Get the stack of hundreds."

I stared at him.

"Please," he added.

Please? As in pretty please? What time was it? No Hair's hazmat mask was riding his chin and he wasn't threatening to wring my neck if I didn't reach for the dirty money. Testing my theory, I said, "You get it."

He said, as calmly as if we were swaying in hammocks tied to palm trees watching the sunset and not packed on a cold hard underground step overlooking a sea of dead bodies, "But you're closer. If you don't mind."

"It must be closing in on five o'clock," I said.

"It couldn't be," Baylor said.

"It has to be. Because this one," I pointed at No Hair, "isn't threatening to hang and quarter us." I leaned and reached for the hundreds. I handed them to No Hair. "Get back to your story, Baylor. And make it quick. I don't have all day."

No Hair stood and nonchalantly said, "You kids settle down."

I rolled a hand at Baylor. As in, keep going and make it quick.

He said, "I was eating a bad omelet full of asparagus. Or artichokes. I get them mixed up."

"One is green and the other one isn't. And if you say one more word about omelets, I will shoot you."

Baylor reached an arm to pat his own back.

He had my gun.

Between us, No Hair stretched, then stepped over two bodies at once.

Baylor seemed to be digging through the minutia of his morning, discarding the details he suspected I didn't want, searching for what I did. I yelled at him again. I might have smacked his arm. No Hair, halfway across the room at the MegaWarm, separating money bricks by denomination, said, "Don't make me pull this car over."

Baylor said, "I don't know where to start."

"The beginning, Baylor."

"I was on my third omelet—"

"Not that far back!"

"If you ask me, Davis, we can talk about this later," he said. "Get in the tunnel," he pointed to the short end, "crawl through, and get us out."

No Hair turned, his fake Starbucks apron bulging with dirty money tucked beneath. "What about Overdose?"

Oh so nonchalantly, Baylor said, "Six o'clock."

"Someone died of an overdose at six o'clock?" I asked. "Someone's going to die of an overdose at six o'clock?"

"How do you know about Overdose, No Hair?" Baylor asked.

"I've been with Bling-Bling's high rollers all day," he answered.

My head whipped between them. "Bling-Bling's high rollers who had breakfast here overdosed? They're going to overdose?"

"Overdose is a game," Baylor told me. "A slot game at Bling-Bling. It launches at six. Five thousand slot machines change to a game called Overdose."

"That's disgusting."

"I need out before six." No Hair patted the money.

If I'd had hackles, they'd have been raised. No Hair's sudden jolly mood in spite of our grim circumstances, his recent lack of contribution in remedying the situation, and his disinterest in anything but packing his hazmat suit with money to play a game called Overdose—still so offensive—was troubling. As a rule, not an exception, but a rule, No Hair couldn't care less about a slot game anywhere—our house, their house, or any other casino's house. He had no interest in gaming outside of the realm of security. Zero. Put it all together, factor in the timing, since we'd passed the five o'clock mark and six o'clock was next, and it might mean we were closing in on the next stage of the synthetic nerve agent too. Compulsive gambling. Somehow—not somehow, rather, by way of synthetic nerve agent—we might have reached Bling-Bling's end game. They'd successfully shut us down providing cover for the final deposition of their dirty money and long dead bodies, and at the same time, if they'd chemically altered brains to impulsively wager with wild abandon at Bling-Bling—cash absolutely everywhere—it could mean the end.

Of everything.

It meant Bling-Bling was cashing out before the casino changed hands.

Before I could react, or begin to react, two things happened. First, a flash of light bounced around the pool pump room. I thought I might have imagined it until the same light bounced off No Hair's bald head. Baylor saw it too and shot his arm out to pin me back so as to keep me from flying out of the car. I'd known since the steel box had broken away, then the money and bodies began piling up in the pool pump room instead of making their way to be processed at the Bellissimo, that someone would eventually investigate.

That time had come.

Next, we heard the distinct sound of a two-way radio alert from the Bling-Bling end of the tunnel. Then a voice. A man's sandpapery voice I knew. It was Dunk, the pool construction foreman. He spoke from deep inside the tunnel, but given the surround-sound amphitheater qualities of the pool pump room, we could hear him. He rasped, "I found it."

And with that, I knew it was time.

I had no choice.

There was no other way out.

I stood quietly and picked my way over bodies and past No Hair to get to the Bellissimo tunnel opening, then turned around to Baylor, who was at the steel-box ramp and at the ready with my Ruger. "Baylor," I whispered. "Help me up."

He holstered my gun at his back, took a giant step over three bodies, then dropped to a stoop. With my hands on his shoulders, I landed a foot in his interlaced hands. He hurled me through the air, cheerleader style, where I barely caught the dark opening with my fingertips. Loose dirt and debris broke away and hit Baylor's upturned face. He sputtered and shook, then caught both my flailing feet in his palms to push while I pulled until I was halfway in. The only smell was that of damp earth. The only light was that of the glimmer of freedom a hundred feet away. I grabbed both sides of the slick rubber of the conveyor belt to hoist myself in. I crab-crawled as fast as I could. I eased to the edge of the end of the tunnel. Before popping my head out, and after wiping no telling what kind of creeping crawling creatures from my face, probably tarantulas and scorpions, I scanned the area and realized just who'd been in charge of pool construction at the Bellissimo.

No one.

Absolutely no one.

Upon first glance, it was deserted, except for two cement trucks on the other side of the huge hole, poised to release their loads. From my vantage point, with gritty dirt still obscuring what was partial vision to begin with, they appeared to be driverless.

To my left was what used to be Splash, the Bellissimo's poolside restaurant, now home to a fake Starbucks truck, brewers of carotene-laced coffee drinks and robbers of casinos. It looked empty. To my right were ten of our old private cabanas, battered, side by side, and they'd clearly been repurposed for makeshift offices and cash cages. Several held Bellissimo cash cages, used to move money around our casino. Both the offices and the cages were empty.

Above me, there was two feet of unstable earth that would never give me purchase, and past that early evening light filtering through the tent. The first for me in hours. Below me? Air. Thin air. Somewhat fresh air. At least ten feet of it.

The pool.

The hole that would be a pool.

I could see the muck and mire of what must have been the baby octopi swamp at the very bottom. Around it, sand. Wet gray sand. The layers of sand grew darker on their way up as it mixed with dirt all the way to the top, which was all dirt, the same dirt I was in. And it was only as the dark sand gave way to darker earth that I caught a glimpse of the galvanized pole missile that started everything when it sailed off Bling-Bling's roof and struck our pool in the dead of night. It had been relocated from its upright position and lodged horizontally in the sand and dirt two feet above the octopi nursery and lifetime of dead air away from me on the other side. It looked to be at least twenty feet long, one glinting end protruding from one side of the pit, the other end visible on the opposite side, the middle buried in dirty sand. There was no going left, right, up, or across to get to the pole, which, if I could dislodge and reposition, might give me enough leverage to free myself, but it felt a world away as there was no easy way to it. Which left me only one choice. I had to jump out of the tunnel, land in the baby octopi nest, then wade through the muck to the pole. While desperately trying to figure out how I was supposed to accomplish all that from my supine position, Baylor's muffled voice interrupted from far behind me. "Davis. Are you okay?" Quickly followed by No Hair's muffled voice. "Can you see Bling-Bling's casino?" I turned my head and yelled down the tunnel. "I'm fine, and no, I can't see Bling-Bling's casino from our pool deck. What in the world kind of question is that?"

I jumped.

Friday, 5:15 P.M.

No. I didn't.

I slithered.

I didn't have enough clearance in the tunnel to maneuver my legs beneath me to jump, so I slid out, headfirst, then tumbled down the dirty sand. The more ground I covered on the way down, the firmer it became beneath me, all the way to packed tight when my feet finally followed the rest of me out of the tunnel. With every drop of blood in my body having pooled in my head on the vertical ride down, I grabbed what might have been a tree root to right myself. The tree root, if it was a tree root, because once I had a grip on it I realized it might have been a petrified sea creature, wasn't anchored to anything, causing me to unintentionally plunge another foot deeper into the huge hole before I could get my arms in front of me to stop. At which point I was finally able to sit up. Swallowing screams and wearing head to toe dirt and sand camo. No one would look at the vast hole in the ground and point. "Look. There's a woman." And the worst part of being as far down as I was, past the assault on all other things physical, was the aroma. If it were a scented candle, it would be called Marine Decay. I couldn't tell if the odor was more from the sand around me or the baby octopi's home below, but if I'd stumbled upon a magic lamp just then, I'd have asked for a phone first, for the smell to go away second, and third, considering how far I was from the galvanized pole I somehow intended to both reposition and vault, I'd ask for a ladder.

I stopped to catch my breath, burrowing my backside into the packed sand to create a small ledge and knocking what grime I could from my face. My good eye darted and my mind raced, my thoughts jumbled and disconnected. Why was the pool deck deserted, deathly still, and quiet? On what was obviously a big day for the money laundering and body disposal teams that called themselves a pool construction crew, they were nowhere to be found. Why wasn't there at least one live body waiting on the receiving end? Why were there no operators in the two concrete trucks poised to pour? Were they showering away their felonious day on the fourth floor of our hotel? Packing their personal belongings before they made their great escape? Was everyone in the whole wide world at Bling-Bling waiting for Overdose? Not like I wanted anyone to be there considering my sitting-duck state, but where was everyone?

Across the hole and on solid ground above me, the mixing drums of the concrete trucks rolled.

Above me, at least halfway if not more into the Bellissimo end of the tunnel, otherwise I'd have never heard him from as far down as I was, Baylor yelled, "DAVIS!"

I tipped my head back. "Where's Dunk?"

"WHO?"

"The man we heard in the tunnel!"

"The tunnel collapsed. He's stuck in it. Where are you? I can't see you."

"Look down! I'm in the pool pit!" I yelled up, the vast maw of dirty sand swallowing my voice. "Where's No Hair?"

"Stuffing money in his socks!"

"Stay where you are! Give me ten minutes!"

Below me, the murky water gurgled. Probably because I'd disturbed so much earth on my way down and it was still breaking loose in chunks and bricks to roll into the muck. And having somewhat acclimated to its proximity and its fumes, I stopped to study the pool of thick dark water, hoping to gauge how deep it was and wondering if I might be better off taking the long way around through the dirty sand to the galvanized pole. It was then I saw the edge of something solid peeking above the surface. Something inanimate. Conical at one end, leading to fairly wide, then tapering again at the other end. And had I not just been in the pool pump room with twenty shapes just like it, I wouldn't have had a clue as to what it was. I'd have thought it was a gargantuan baby octopus that had grown and flourished in the vast nothingness at the bottom of the pool pit, and I'd have scrambled up the sand to get away from it in record time. But it wasn't alive at all. It was, in fact, another dead body wrapped in the same clear tarp and secured in the same four places with the same black rope. I dislodged rocks from the sand around me and began tossing them at the body bag enough for it to submerge, then resurface, and each rock, especially the ones that actually landed on the body bag instead of left or right of it, served to rinse away a little more of the surface slime until I could make out details. Such as the lack of bones. It wasn't a corpse that had been decaying for years. It was a much newer model. I moved to my left because I'd run out of rocks, and on my first dig found something solid that might have been a real tree root that time. After wrestling it out of the packed sand with the very last ounce of strength I had left in my body, I used it to help me stand and gain footing. Once I was upright and rooted to the earth myself, I stretched far enough to use the root to catch the edge of the body bag and pull it closer. I used the root one last time to give the body bag a final rinsing plunge. It surfaced face up that time, staring at me. It was wearing a hospital gown. It was Jimmy "Tick-Tock" Russo.

No one had seen him because all that time he'd been dying in the basement hospital room at Bling-Bling.

And his daughter, Ponytail, intended to lay him to rest in concrete at the bottom of our pool.

I might have continued to stare at his body until I understood, which might very well be never, had I not heard the distant sound of a dog barking.

My dog barking.

Candy. My Candy girl.

Who could find anything.

She'd found me.

The muted pound of rubber-soled shoes followed the increasingly loud barking until I saw Candy across the vast pool pit, standing on what used to be the Bellissimo's pool deck, between the concrete trucks. Wildly wagging her tail. My daughters, my mother, and Starling Halter fell in line behind her. Starling, wearing an OCU Kevlar vest, took in the scene before taking a step back and speaking into a two-way radio. "I found her." She went on to say, "Found Tick-Tock too." She spotted Baylor's head poking out of the tunnel. "And bonus, I found Baylor."

Bex and Quinn, blonde curls dancing, waved and squealed, "Mommy! Mommy! Mommy!"

My mother, who was holding Bex and Quinn by their shirt collars, yelled over their heads, "Davis Way Cole, you are absolutely filthy!"

I yelled back, "Mother, what are you doing here?"

"Where is it you think I'm supposed to be, Davis?"

She was supposed to be at Bling-Bling.

If Bling-Bling didn't have my mother, who did they have?

Eugenia Winters Stone.

I'd have asked where Fantasy was, because we hadn't spoken in hours, and I'd have asked where Dr. Winford Wurtz was, because No Hair desperately needed a double dose of whatever cure the good doc had, and I'd have asked where Ponytail was, praying she wasn't still in my home with Bianca Casimiro Sanders, and I'd have asked someone to please contact July and find out what document she was holding at her parents' house in New Orleans, but I think I passed out before I could.

Friday, 5:30 P.M.

A lone news reporter at the back of the press pack congregated on the Bellissimo front lawn noticed three Biloxi Search and Rescue vehicles quietly arrive and park on the street. Far from the action. Only the one reporter noticed. The rest were busy watching the last of the Bellissimo evacuation while shoving microphones into Biloxi PD, SWAT, and FBI faces seeking any tidbit of news as to who issued the bomb threat against the Bellissimo, what the bomber's demands were, and were they far enough away from the blast to both get the story and avoid bomb debris. "Probably not," an FBI spokesperson said. "If I were you, I'd run."

"What's that supposed to mean?" a reporter shouted out.

"It means to put one foot in front of the other in rapid succession and get as far away from here as you can," the FBI spokesperson responded.

While all that was going on, the reporter at the back who'd spotted the Search and Rescue response vehicles watched the crews unload, gear up, and sidestep the big crowd to stealthily make their way around the building. The lone reporter, none other than Prime Eight's Spider Gibbons, followed. With his camera. Not that any of his media cohorts noticed. They were too busy shouting questions at the authorities. Had the Ferraris been evacuated from the showroom on the mezzanine? How about the thirty-million-dollar two-hundred-carat white diamond on loan from Christie's Auction House and on display at Rock's, the Bellissimo's fine jewelry store? What about the owners, Richard and Bianca Sanders? Were they in residence? Spider wasn't a bit interested in the answers, as he was the one who'd accidentally started the bomb rumor an hour earlier when he'd wondered aloud where everyone was. "It's like someone called in a bomb threat," he said. The reporter beside him only heard the last two words—bomb and threat—and from there, it spread like wildfire.

Spider slipped away and stealthily followed the rescue crew and their gear around the east perimeter of the property to the large tent behind the hotel. He slid in right behind them, temporarily paralyzed by the chaotic scene that unfolded before him, and wondered if a bomb *had* been detonated. He snapped to quickly, hugging the building and hiding behind sparse and untended landscaping, then sneaked onto what he thought was an unoccupied Starbucks truck parked on the west corner of the pool deck. He settled in for an exclusive, pocketing a lonely hundred-dollar bill he found on the dashboard and helping himself to an unclaimed room temp double espresso he found on the mobile kitchen's prep counter. Then raising the large metal window on the side of the truck carefully and only high enough for his camera to peek out, he hit the red "record" button.

He sipped his cold espresso and filmed Baylor being assisted from the edge of the tunnel, then pushing his way through the rescue team and running as fast as he could. Probably to New Orleans. Spider filmed No Hair in all his hazmat jumpsuit glory, liberated from the pool pump room by way of the Maintenance door after the concrete truck against it was backed away, then seemingly having a fit. Shouting, refusing water, defensively guarding the money he was harboring in his hazmat suit, shaking off all attempts to assess his physical and mental state, and punching one guy in the face. Spider filmed me as I was lifted from the pit with a Class III rescue harness, looking for all the world like something out of a horror flick. Spider filmed it all. Including a stout man in a Bomb Squad windbreaker so covered in dirt he had to have taken part in the pool pump rescue, who was leading my daughters, my mother, and my dog into the Bellissimo. And Spider filmed the woman who'd put him on the map, Starling Halter, in her OCU Kevlar, pointing fingers and shouting orders at the Kevlared people who'd joined her, all of them fielding calls right and left on their two-way radios and cell phones. Spider finally made his presence known just as my feet hit solid ground when he threw the coffee truck window all the way open and stuck his orange marmalade face out. "DID VICTORIA ELISE FABRÉ DO THAT TO YOU?"

She hadn't, but with the total lack of journalistic integrity that was his modus operandi, Spider ran with his story, immediately posting it on his website and social media pages to an instantaneous twenty-five thousand local views. "New York Times Bestselling Author Viciously Attacks Mother of Twins Responsible for Daughter's Heinous Haircut." And the image of me he chose to share with the fabricated story, in which Spider reported that Victoria Elise Fabré tried to bury me alive after beating me to an absolute pulp, immediately picked up by Associated Press, was not only the worst picture of me ever taken, it was the worst picture of anyone ever taken. I was completely unrecognizable, so much so that the image of me caked in dirt and sand being lifted from the pool pit, my limbs dangling, what was left of my clothes in tattered strips blowing in the breeze, my head tipped back in relief, looked like someone being pulled from the depths of a war fought in hell. As the image began circulating, it wasn't long before one of the reporters in the crowd in front of the Bellissimo said, "That's not the twins' mother. That's Bianca Sanders." The man next to him studied the photo. "You're right." The woman next to him said she knew for a fact Victoria Elise Fabré was jealous of Bianca Sanders. The woman next to her thought the assault had possibly happened during a psychotic break, something she'd heard the bestselling author had a history of. The man next to her suggested attempted homicide charges were in order, and within five minutes phones buzzed with more breaking news. Victoria Elise Fabré was wanted for questioning in connection with the vicious aggravated assault of the Bellissimo Resort and Casino's First Lady, Bianca Casimiro Sanders.

It was true. Not that Victoria Elise Fabré tried to bury Bianca Sanders alive during a psychotic break, but that the poorly lit photograph featuring my profile rising up from the ashes of middle earth resembled Bianca Casimiro Sanders more than it did me when factoring in how long I'd been Bianca's celebrity stunt-double, because at that point in my doppelganger career, ninety-nine percent of the photographs out there of her were actually of me. Sporting sunshine blonde hair and poison green eyes. But distribute a photo of me with my almost-red hair caked with dirty sand and my caramel-colored eyes closed—one purposefully, the other of its own accord—it looked to the public like a photo of a seriously compromised Bianca Casimiro Sanders. I hadn't been out of the pool pit ten minutes when a BOLO was issued for Victoria Elise Fabré.

On one side of the pool deck, Starling picked her way around the line of plastic-wrapped mummies retrieved from the pool pump room to shut down her buddy, Prime Eight's Spider Gibbons, and stop him from live streaming footage that might seriously jeopardize her case for a second time, just as Bradley, from the other side of the pool deck, fought his way through feds and rescuers to get to me. Then froze. He didn't swoop me into his arms and shower me with kisses. In fact, he stopped cold and stared at me, his mouth agape, the color draining from his face. He stammered out my name a few times, weakly at first, then incredulously, then indignantly. Surveying the EMT crowd attending me, he demanded, "Who did this to her?"

I was the only one who answered. "How could you!"

"How could I what?"

"Send Eddie Crawford to pick up our daughters!"

"Would you rather them be bald?"

No. No, I wouldn't.

He swept an arm toward the Bellissimo. "You need a shower."

Boy, did I ever.

And as we made our way into the building—ghost town— and after he acknowledged I'd been right about Bling-Bling all along, I was either asking him a question or answering one of his. We traveled a long empty hall, me leaving a sandy dirt trail, until we reached the end, where he kicked through the locked door that led to the outdoor venue dressing rooms reserved for visiting poolside acts—deserted—where I could take said desperately needed shower. After telling him I'd just found Jimmy "Tick-Tock" Russo's body, plus how Bling-Bling had been laundering their dirty money through our casino, and that Jimmy Russo's daughter, Ponytail, who, as it turned out, owned Good Pills Biopharmaceuticals, was singlehandedly responsible for everything that had happened to us that day, starting with sneaking her hiccup conference through our back door and ending with her attempts to eliminate the last of any evidence that could possibly be used against her operations in the future, I said, "She's been at our house most of the day, Bradley. Our *home*. For all I know she might still be there. And she thinks Baylor is her brother."

"He might be." Bradley caught what was left of my t-shirt in a waste basket as I sailed it through the air. "What's left of your bra too, Davis. Everything."

"How do you know that?"

"How do I know what?" Then, "Shoe," he said. "Toss your shoe."

I looked down to see the shreds of charcoal canvas where there had previously been a white tennis shoe on my left foot and a shiny speck of California Raspberry in a sea of dark greige dirt on my right, recognizing the California Raspberry peeking through as the color of polish on my toenails, and wondering where the shoe that should have been covering it might be. "How do you know Baylor might be her brother?"

"I don't know it for a fact. What happened to your eye?"

To which I said, "Where are our daughters and my mother? Where did the dirty man in the bomb jacket take them? Where are Bexley and Quinn?"

To which he said, "I flew back to Biloxi in Vernon Wilson's King Air 350 with the mayor. She briefed me."

"You flew in the governor's plane?"

"I did."

"What does that have to do with Bex and Quinn?"

"I was answering your first question."

I stopped dead in my tracks. "The mayor?"

"Celeste Reed. Our mayor," he said, "who doesn't have anything to do with Bex and Quinn that I know of, and she isn't a mayor at all."

"Let me guess. She's with the Organized Crime Unit out of Chicago."

He nodded while turning on a shower full blast then gathering all the shampoo and bodywash from the two shower stalls on either side to join the soaps already there. Which probably still wouldn't be enough. "And the girls along with your mother and Candy are being escorted to Fantasy."

Relief blanketed me. Poured over me. Found its way to every cell in my body. My daughters, my mother, and my partner were okay.

"Where?" I asked, opening the shower door while he slammed drawers and cabinet doors several feet away searching for towels.

He said, "Found them," just as I stepped under the spray and let out a horror-movie scream. He dropped the towels and ran my way. "DAVIS! WHAT? DAVIS!"

Through chattering teeth, I said, "NO! HOT! WATER! WHERE?"

"WHERE WHAT?"

"WHERE IS FANTASY? WHERE IS THE DIRTY MAN IN THE BOMB JACKET TAKING BEX AND QUINN?"

"Home, Davis. Upstairs. Our home. You asked him to."

Panic blanketed me. Poured over me. Found its way to every cell in my body. I hadn't spoken to the dirty man in the bomb jacket. I hadn't asked him to take anyone home. Not with the strong possibility of Ponytail still there. Which meant the dirty man in the bomb jacket wasn't on the bomb squad at all. He was a dirty pool construction foreman named Dunk who'd either crawled out of the collapsed end of the tunnel or had been pulled from it by the search and rescue team who wouldn't have known to detain him. Then helped himself to a Bomb Squad jacket. And if he was escorting my daughters and my mother to my home, it meant Ponytail was still there. And would be barricaded with all of them—my daughters, my mother, Fantasy, Bianca Sanders—and with her partner Dunk's arrival, she'd have backup.

Friday, 5:45 P.M.

Fifteen minutes later, Starling Halter asked us, "How many ways are there into your home?"

In those fifteen minutes, after I'd sent as many pool pit leftovers as possible down the sink drain with the help of hand soap, a dozen washcloths, and freezing cold water, then dressed in a Bellissimo spa robe and stuffed my hair into a Bellissimo ball cap, we'd learned that after an extensive investigation by bomb squad resources from five counties, including a large team from next-door Orleans Parish in Louisiana with enough bomb-sniffing dogs to open a kennel, there were no signs of the bomb anywhere in or around the Bellissimo that they were unable to verify in the first place. And we'd learned that Jimmy "Tick-Tock" Russo, after suffering a series of mild strokes immediately after being acquitted of bribery, kidnapping, witness tampering, murder, money laundering, counterfeiting, embezzlement, drug trafficking, and every other charge the RICO Act could throw at him, decided to clean up his own act, make amends, and get as far away from Chicago as he could. Both from the feds and from his sorry excuse for a family. He had no intention of letting his blood-sucking ex-wife, who'd personally made the last four decades of his life a living hell, or, for that matter, their daughter, Blake, follow him south. She was just as greedy, power-hungry, and money loving as her mother. He broke the news to his daughter, Blake Russo, that he was retiring and moving away, then gifted her—no strings attached, except the lingering loom of federal strings—everything left of his local operations that had been legitimate enough to survive the trial. They included an over-the-counter biopharmaceutical research, manufacturing, and distribution operation, four established and extremely profitable construction companies, one specializing in luxurious outdoor venues, and two hundred hot dog stands. Thinking that would keep both money-grubbing women happy. Mostly because the hot dog stands were cash cows. Surely they'd be too busy counting their money to bother him. He was seventy-six years old, in failing health, sick of the fight, sick of the women, sick of his lawyers, sick of looking over his shoulder, and wanted it all to stop. So he could set about putting his affairs in order. One in particular. The affair he'd had in New Orleans three decades earlier. It was time for Jimmy "Tick-Tock" Russo to do right by the child he'd abandoned before it was even born. He hired ten top-notch private detectives from ten different reputable firms giving them all the same instructions: locate a child born three decades earlier to a brunette dancer on Bourbon Street who went by the stage name of Coco, offering a fifty-thousand-dollar bonus to the discreet inquirer who produced the results first. Ten days later, three different detectives were waiting outside his office when he arrived at nine a.m., all three with dossiers on the same young man believed to be Tick-Tock's biological son. Which cost him a hundred and fifty thousand dollars. And brought on another stroke. That one, more serious.

Jimmy "Tick-Tock" Russo had very little time left.

Upon finding Baylor in Biloxi, and in the casino industry, he was pleased to find Southern wheels much easier to grease than Windy City wheels, never suspecting they were the wheels of justice. That generally greased themselves. Especially when there was something in it for them. And the Jimmy "Tick-Tock" Russo case had more than something in it for them—retribution, revenge, and saving face. The first thing Tick-Tock did after purchasing and making plans to develop the property next door to the Bellissimo was to make out a new will. The second thing he did was call his ex-wife, Hilda, and his daughter, Blake, to tell them about the new will, specifically to let them know there wasn't one red cent in it for them. The Biloxi holdings would be left to his other heir. A surprise son. Who he intended to build a casino for. His plans were to spend the next six months establishing the casino, and at the end of the six months, turn it over to his long lost boy, then retire for good. He advised the women to be good stewards of what he'd already given them because there would be no more, and he asked that they let him live out the rest of his life in peace. The third thing he did was have his final stroke, which wasn't peaceful at all. It was the stroke that put him on life support for the next eight months. The stroke from which he never recovered. He died—the actual time and cause of death had yet to be determined—having never laid eyes on the man he believed to be his son.

Our Baylor.

Upon hearing the news of his incapacitation, then consequently learning the black suits knew nothing about Jimmy "Tick-Tock" Russo's old son or new will, his daughter, Blake, happily swooped in to fulfill her father's Biloxi wishes. She slammed the casino together, slapping her father in a hospital dungeon, and took her seat on the Russo Crime Family throne. And as soon as she milked her stepbrother's inheritance for everything it was worth, then took him and the casino out of play before ownership could be transferred, and at the same time destroying every shred of evidence that could ever be used against her Chicago enterprises in the future, she fully intended to swoop out.

And she would.

If we didn't stop her.

The feds detected one weak heat stamp emitting from the private elevator that led to our home.

"Any idea who this could be?" Starling asked.

Bradley answered, "Our surveillance is inoperable. I have no idea who it is."

I answered, "No."

The feds found three heat signatures in our home: two stationary and one creeping up and down the east wall.

"This small heat stamp on the east wall." Starling pointed. "Do you have a robot vacuum?"

Bradley answered, "A what?"

I answered, "No."

Five heat signatures were visible above our home in the Penthouse, the Sanders' residence. Three, most likely, were Bianca's staff. Her personal maid, her personal chef, and Jules the esthetician. Who'd turned Bianca's face green. We couldn't identify the other two.

"Does Bianca Sanders entertain?" Starling asked. "Could it be friends?"

Bradley answered, "I doubt it."

I answered, "No."

Two of the three heat stamps in our home were surely Ponytail and Dunk. The third could have been Fantasy. Or Bianca. Or my mother. But why would any of them be alone and why would any of the three be wandering the east wall? It made way more sense that Fantasy and Bianca would be together—Fantasy wouldn't leave Bianca—and had somehow managed to escape to the Penthouse, making them the two unidentifiable heat stamps there, but I couldn't see the third heat stamp in my home being my mother. Alone. And wandering the east hall.

Where was everyone?

Who was stuck in the elevator?

Where were our *daughters*?

Bradley and I sat across from Starling Halter and Celeste Reed, who'd donned Kevlar too, at one of many long banquet tables set up in the Bellissimo lobby. Harried activity was all around us, including a team that was camped out at the front desk singularly devoted to finding Dr. Winford Wurtz. What everyone could only hope was the last stage of the nerve agent effects, the one in which all gaming inhibition flew out the window, was causing enough problems at next-door Bling-Bling to drain all local resources—traffic was at a standstill because of the Bling-Bling marketing jingle broadcasting on a loop through long-range Bluetooth portable speakers at the main entrance Pied Pipering people in, resulting in over-capacity crowds, fights breaking out, and extensive property damage—therefore distracting from and impeding investigations at the Bellissimo. If the scientific feds could find Dr. Wurtz, who they believed might still be somewhere at the Bellissimo, and if he could tell them how to negate the final effects of the nerve agent that appeared to be ridiculously contagious at Bling-Bling, they could put a stop to it. Meanwhile, Bradley and I numbly stared at monitors showing the heat stamps, not seeing anything small or wiggly enough to represent our daughters, and the terror between us reigned supreme.

"What about our dog, Candy?" I asked. "Do you see anything that could be Candy?" Even Bradley responded incredulously. That I would worry about the dog with so many lives at stake. "She would *not* leave the girls, Bradley. She just wouldn't. Wherever Candy is, that's where the girls are."

He didn't disagree.

Several essential Bellissimo employees—maintenance, finance, and operations—were called in. Our system was restored, our empty casino and hotel secured, and soon we would have hot water. Someone passed me a large cup of coffee I couldn't swallow, an ice pack for my busted eye, and a new clone of my old phone. While we waited on additional equipment for the SWAT teams who would breach our home from the roof, and while Bradley identified our front door, service door, balcony, lanai, deck, and interior elevator on one monitor, and while Starling tried to place who might be where by moving color-coded dots with initials representing everyone in question on the other monitor, I instinctively turned on the phone. Bex and Quinn knew my number by heart. Maybe they'd picked up a phone and called. But nothing in the hundreds of text messages, alerts, voicemails, and missed calls landing on the new phone, one on top of the other, looked like it could possibly be from them. There were six text messages from Cricket Robinson at Willow School for Exceptional Children, five from my mother, four from Fantasy, three voicemails from my father, and the following two hundred incoming received were either security alerts or messages from internal departments within the Bellissimo. I'd missed them all. But nothing that looked like it might be from our daughters.

"What about this area?" Starling used the eraser end of a mechanical pencil to circle a spot on our digital home map. "We aren't picking up anything here."

"That's an enclosed playground," Bradley told her.

"Enclosed by what?"

"Four inches of hurricane-proof tempered glass."

"Why isn't it on the blueprints?" she asked.

"Because it's new."

"Where's the access?"

"One through the den and another through the girls' indoor playroom."

"Spoil your kids much?" She tipped her head back. "Someone find out if heat signatures can be identified through four inches of tempered glass!"

She showed Bradley a Google Earth image of the same enclosed playground. "Why does it look like a jungle? Why can't I see through the trees? How did you even get trees that far up in the sky? And am I looking at a high-rise *beach*?"

I started with the messages from Willow School for Exceptional Children and read quickly and straight through, the first one logging in at 2:35 that afternoon, just after the school released my children to Eddie the Idiot Crawford.

Davis, Cricket began, *turn around. You didn't sign the girls out in pickup line, and as you very well know, your signature is required. And by the way, no one appreciated your peel-out exit. You almost mowed Mr. Honey down. And you destroyed a whole line of his pickup lane cones.*

The next message was five minutes later. *Davis, upon reviewing pickup line security video, it would seem there was a small misunderstanding. It is imperative you call at your earliest convenience so we'll know your daughters are with you.*

The third message from Cricket hit my phone twenty minutes later. *Davis. Mrs. Wellesley is requesting you return to the school as soon as possible so that we might share new information that has come to light about Eliza Fabré's unfortunate haircut.*

The fourth message arrived a half hour later. *Davis, it's me! Cricket! Again! Just making sure you received my message that we need to talk! Please call! Hope you're having a super-duper day and look forward to chatting with you!*

The fifth landed fifteen minutes later. *Look, Davis. We're sorry. Mrs. Wellesley is sorry. Eliza Fabré is sorry. And our Board of Directors, collectively, are sorry. I can't say Victoria Elise Fabré is sorry, but I can say I'm certain she'll get there, and when she does I'm sure you will hear a sincere apology from her too. We have learned that not only did Eliza cut her*

*own braids and give them to Bexley and Quinn so they could
have pretty dark hair like hers, which, if you think about it, is
very sweet, she's also confessed to being responsible for several
other baffling incidents at school previously thought to have
been Bex and Quinn's fault. Eliza has been in the office with me,
Mrs. Wellesley, and our Early Childhood Behaviorist, Cristina
McKee, and much has been learned about her tumultuous
relationship with her mother. Eliza takes full responsibility for
her actions and is so remorseful that she insisted we enjoy the
chocolate truffles she brought for your family in exchange for
your rabbit. Apparently, the rabbit-truffle trade was the result
of an earlier playground negotiation between the girls we
knew nothing about. Those little wheeler-dealers! The truffles
were prepared by her mother's private chocolatier. And they
were   melt-in-our-mouths   delectable.   We   have   already
contacted our staff child psychologists, Drs. Tate Escobar,
Stanley Sawyer, and Martha Friedman, who are putting a
program together for our entire student body to discuss the
dangers of bartering personal belongings, and we are
prohibiting the playing of Truth or Dare from this moment on.
Eliza's a sweet girl, Davis, and very much wants to explain and
apologize to you, Mr. Cole, to Bexley, and to Quinn. We look
forward to sitting down with you and your lovely girls, who, it
would seem, are as innocent as the day is long. And please
don't forget I still have your birth control pills.*

The last message from Cricket logged in an hour and a half
later. *Davis, forget about coming by the school. Mrs. Wellesley,
Miss McKee, and I are at the Biloxi Memorial emergency room
with listeria food poisoning from the chocolate truffles. Don't
worry about Eliza Fabré either. That brat will never darken
the door of Willow School for Exceptional Children again. Good
luck with your birth control pills.*

Starling asked, "What do you make of this?" She tapped the monitor with a pencil. "The two heat stamps that haven't moved."

I glanced up from my phone. I leaned in. "That's our living room. That's our sofa."

"The two people on your sofa appear to be compromised."

"What's your definition of compromised?" Bradley asked.

"I'm suggesting they have a gun or some other manner of threat on them, Mr. Cole. They haven't moved. One is large, one small. The small one could be the mother."

"My mother?"

"Davis," Bradley put a hand on my robed knee, "we're doing everything we can."

"Back to this roving heat stamp on the east wall," Starling said, sending me back to my phone to read my mother's text messages I'd missed, praying she didn't have a gun on her but that she did have a phone. And there'd be a message from her saying she was on her way home to Pine Apple with my daughters. Where life was simpler. And hauling off with my daughters without saying a word to me beforehand would be something my mother wouldn't hesitate to do, considering it well within her self-appointed rights as their grandmother, and given the circumstances, very welcome news. I started with the first message I'd missed, half an hour after the one above it I hadn't missed, the one telling me my farther's trampoline had the pickups and the lice doctor, by which she surely meant nice doctor, had a cure in his hotel womb. At one forty-five she wrote, or dictated to her phone, rather, *Tavis, we are licked in the lice doctor's hotel womb. We can't Aleve.*

The second message from my mother I'd missed said, or tried to say, *Tavis, Franticly called to said she wood fescue us but a mans with stained Vogel cords showered up insteads. He tacks like him eats rockers for wreakfast. Whore R U?*

If he had strained vocal chords to the point of talking like he ate rocks for breakfast, I knew exactly who he was.

Dunk.

Ponytail Russo's partner.

The third message, only a half hour earlier, which was shortly after she'd been escorted from the demolished pool deck with the girls, said, *Tavis, I half putt my grandditrers and Ur dig Candies in times route. Whit they knead R a whacks or too on their little buttons if U axe me. Ur crazed dig Candies distant liked the mans whoop tacked us to your mouse. She bracket him in the corners of the alligator and barkleyed at him loud. He spayed, "Shit yup, dig," and thin I no who he whiz. The mans hoot eatery rockers for wreakfast. He tried to knick your dig. Thin your dig Candies bite him. Thin Exley And and Carolina Quinton knicked him bee cause he tied to knick their dig Candies butt they knicked him in his privateers. His familial jewelry. He is pissed out in the alligator. You butter git tome fastidious.*

I shot out of my seat. "LOCK DOWN OUR ELEVATOR!" I interrupted everything happening in the lobby. I shook my phone above my head. "LOCK DOWN OUR ELEVATOR!" I went back to my mother's messages for the fifth and final one I'd missed, ten minutes earlier. *Have you seen the babbitt?* Still on my feet, I shook my phone in the air again. "THE ROOMBA IS A RABBIT!"

At least a hundred people in the lobby froze.

The vast room grew eerily still.

Until Celeste Reed delicately cleared her throat.

I slinked back down to my seat.

"Davis?" Bradley's voice was gentle. "Do you need a doctor?"

"THE DOCTOR!" I jumped straight up again, so fast that time my head swam. "DR. WINFORD WURTZ! THE ROOMBA IS LOOKING FOR THE DOCTOR!"

Bradley's head whipped around. His voice rose as he shouted across the room, "Could someone get the EMTs?"

"Bradley." I leaned in and slapped the table to get his undivided attention. "The dirty man in the bomb jacket who walked Mother, the girls, and Candy home. He's the heat signature in our private elevator. He's passed out. Bex and Quinn kicked him in the you-know-whats."

"No, Davis. I do not know whats."

"His man parts."

Bradley blinked. And blinked.

"The heat signature that looks like a robot vacuum," I went on, "is the rabbit. The rabbit is trying to get to the doctor. Dr. Winford Wurtz. Who must be on the other side of our east wall at Jay's place."

The whole time we'd been trying to figure out how to sneak into our home to find our daughters without suffering death by Ponytail and Dunk in the process, and there it was. Jay's place.

Bradley collapsed in relief.

Celeste Reed said, "Who is Jay?"

I tried to think, speak, and run for the service elevator at the same time, knowing I had to get to Fantasy's messages at some point, but before I could do anything my phone rang in my hand.

It was Baylor.

The four of us who were halfway out of our seats on our way to the service elevator that would take us to Jay's place sat back down. I placed my phone in the middle of the table. I answered in speaker mode. "Baylor?"

"Davis. My thing."

"What?"

"My thing I forgot. Remember I told you I had a thing today and I couldn't remember what it was?"

"Baylor—" I would have told him then wasn't the time for him to tell me he'd forgotten Little Dude's Baby Mozart or Infant Literacy or Tiny Yogis class, but he didn't give me the chance. "My anniversary," he said. "I forgot today was my anniversary. Remember? When we all flew to St. Barts so me and July could get married?"

Starling Halter threw her hands in the air and directed all her frustration at Celeste Reed, who said, "How was I supposed to know to look for a marriage license in St. Barts?"

"And, Davis, guess what else?" Baylor's voice rang out from my phone. "Just guess."

I dropped my head. "Not this again. Baylor—"

"We're going to be neighbors!"

"What?"

"Old Man Russo? He left his casino to me in his will. It's mine at midnight tonight. I'm on my way back from New Orleans with July, Little Dude, and Old Man Russo's last will and testament. When I get there, I'm going to say, 'Howdy, neighbor!'"

His call and his news might have brought on a "Don't start celebrating just yet, Baylor," or a panic attack, or at least a moment of silence, but we didn't have a moment to spare.

We ran.

I checked Fantasy's messages stuffed in the service elevator with Bradley, Starling Halter, Celeste Reed, and two additional feds—too stuffed in the service elevator, considering Starling had chosen heavily-armed federal linebackers to accompany us—on our way to the catering kitchen on the twenty-fifth floor.

Fantasy's first three text messages were relatively brief. *Bianca stopped speaking English. Maybe it was English, but it was deranged English. You've heard of word salad? This was word goulash. I mean it, Davis, she's crazy talking. About applesauce, snowmobiles, and Miley Cyrus. What do you make of that? She finally shut up and started banging her head against the wall. She was totally out of control. Flailing all over the place would be a good way to put it. She's broken about everything you own and not necessarily on purpose, but because she's possessed. I need an exorcist ASAP. Do you have a straitjacket anywhere? Where are you?*

When she'd asked, I'd been trapped in the pool pump room was where I was.

Her second message said, *Bianca's dancing now. First it was interpretive dance, and from there, the hokey-pokey, with her left foot in, then her left foot out, then shaking it all about. Wait till you see the video. Now it's Celtic stomping. Think Riverdance. Where are you?*

When she'd asked that time, I was still in the pool pump room was where I was.

Her third message was more of the same. *Bianca has lost her very last marble. She stopped dancing, but now she's having BABY COWS about your decorator, threatening to kill him or her, and about Wednesday, on and on about how she wants Wednesday—the day of the week Wednesday—stricken from the calendar, and about every thirty seconds, she fires ME. Not you. ME. I don't even work for her. I thought I heard your mother sneak in with the girls and assumed you were with them, but WHERE? I can't leave Bianca long enough to track you down. Come on, already. Please, please, please get here and help me with Bianca. Where are you?*

When she'd asked for a third time, I was still in the pool pump room was where I was.

Her fourth message was a voicemail. A four-minute-long voicemail I might have listened to after we made it to Jay's place, from which we'd be able to enter our house without being shot so we could secure our daughters and my mother, because Ponytail would never see us coming via that route, but it could only happen if we ever made it to Jay's place. The service elevator's doors were in the process of closing when a hand caught the door sensors by waving them open again. Another linebacker fed, out of breath and armed to the teeth, squeezed in. The elevator took off, but when the third linebacker took a step back to join his linebacker friends against the elevator car's wall, he threw it off balance. The elevator came to a grinding stop between the sixth and seventh floors. The automated woman who lived in the panel control said, "Weight limit exceeded. Weight limit exceeded. Weight limit exceeded."

"Everyone stay right where you are," Bradley said. "Don't even breathe."

Starling had her phone to her ear. "No signal."

Celeste Reed tried her two-way radio. Nothing but static.

The two women turned to Bradley, who said, "It's a twenty-five-year-old service elevator built for nothing heavier than a housekeeping cart that's stuck between floors. Our best bet is to distribute our weight more evenly and get the car moving again on our own."

While they decided what course of action might circumvent the snapping of the cables from which we were dangling, leading to a conversation about the linebackers spreading out and lying down, I listened to Fantasy's voicemail. So I'd be distracted as I plunged to my death before securing my daughters and my mother. *Hey,* Fantasy had said half an hour earlier. *Listen, I think I have to go to Bling-Bling. Bianca is dead set—seriously, I've never seen anything like it—on going to Bling-Bling. I unplugged the keyboard and mouse from your television trying to figure out what in the world was happening with all the sirens, and every commercial between horrific news—I mean it, Davis, every commercial—was the Bling-Bling jingle and* casino footage of a new game there that launches at six. *Overdose*. There are three levels: Low Dose, Maximum Dose, and Lethal Dose—HAVE YOU EVER? IT'S DEPRAVED!—all leading to a bonus round at midnight. The Overdose round. Which, clearly, was meant for the Good Pills Convention. What do we make of THAT? I'll tell you what we make of that. Good Pills was originally booked at Bling-Bling is what we make of that. You know I can't let Bianca go alone. And there is no stopping her. Ponytail said she'd be fine until we got back, and it's not like she can go anywhere anyway until you come home. If you ever come home. So here I go next door with Bianca. You'll be happy to know she's finally wearing clothes, so to speak. For some reason, the penthouse is in lockdown mode, so she went to your closet for clothes. If you can talk yourself out of custody for trying to kill your idiot ex-ex-husband for whatever it was that happened with Bex and Quinn, which is the only reasonable explanation I can come up with for why you haven't shown up yet, come rescue me at Bling-Bling and help me haul Bianca's gambling ass back home. We'll be easy to spot. I'll be the tall one. She'll be the one wearing a track suit of yours advertising Willow School for Exceptional Children on the front, the back, across the butt, up and down both sleeves, both legs, and everywhere else that stupid school could get their stupid name. I can't imagine why you aren't answering other than in jail for dismembering Eddie, how Baylor is faring, why No Hair hasn't checked in, or where in the whole wide world anyone else is. P.S. Don't let your dog eat pineapple pizza again. He's gassy as all get-out. He's gotta be choking Ponytail to death. She hasn't said a word, unless it was one of the million words she's said to her watch. Not that I could hear what she was saying between Bianca dancing, or slamming herself into walls, or trash talking Wednesday, or through your dog's eight miles of fur. Remind me to ask Ponytail if she *remembers where she got her watch. And if it comes in different colors. We need watches like that. XO*

By then, the federal linebackers were strategically placed and prone. Bradley told Celeste Reed, who was closest to the elevator panel, to push twenty-five. For the twenty-fifth floor. Which would lead us to Jay's place. She might have been aiming for twenty-five, but her finger landed on the arrows pointing away from each other instead. The open-the-doors button. A command the elevator obeyed, but not completely. The doors parted but didn't open all the way. About a foot. Maybe only ten inches. Between the sixth and seventh floor.

"Now what?" Starling asked while peering into the dark unknown through the partially open doors.

"Give me a minute," Bradley said.

I took the minute to listen to the messages from my father, which would also distract me from death by elevator. I hadn't taken any of his calls and he was probably borderline frantic. First up, that morning, or in other words a lifetime ago, he'd said, *Davis, honey, your mother is on her way to you. Call and I'll try to explain.*

His next message, several hours later, said, *Sweet Pea, I'm watching breaking news from Biloxi and I'm on my way.*

His last message, two hours later, said, *Davis, I've tried to talk to your mother several times. She's answered my calls, but only to say things like my cheating heart would tell on me and her boots were made for walking, then immediately hanging up. After my last attempt, my phone rang five minutes later with an incoming call from an unknown number in your area code. I answered, thinking it might be your mother calling me back, but it was Eugenia Winters Stone. Davis, that's a long story. One I'm sure we'll all laugh about one day. And a story that will have to wait. Somehow, Eugenia found herself detained at the new casino next door to you. She needed help.*

At the time, I was still more than a half hour away and couldn't reach you, anyone else, or even the Bellissimo switchboard, so I called your Biloxi homicide friend, Sandy Marini, who for some reason was already at the Bellissimo. At your pool, she said. I have no idea why. Detective Marini managed to retrieve Eugenia from the casino next door. I met up with them at the Bellissimo side entrance. Detective Marini let us in but couldn't escort us to your home because your private elevator was inoperable. She escorted us to the Sanders' Penthouse instead and told us to stay put until we heard back from her. At that point, Eugenia was nothing short of hysterical, which alarmed the Sanders' new chef, who wasn't familiar with me, much less Eugenia, and following protocol he pressed the panic button locking down the Penthouse. We are here and will remain here until someone with the proper credentials arrives. Davis, none of this is why I'm leaving you such a long message. Your mother finally called me. A call I missed, as Eugenia and I were in the elevator with Detective Marini at the time. Apparently, Bexley and Quinn had some manner of altercation with a man who tried to kick your dog. My feisty granddaughters kicked back with what sounds like painful results. Your mother sent them to their room to think things over. A moment later, realizing it was entirely too quiet, she stepped in to find the girls had sneaked to their playroom, which, unbeknownst to her, led to their new outdoor playground, leaving her a note of sorts, a drawing of a rabbit holding an I'm-Lost sign, which she interpreted as meaning the girls had gone outside to look for their rabbit. I didn't know the girls had a rabbit. And now your mother can't locate them. She claims Bexley and Quinn are either hiding in the woods or have gone next door. Is the landscaping of the girls' new playground that thick, Davis? Obscure enough to hide the children? What, other than the celebrity suite, is next door? Can the girls enter the celebrity suite from their outdoor playground? I called your mother, and all she had to say to me was we couldn't go on together with suspicious minds and that I couldn't eat crackers in her bed anytime, which said to me the situation with the girls may have somewhat corrected itself. In an effort to find evidence of just that, and with the new chef's blessing, I explored the Penthouse balconies to hopefully get a view of the girls' playground. Which leads me to why I'm really calling, Sweet Pea. Nothing I've relayed so far feels as urgent as what I observed from the Penthouse's southwestern-facing patio. The one that wraps around the Sanders' formal living and dining rooms. I fear there is imminent danger at the crowded casino next door. A three-foot-wide and several-hundred-foot-long strip of topsoil leading from the back of their property all the way to yours has given way. Collapsed. And the ground around it is eroding quickly. In the past half hour, the ditch between the two properties has easily grown to six feet wide and ten feet deep leading straight to the foundation of the new casino. Equipment has been brought in. But rather than shoring up what appears to be great instability to the foundation because of the sinkhole beneath it that won't stop growing, the excavation and backhoe equipment operators appear to be attempting to finish the job, as in eroding the foundation of the building even further. It looks as if an entire construction crew is intent on purposefully destabilizing the building. Davis, the casino next door to you needs to be evacuated before the lower floor gives way, which will imperil the many floors above. Most of my calls to your local authorities aren't being answered, and the calls that have been answered have been unproductive. If I weren't seeing it with my own eyes, I wouldn't believe it either. Everyone in the casino next door needs to exit immediately. If your casino and hotel weren't deserted, I'd strongly advise the Bellissimo to evacuate as well.

Bottom line, Sweet Pea, unless someone intervenes, and at the rate the inexplicable excavation is going, the entire edifice might not be standing at midnight.

"She's barefoot. And wearing a bathrobe."

It was my husband's voice breaking through my terror. Explaining to Starling that he didn't want me to crawl through the opening, then somehow drop to the sixth-floor landing or hoist myself up to the seventh-floor elevator landing in the dark, find a way to open the elevator doors while dangling midair, then free us.

"No one else is small enough," Celeste Reed said.

Knowing we didn't have one single second to spare and having not one ounce of patience left in my entire being, I reached for the elevator control panel and pulled the red emergency button so hard it came away in my hand. An alarm so shrill and loud it immediately threatened to burst all our eardrums had all three federal linebackers on their feet, which upset the balance of the elevator car for a second time, but in a good way. The doors closed, the elevator lurched into action, and it stayed on course to its original path to the twenty-fifth floor.

When we reached the catering kitchen that would lead us to Jay's place, we stopped cold, stunned to find it occupied. My mother was quietly perched on a stool in the middle of the fine china mess I'd made earlier when I'd tipped over a cart. Not a single hair on her head was in place; she looked like she'd lost an argument with a light socket. Her eyes were glassy and wide, and almost popping out of her head, as if she'd seen a ghost. And she had her arms wrapped around the fire extinguisher sitting straight up in her lap as if it was an emotional support lovey. My papier-mâchéd daughters were across the room on matching stools at the catering kitchen sinks with what looked like a five-gallon drum between them, simultaneously showering each other with flour and blasting each other with water from the kitchen faucet sprayers. Most of our goldendoodle, Candy, was inside the pantry. No telling what she was eating. We could only see her tail wagging. The rabbit was on its back, paws sprawled, whiskers twitching, asleep on the stainless-steel prep table.

With no emotion whatsoever, staring off into space, my mother said, "Davis, you have ruined these girls."

"Mother." I gently pried the fire extinguisher from her. "What happened?"

"My granddaughters played scientist upstairs."

"At Jay's place?"

"Yes." She sighed. A long weary sigh. "Someone should call and tell him."

"Is that why you're here?" I asked. "In the catering kitchen? There was a fire at Jay's?"

"I put it out."

"Then came here? To the catering kitchen? Why?"

"To hide."

"What are you hiding from?"

"I'm hiding from your life, Davis. I can't take another minute of it."

"Mother, where's the doctor? Is he hiding too?"

"He is." Without looking, she pointed to the butler's pantry lift. "He's hiding from your house guest. The woman under your dog."

I stepped over to the butler's pantry lift, and there was Dr. Winford Wurtz.

Again.

That time with what looked like fire soot on his nose.

"Dr. Wurtz?" I helped him out. "What are you doing?"

He straightened his tie, dusted his lapels, and adjusted his glasses. "Waiting for zee stormz to pass."

In the big scheme of things, it wasn't the worst place at the Bellissimo to wait out a storm.

"Dr. Wurtz, what can we do to stop the effects of the nerve agent at the casino next door?"

"Zee levelz reached?"

"No inhibitions," I said. "Reckless gambling."

"Ah," he said. "Zee end."

Very welcome news.

"What can we do to stop it?"

"Zee shockz therapiez."

"We can't go through Bling-Bling zapping people."

"Zee hypnozeez."

"We can't hypnotize thousands of people either."

"Zee decomprezzion chamberz."

"I don't really know what a decompression chamber is, Dr. Wurtz, and even if I did, and if we had one, I doubt we could get thousands of people in it."

"Zat being the caze, you must eliminatez zee targetz."

"Zee whatz?"

"Zee objectz of zee affectionz."

"He means the game, Davis." Bradley said it from across the catering kitchen where he was pulling the girls out of the flour and the dog out of the pantry. "Take the game out of play."

"You are correct," Dr. Wurtz said. "Eliminate that upon which zee dezirez are focuzed."

That we could do.

Starling, at the door with her crew keeping their distance from the mayhem inside, or maybe just avoiding our gooey daughters, and having called EMTs to retrieve Dunk from our private elevator, sent the federal linebackers to assist. "Make sure he's shackled to the gurney and one of you ride to the hospital with him."

Celeste was on the phone too. "Pull the plug on the Overdose game at Bling-Bling. At the same time, lower the lights, kill the music, but leave the PA system up so we can evacuate in as orderly a fashion as possible."

Ending both their calls, they set their sights on me. Starling said, "Wait here. I'll have someone let you know when it's safe to go home."

"That won't work," I said.

"I know how to take someone into custody, Davis."

"My dog won't release her to you, Starling. He'll only release her to me."

"Cotton?" Bradley's head popped up. "You asked Cotton to watch her?"

Five minutes later, I strolled through my front door. Barefoot, wearing a bathrobe, sporting a shiner, and I needed three hot showers. I yelled out a singsong greeting. "Ponytail, it's me! Davis! I'll be right with you!" I caught a terrifying glimpse of myself in the foyer mirror and almost took a left for my bedroom for the first of the three showers I desperately needed, but I only stepped into the adjacent sitting room long enough to retrieve a .22 from the gun safe. Because I felt bad for my dog. Who'd been on guard duty for hours.

I nabbed a straight chair on my way through the living room. I placed it two feet from Ponytail and sat down. I put the .22 in my lap. "Cotton, leave it." And leave it he did. Cotton hurled himself off Ponytail and ran down the hall to Bex and Quinn's playroom on his way outside.

Ponytail cleared her throat, smoothed the skirt of her power suit, crossed her legs, then raised her eyes to meet mine. Her face was a clean slate. Drained of all color. Her gaze was dull and dead. Her ponytail was past disheveled. If she was relieved to be out from under Cotton, whose resting body temp was somewhere in the four-hundred-degree range, she didn't let on.

If she was surprised to see I'd survived, albeit the worse for wear, she didn't show that either.

"So, you really liked being an only child, huh, Blake?"

She stared straight through me.

"Your partner, Dunk, is in custody. Everyone else, and I mean everyone, is in the process of being arrested. We've secured the dead bodies and the last of the Chicago money. Bling-Bling is being evacuated, closed, by order of the county sheriff, and I feel certain it's only a matter of very little time before the building is condemned."

She didn't even blink.

"Your father's body has been retrieved and will be properly buried."

She finally moved, but only to place her elbow on the arm of the sofa and slowly tilt her head to rest her cheek in her cupped hand.

I matched her movement, but only to place my hand on the .22 in my lap.

"It's over, Blake. You know that. But before the feds haul you away, which will be any minute, could I ask you something?"

Her palm all but caressing her cheek, her fingers creeping up to rub her temple, she finally spoke. "Sure."

"Did you accidentally dose yourself? Were you really asleep? Did you have amnesia?"

She slowly turned her head to the left, which put her chin in her palm, but not to contemplate her response. Or to admire my living room wall. She did it so I wouldn't see her using her teeth to pop off the face of her unbelievably smart watch. I sailed through the air so fast the gun flew out of my lap, and I landed on her so hard the sofa flipped. "Oh, no you don't, Ponytail." I pinned her down with her left arm stretched as far as it would go, and the thin red tablet that had been hiding inside her watch dropped and rolled across the floor. Panting, my heart beating out of my chest, I looked up to see Fantasy and Starling, weapons drawn, in my living room doorway.

"Davis!" Fantasy said. "You're half naked!"

I rolled off Ponytail. I stood. I gathered my robe and my wits about me. I retrieved my .22. "She's all yours, Starling." I pointed to the red dot on the gray floor. "And process that first. Bag it, tag it, and search her for more suicide pills."

By then, Starling had her cuffed and on her feet. "Trying to take the easy way out, were you?"

"While you're at it, Starling, get rid of everything else that even looks like medicine. Every pill, every tablet, and every capsule under my roof. Except the Children's Tylenol. And the dogs' heartworm prevention chewies. And my husband's Claritin. Leave that too."

Over her shoulder, as she handed Ponytail off to the intake team waiting in the foyer, Starling said, "Is that all, Davis? Want me to unload your dishwasher while I'm at it? Start a load of laundry? Got any ironing?"

"She's kidding." Fantasy put an arm around me. "She's probably never seen an iron." I rested my head on her shoulder. "Let's get you cleaned up, Davis. I'll make coffee while you shower, then we'll do something about your eye."

"What?" I asked. "A raw steak?"

"I was thinking we'd ask the old Albert Einstein doc. I bet he knows a black eye trick or two."

"No," I said. "In a million years, no."

Six Months Later

DNA test results were back within three weeks of that fateful day, and there was no familial match. Not one marker. Baylor was not Jimmy "Tick-Tock" Russo's son. But the Probate Court ruling came back the same week, and after validating the will, determined Baylor to be the legal and sole owner of Bling-Bling. He let the Organized Crime Division of the Department of Justice in first, and once they had everything they wanted, which was very little additional evidence and most of the cash on hand, Baylor used what was left to deconstruct Bling-Bling in the same fashion Ponytail had constructed it: piece by piece and pod by pod. He donated the guest room pods—structurally sound as single units and stacked no more than two high—to the Roof Over My Head homeless shelter in New Orleans. He sold off what he could of the remaining contents, including two small jets, multiple vehicles, mostly limos, along with furniture, fixtures, art, and restaurant equipment, to pay for the deconstruction, cleanup, and restoration of the beach.

It took forever.

The Bellissimo closed to wait forever out. For one, the Gaming Commission shut us down until they investigated and were satisfied we weren't culpable in the money laundering that had happened in our house and under our noses. For two, everyone needed to take a breath. For three, we wanted our pool back. But mostly, because trying to keep the Bellissimo open during the demolition of Bling-Bling would have been just as dangerous, distracting, and even messier than the construction was.

Once the initial dust settled, most everyone else went back to their corners—Starling Halter and Celeste Reed to Chicago, Dr. Winford Wurtz, his research, and his rabbit all the way back to Germany, and Eugenia Winters Stone back to Pine Apple in MY new car, with Eddie the ABSOLUTE IMBECILE at the wheel, where she promptly resigned from her seat on the City Council. Everyone else went to prison. The black suits, Dunk and his entire money laundering crew, and, of course, Ponytail. The only mobster who caught a half break was the squirrely black suit, Tony Francesco, Bling-Bling's VP of Security, who'd called me and Fantasy old girls, who'd spied on Baylor harder than Baylor had spied on Bling-Bling, and who'd never liked Ponytail. His final act of gangster loyalty had been to make sure Jimmy "Tick-Tock" Russo's last will and testament made it into the right hands.

The first thing we did was go on vacation. Within twenty-four hours, Bradley and I were on the road with Bex, Quinn, and the pups. Destination? The Peppa Pig Theme Park in Winter Haven, Florida. We stayed a week, which wasn't without its challenges, considering Bex and Quinn spoke with English accents the whole time, just like Peppa Pig, for which we needed an interpreter, and Cotton ate a nine-thousand-dollar sectional sofa in the twelve-hundred-dollar-a-night Airbnb we were staying in while his teenage dogsitter floated in the pool with Candy. Who was on her own float. We left Peppa Pig Theme Park saying never again, then drove to Pine Apple where we dropped off the girls and the dogs with my parents. Bradley and I spent the next ten glorious days in our own luxurious villa in the Maldives, hardly seeing another soul, and had it not been for missing our daughters and our dogs, plus the fact that I needed to start the application and interview process at prospective preschools all over Biloxi, we might have stayed another ten days. We might have stayed another ten weeks.

My team officially reported for work a month before the grand reopening. Much had changed. For one, we stepped into No Hair's office and almost passed out. He wasn't wearing a tie. He told us to get used to it. He was tired of having a noose around his neck. Baylor, having completed all phases of demolition, cleanup, and beach restoration next door, had been tasked with transforming the property into a five-star beach experience for our guests. He was given all the leeway he wanted, which was only fair, considering he'd donated the land back to the city, who in turn donated it to the Bellissimo. The first thing Baylor did was name it Little Dude's Sandbox. (So off brand, but no one said a word.) Fantasy, after working full-time while the hotel and casino were closed overseeing the construction of our new pool—very on Bellissimo brand, and made me feel like I was back in the Maldives—was preparing to step up and fill in for me as lead of our team, because by that time, I was five months pregnant.

It's a boy!

DOUBLE WHAMMY

Gretchen Archer

A Davis Way Crime Caper (#1)

In case you missed how it all began...

ONE

A little unemployment goes a long, long way, and after more than a year of it, applying for every available position in L.A. (Lower Alabama), I took a right and tried Mississippi. At the end of the road I found Biloxi, where instead of applying for fifty different jobs, I applied for the same job fifty different times.

My final interview, like the dozen before it, began in a posh corporate office with an executive assistant at the Bellissimo Resort and Casino, Natalie Middleton. From there, the others had gone in several different directions. There'd been a marksmanship test with long-range pop-ups (I aced it), ink-blob and dot-to-dot psychiatric profiles (not sure how I did on those), and an extensive photo shoot with costume changes, tinted contact lenses, and wigs. I couldn't wait to hear what my last interview act would be.

"You'll be meeting with Richard Sanders," Natalie said, "our president and CEO. The final decision is his, and it will go quickly."

I'd applied for the job six weeks earlier. It was two hundred miles from where I lived. Most of the interviews had been all-day ordeals. It had already not gone quickly.

Richard Sanders' office had museum qualities: everything was quiet, valuable, and illuminated. Natalie directed me to a leather chair. "He'll be right in."

Right in, for the record, was almost an hour later.

I'd just helped myself to a fifth Red Hot cinnamon candy from the crystal bowl on Mr. Sanders' desk when a hidden door on the right side of the room slid open and a man stepped through, then froze, staring at me as if I was a ghost. I wondered who he was expecting. From the look on his face, not me.

He cleared his throat, then cautiously crossed the room with a guarded smile, hand outstretched. "Richard Sanders."

I skipped around the candy. "Davith Wathe."

He took his seat behind his desk and reached for the folder in front of him. I could see the right angles of a stack of photographs. Of me. The dress-up interview.

I sat up straighter, looking for somewhere to lose the candy. I gave him the once-over while he looked at the photographs, the whole time discreetly working the candy at top speed, the roof of my mouth on fire. Mr. Sanders was in his early forties, six-two, strikingly fit, blond, and either perpetually tan or just back from the Bahamas, since it was the dead of winter and he had a late-July glow about him.

He looked up. Baby blues. "Davis?"

The cinnamon disk burned going down. "Family name."

"Davis Way," he tried it on. "And you're from Pine—?"

"Apple." The hot candy brick was stuck sideways in my throat.

"Two words?"

"Ach." I discreetly pounded my chest. "Garkle."

"Are you okay?" he asked.

I was anything but.

He pushed a button on his phone. Two seconds later Natalie returned. She gently patted me on the back, then landed one between my shoulder blades that almost knocked me into the next week. She poured me a glass of water while he slid the candy dish out of my reach. As soon as it appeared I would live, Natalie said, "Well then," and disappeared, leaving me alone with Richard Sanders again.

"Why don't we start over, Davis?"

"That'd be great."

"Where is Pine Apple, Alabama?"

"South of Montgomery."

Other than the Red Hots, the real-live Monet on the wall, and the expensive Oriental rug under my feet, I was in very familiar job-interview territory. I'd applied for everything with a heartbeat, and the resulting interviews had all had common elements. First, my name threw people off. In my thirty-two years it had been pointed out to me thirty-two thousand times that Davis Way sounded more like a destination than a person. After that, potential employers liked to suggest that I'd written down my hometown incorrectly. My resume clearly stated my credentials, including two college degrees, one in Criminal Justice and the other in Computer and Information Science. As such, would I really forget where I lived? Next, he would bring up my size, because I was considered undersized in general, but especially so for the line of work I was in. (I'm five foot two.) (And a half.)

He surprised me when he asked instead, "How large is the police force in Pine Apple?"

"There are two of us." There were two of us. Surely he'd read that far.

"Is there a lot of crime in Pine Apple, Alabama?" He leaned back, elbows to armrests, his hands meeting mid-chest. He rolled a thin platinum wedding band round and round his left ring finger.

"The usual," I said. "Domestic, vehicular, theft. We double as fire too."

"So you've had EMT training?"

"Yes."

"And you write computer programming?"

"I'm not sure I'd go that far," I said. "Pine Apple's a small country town, not exactly a hotbed of criminal activity. I had a lot of time on my hands and spent most of it on the computer."

"It says here you rewrote the program for incident reporting nationwide."

I hadn't put that on my resume. What else did it say there? "Not so much, Mr. Sanders. I only eliminated the inefficiencies of the old program and it went viral."

"Why do you want to leave Pine Apple, Davis?"

Oh, boy.

"You know what?" He looked at his watch. "Let's save that for later."

Yes. Let's.

He started up with the wedding band again. "I'm going to say something that could be construed as politically incorrect." He made direct eye contact. "With your permission, of course."

"Sure."

"I have a thirteen-year-old son who has at least five inches and fifty pounds on you."

There it was. "Is he my competition?"

Richard Sanders unexpectedly laughed. "Not hardly. Maybe if we were looking for someone to play Xbox."

"For all I know, Mr. Sanders, you *are* looking for someone to play Xbox." I surrendered. "I've been interviewing for this position for six weeks now, and I still don't know what it is."

"I don't either."

Could we get someone in there who did?

"Did Paul and Jeremy not go over it with you?" he asked.

"Who?"

"Paul and Jeremy," he said. "My security team."

I had nothing.

"Big guys," Mr. Sanders said.

Ah. Those guys. I remembered. The two mammoth men from my tenth interview I'd been trying hard to forget. One had no hair and the other had the biggest, brightest teeth I'd ever seen in my life. The bald one wore strange neckties and the one with the teeth dressed monochromatically—everything, tip to toe, the same color. Natalie introduced them as if I had no idea who they were. As if they hadn't been following me around since my first interview. I'd spotted one, the other, or both giants every time I'd been there. They'd jumped on elevators with me, the bald one had been at the shooting range, and the one with the teeth had actually followed me all the way home once. But on the day I officially met them, I played along. Nice to meet you, large total security strangers.

Then they drilled me for three solid hours on subjects far from security. My waitressing skills, or rather my lack thereof, had been heavily discussed. How did I feel about gambling? (I felt like you shouldn't do it with other people's money.) Would I care to explain that? (No, thank you.) How did I feel about hundreds of pounds of dirty linens? (Opposed.) How about scrubbing shower stalls? (Again, opposed.) Did I know or had I ever known or had I ever seen photographs of someone named Bianca? (No. Wasn't that a breath mint?) How many times had I been married? (None of your business.) Could I type? (How many fingers were we talking about?) Had I always been a redhead? (I wasn't one of those pale, freckled, flaming-red redheads. My hair was a coppery-caramel color, and my eyes were the same color, only darker.) Had I ever been convicted of or committed a felony? (Which one? Convicted or committed?) Either. Both. (There's a big difference.) Let's hear it. (I'd like to use a lifeline.) Did I have culinary skills? (Could I cook Pop Tarts? Yes. Do I know what to do with a dead chicken? No.) Had I ever held a customer service position? (Not specifically. More no than yes. Okay, no.) The hairless one asked me if I could operate an industrial vacuum cleaner. I didn't know such a thing existed.

If I thought I knew what the job was before those two, I sure didn't know after. And there I sat in my final interview with the president, and *he* didn't know.

I picked up my purse.

"Wait," Richard Sanders said.

I put down my purse.

"It's a new position, Davis, and a highly classified one. If I knew exactly what you'd be doing on a day-to-day basis, I'd tell you."

Finally, some bottom line.

"You'll be working undercover throughout the casino and hotel, and if you want to know more than that," he said, "you'll have to agree to the terms."

"Are you offering me the job, Mr. Sanders?"

"Do you want the job, Davis?"

I wasn't sure I wanted it. I was very sure I needed it. "The terms," I said, "what are they?"

"In a word? Discretion." He steepled his fingers, then used

them as a pointer. "Your job is to be discreet."

"And?"

"Use discretion," he said.

Use discretion while being discreet?

"Don't talk to anyone on or off this property about your job," he said. "And don't reveal your identity under any circumstances."

"When do I start?"

"How soon can you start?"

"I'm good to go, Mr. Sanders. You say when."

"Today's as good a time as any." His hand went for the phone. "You can start now."

My eyebrows shot up. I didn't mean that very minute. I was thinking Monday. Or the Monday after that.

"Do you need time to think about it?" His hand hovered over the phone. "Because the iron is hot now."

Wait a minute. No one had said a word about ironing.

"Davis? Do you need a little time?"

Yes. "No."

"Good." He smiled. "Welcome to the Bellissimo."

And with that, I was well on my way to prison.

Gretchen Archer

Gretchen Archer is a Tennessee housewife who began writing when her children, seeking higher educations, ran off and left her. She lives on Lookout Mountain with her husband and a misbehaving sheepadoodle named Kevin. *Double Dose* is the eleventh Davis Way Crime Caper. You can visit her at www.gretchenarcher.com.

Made in the USA
Monee, IL
26 January 2024

52438453R00154